DEVIL MADE ME DO IT

SAVANNAH BLAIZE

ACKNOWLEDGMENTS

I wish to acknowledge all the authors, friends and family who have encouraged me, throughout the long and arduous process of downsizing my home and then relocating to an apartment, to finish Lucia's story and bring it to print. Especially Heidi Catherine and Beth Prentice who are wise, encouraging, and knowledgeable, and have individually been a "Devil-send" to me. They are my sisters-in-crime and I love them dearly.

A special mention to my beautiful friends Joanne Foster, Kamilla Zwolak, and Enisa Haines who edited this book very quickly during the Christmas & New Year period, when the chips were down to complete it by the start of 2024. It takes an army of caring friends to bring my words to you, my precious readers, and believe me I am very grateful.

My Sparkle Sisters, the crystal we picked as a group was malachite. It was very fitting if you read the meaning below. It fits very well with the story:

"Malachite is the essence of joy, a Stone of Transformation, because it helps reveal and heal emotional pain by absorbing the pain into itself."

DEVIL MADE ME DO IT

PROLOGUE

LUCIA

*I*f I had been born a male my destiny would have been a forgone conclusion. Sure, being female has its advantages, but all the good jobs are given to men. All the power is bequeathed to them from birth. This hardly seems fair. Not in my book anyway.

My father decided my brother was the perfect candidate to step into the family business, learn the ropes, walk the walk, and talk the talk. I intend to change that notion. Who better than a woman to beguile, coerce, deceive, entice, persuade, and seduce the weak humans? Who better to bring the world's degenerates to their knees than a woman who knows what she wants and will go the extra mile to get it? I grew up knowing I wasn't like other children, and that I had powers and abilities which I had to keep secret from the world. No one could even be allowed to guess that I was different. If anyone put two and two together and came up with six, they suddenly had a memory loss. My father made sure of that.

My name is Lucia Nightingale, and I am the daughter of Harper

Ericson and Luc Nightingale, who also happens to be the Devil, Lord of the Underworld. To the outside world I am Lucia Ericson, because my father wants me to be protected from those wishing to harm me, in this world and the next. My family is like most families, we have our good days, and we have our bad days. Although I'm certain that our bad days far outweigh the general population's worst days. Sure, we have skeletons in the closet. Doesn't everyone? There are things we don't want the world to ever find out. But we keep our secrets close to our chest and we love and protect each other no matter what.

When my brother rejected the role of successor, my father reluctantly trained me for the role. Now I must prove I'm up to the task, *the* better woman for the job, so to speak. The moment I turned eighteen my life changed, and my body changed in ways I could never have imagined. Like a butterfly I emerged from my human chrysalis, I grew my stunning iridescent wings, and transformed into the strong and powerful She-Devil I was meant to be.

1

LUCIA

NEW YEAR'S DAY 2018

"*D*omenic does not want to do this. Allow him to be with his family. I will step up and be your successor," I announced. But my father does not want to listen.

I raised my arms and transformed the flower garden by the wall into rocks and lava. I lowered my arms to change everything back. When I pointed my finger at a large established tree, and sent it skyward, he began to see I was capable of more than he had imagined.

"You've been developing these talents from me in secret. Why?"

"Because you have always treated me like a child. I am a woman now."

"You are a child. *My* child."

"I am no longer a child. I am eighteen, born on this very day, at this moment. I feel a change in my body already. I deserve a chance to prove that I can do this." My thoughts and speech are halted by excruciating pain, and I am driven down onto one knee on the grass.

The pain ripping through my partially human body was only bear-

3

able because of the euphoria I experienced once my fledgling wings expanded. I was acutely aware that my bones were growing in density and strength, my limbs extending, my figure changing, and my face itched as if tiny creatures were running rampant, madly realigning my features.

I shook my head at the sudden magnification of sounds, celebration and revelry from houses far, far away piercing my brain. The tiara I wore fell to the ground, my hair tumbled down around my shoulders, the bangs covering my forehead. My clothes felt so tight. I look down amazed at how large my breasts became, swelling and pushing at the confines of my dress. I saw the seams of the garment straining to accommodate this growth spurt.

A new sense of awareness gripped me. I stood straight and tall and lifted my chin proudly. I grew into a better version of myself, an older more confident version. It's as if the wisdom of a thousand years of mankind had settled within my brain.

"This is who I am. No longer a little girl. I am Lucia, daughter of Luc Nightingale, King of Hell. Powerful in my own right. I am ready to be trained as your successor. Believe me I will make one Hell of a Queen of the Underworld." I hardly recognized the strong confident and commanding voice emanating from my own lips.

My father walked forward. We stood face to face only inches apart. "I had no idea that on this night I would discover a new side to you, Lucia. This show is impressive, but it will take much more than this to persuade me you are able to take my place."

"I can assure you this is no *show*. This is who I was meant to be. I have emerged from the human form in which I began life. I am no longer the person I was. Look into my heart and tell me you cannot see this."

My father tried to stare me down, and although it was difficult, almost painful to be caught and held in his gaze, I could not lower my eyes.

"Maybe Lucia is better for the job. You may not be impressed by this change in her appearance, but I'm blown away. I had no idea that this stunning creature was inside you Lucia, waiting to burst forth. I feel rather silly calling you little sister now," Domenic said.

"Believe me I had no idea either. But now that I have transformed, it doesn't change the fact that I will always be your little sister and you will always be my dependable big brother. I appreciate your support more than you know."

A noise in the shadows beside the patio door had my attention now, where I knew my mother and sister-in-law were patiently waiting. "Mom, it's okay. You can join us. And you, too, Sophie." I turned to watch them approach. Sophie held my mother's arm. For support or out of fear? I wasn't sure.

"Lucia. I don't know what to say." Even in the moonlight I could see that all the color had drained from my mother's face.

I turned and addressed her. "I know this must be a shock, but it's been a long time coming. I have been aware of subtle changes for a while now. New abilities, a change in mindset, more determination to make my mark. I didn't know this was going to happen though." I spread my arms wide. My wings lowered and folded behind my shoulder blades.

"You can't possibly mean it Lucia. You can't take Luc's place. You are my youngest child. I can't bear the thought of you going to...to..."

"To hell? But you could accept Domenic replacing my father?"

"I have *never* accepted that fact. I had always hoped that it would never happen, and that it would never come to this."

"I want to spend more time with you here Harper. I've made myself clear from the beginning." My father turned toward my mother.

"But sacrificing our children to do so... I can't bear it." My mother covered her face with her hands.

"Mom. I am not sacrificing myself. I was born to this. If I had been a boy, we would not be having this discussion. It would be accepted as the natural order."

"Aren't you afraid, Lucia?" Domenic asked.

"Strangely enough no. I'm excited by the prospect of having a purpose."

My father walked over and put his arm around my mother's shoulder, pulling her into an embrace. Sophie left my mother's side and took Domenic's hand.

"Our guests will be wondering where we are," Domenic said.

"I've paused everyone in the house," my father replied. "Lucia, you cannot return to the house in this body. Can you reverse to the eighteen-year-old girl the guests will expect to see?"

"I'm not sure. Let me try."

I had been able to subtly change my appearance before. But I had never tried such a big transformation. Parts of me did not want to conform to the mental command. It was taking a great deal of physical fortitude to return my body to what it once was. I knew my father could do this easily. I redoubled my efforts. At last, I stood as I did before. My wings had retracted into my back. My dress was not threatening to rip apart. I pulled my hair up and twisted it onto the top of my head and tucked it into a bun. I picked up the tiara and shoved it into place.

"Okay I think this is satisfactory. What do you think?" I asked.

"Your face," Domenic said. "It's too... It's older."

I adjusted my features as best I could. "What about now?"

"Pretty good," Domenic said.

We all stepped onto the patio, and my mother opened the door. Everyone was frozen in place. My father snapped his fingers, and people began to move about, as if a switch had been flipped on. He walked over to the bar, picked up a glass of champagne, and tapped the side of the glass with a spoon. All eyes turned to him.

"I have an announcement. Lucia has accepted a scholarship with a renowned college in Switzerland. This is her last night with the family for a while. Please wish her well in her search for a meaningful career. I expect we will see a more grown-up version of my daughter when she returns home."

"Are you following your brother and going into medicine?" Sophie's mother, Kate, asked.

"No. One doctor in the family is enough," I replied.

"I own a chain of Luxury Hotels here and in Europe. Lucia has shown an interest and wants to take over the business from me one day. She will be learning all the basics of hotel management, starting at the bottom, and working her way up. I have every confidence that she will achieve her goal, and if she applies herself, she will be rewarded with a management position in my organization in the not-too-distant future."

"Oh, Harper, it's going to be very hard to say goodbye to Lucia too, now that Domenic is married," Kate said.

"Yes, I'm going to miss her terribly."

"But with Domenic and Sophie now living next door and the baby coming soon, I'm sure you will be very busy," I said.

"Being busy won't take away how sad I will feel when you are... overseas."

"I'll fly back whenever I can. I promise." I gave my mother a smile, and she smiled back knowing I would be flying under my own wings.

Aimee brought around more trays of hot food, and Cameron refilled the champagne glasses. Everyone appeared to be having a lovely evening, but each time I caught my mother's eye, I could see the sadness reflected there.

Mom, it's okay. I'm not going to be gone for very long I promise. I'll come back as often as I can, and I will be in contact with you all the time. Remember we can talk like this any time now. Although I'm not sure if the same can be said when I'm in the underworld.

Lucia, I'm still trying to get my head around your transformation. I wasn't prepared to see you add at least ten years onto your appearance and change right before my eyes into a more mature woman. I wasn't prepared for the wings either.

Oh Mom, we'll work it out, don't worry. Our family always works it out.

Sophie made her way around to say goodnight to the guests and excused herself. She was looking pale and tired and had been on her feet too long in the last twenty-four hours. Aimee took her arm and walked with her upstairs. That was the cue for everyone else to decide it was time to go home. Domenic walked the guests to the front door where co-incidentally Cameron was waiting with the stretch limousine.

I helped to clear away dishes and glasses, and when Aimee came back downstairs, she insisted she finish cleaning up, and sent us all out of the kitchen. It was time for us to leave too. I kissed Domenic goodnight, linked my arm through my mother's, and we walked through the adjoining gardens back to our own house. My father had disappeared after Domenic closed the door on the guests. My mother didn't mention it, but I knew she was wondering where he'd gone.

We hugged goodnight at the top of the stairs and went to our separate bedrooms. It wasn't until I was in the privacy of my own room, with the door locked, and the blinds closed, that I stepped out of my dress and undergarments and allowed myself to transform back to the new me. It had taken a lot of concentration to hold onto the younger Lucia for all that time. I presume it will get easier the more I attempt it. I will have to discuss that with my father. I will have to discuss a lot of things with my father. I have many questions. I wonder what's going to happen next. I know my father is off somewhere trying to figure this out. The announcement about my overseas trip was his way of covering my absence.

With absolute focus, I allowed my wings to open fractionally. It was like flexing my fingers but to achieve it inches at a time took infinite care and extreme effort. I turned around to get a better look at them in the gilt framed mirror which took up most of the wall near the bedroom door. My wings were black and lush, and every color of the rainbow was reflected and glistening on the surface of the silky feathers. There was no room for me to open them up fully in here. I opened and retracted them a few times, folded them back into my body, mainly to get an idea of what was required.

I turned around in a circle, seeing my figure in the mirror from all angles. Full breasts with prominent nipples, high rounded buttocks, tiny waist, ample hips, and impressive, long, shapely legs. A sinfully beautiful body. Which I guessed was the point. This body could persuade a man to give up his soul. And a woman if she was so inclined.

My full lips curved into a wicked smile, and dimples appeared near my mouth. I moved closer to the mirror to inspect each feature. An attractive nose, some might say 'pert'. Large, almond-shaped, mysterious eyes surrounded by full, thick, dark lashes and showcased by arched eyebrows. Cheekbones sitting high in a perfectly symmetrical oval face.

I pushed my hands into my hair. Thick, lush, and as black as coal, it framed my face and curled over my shoulders and down my back. I appraised and admired the flawless skin and the gorgeous features of the woman looking back at me, as if they belonged to someone else. In some ways they did, as I had to get to know this woman in the mirror intimately, to understand how this new body worked.

It was late, or rather it was early, and the sun would be up soon. Naked, I slipped beneath the sheets and stretched out my arms and my legs. I was going to need a bigger bed. Time to try and sleep if I could. I was sure tomorrow would be another exciting day. The immediate family was coming for dinner to celebrate my actual eighteenth birthday.

And I realized then that the new me didn't have a thing to wear!

2

LUCIA

The tapping was getting louder. I pulled the pillow closer, placed it over my head and covered my ears. My supersensitive hearing, however, was not fooled.

"Lucia. Are you awake?"

"Hang on Mom." I rose and pulled a pink cotton robe from the back of a chair and attempted to close the front over my naked body. It barely met in the middle. I tied it as tight as I could and opened the door. My mother had her arms full of clothes, which she dumped on the bed.

"It dawned on me that you have nothing that will fit your new figure. Perhaps there are some items here that might fit until we can go shopping for a new wardrobe. Of course, we can't go shopping on New Year's Day, and your father thought of that. I've got a tape measure, and he's requested I take measurements. He's sending over a selection of dresses for your Birthday dinner, but he doesn't know your size."

"That's very thoughtful. I'd been wondering what I was going to do, or if I would have to attend my dinner in my old body. Where are the dresses coming from?"

"I'm sure your father can get someone to open their shop in Beverley Hills, especially for him."

"Oh, that's wonderful. Designer clothes. This birthday is turning out much better than I thought. Okay let's do it."

My mother started at the top. Bust, waist and hips, then height and leg length from waist to floor. She even made me stand on paper to draw and measure my feet.

"I'll leave you to try on some of my things. Then come on down for breakfast. Aimee is making pancakes with crispy bacon and maple syrup, just for you."

When she left, I picked up an aqua kaftan from the pile, and slipped it over my head. It didn't look as good on me as it did on my mother, but, after trying on a few other things I surmised the kaftan didn't cling as tightly to my body, so it would do. I brushed my teeth, splashed some water on my face, and secured my long hair into a ponytail. I checked out the vision in the full-length mirror. I was only beginning to recognize the tall, barefoot woman in a kaftan obviously too small and too short for her body, staring back at me. It would have to do.

When I entered the sunroom where breakfast was being served, Aimee had her back to me. She turned around and stopped dead, mid-stride, eyes wide and coffee pot in hand. I had forgotten she hadn't seen me in this form last night.

"Aimee, meet the new Lucia," Mom said.

"You said she'd changed, but I wasn't expecting such a big change."

"You'll get used to it. We all will." Mom picked up her coffee and took a sip. "Eventually."

"She looks a lot older and more buxom. Those breasts are popping out of that kaftan. Not our little Lucia now." Aimee walked around me, assessing all angles.

"I know. Not our little girl anymore."

"I'm in the room. You know I can hear you both, right?"

"Sorry child." A small smile curved across Aimee's lips. "I didn't mean anything by that comment. I'm just amazed by the size of them. You look beautiful. But then, you always did look beautiful."

"It's okay Aimee. I guess everyone will have this reaction for a while."

"At least there will be no one here tonight who hasn't seen you. Oh, except Cameron. Perhaps you should warn him Aimee," Mom said.

"I'll do that. Sit, child, and eat your breakfast before it gets cold." Aimee patted my arm and disappeared into the kitchen.

Breakfast was delicious. My appetite had increased but after two servings I pushed back my chair and stood to take the empty plates to the kitchen.

A growl, low but persistent, came from the hall. Max appeared, walking slowly forward, ears pricked up, taken aback by the apparent stranger in the room, but sensing something familiar. He approached, sniffing the air, then my bare feet and his demeanor changed abruptly. He licked my hand and head butted my thigh, as if to say "Whew, it's only you, Lucia. How did you get to be so tall all of a sudden."

"Hello, Max, you devil dog! How are you? Where have you been the last few hours?" I rubbed his silky ears.

"He's been with me." My father walked into the sunroom, holding the lead of another dog, a slightly smaller version of Max. "I'd like to introduce Raven. She's a direct descendant of Max. I thought it would be nice for him to have a playmate, Harper, now that Lucia isn't going to be around as much."

"Two dogs, Luc. Really?" My mother sat back in her chair and folded her arms.

"It's not as if you need to feed them or pick up after them. She's a Hellhound too." He unclipped the lead.

"Come here, girl." She approached me slowly. I stood still and allowed her to sniff and was rewarded with a nudge to my hand. I stroked her sleek head. She really did look like Max.

"I've brought some clothes for you to try for the party, Lucia. Cameron is unloading the car. What doesn't fit can be returned.

Please do not remove the tags unless you are sure you want to keep them. I think you will find something to your liking. I must admit it was a bit of a challenge remembering that the clothes I was selecting were not for the eighteen-year-old daughter I knew just the other day, who only came up to my chest. And by the way I did not select the lingerie. That was a task I was unqualified and unwilling to perform. I left the decision to the store manager. I presume the packages contain everything a young lady would require for the dresses we selected."

"I promise to only keep what I love. I'm sure what you picked out will be lovely. Thank you. I really do appreciate your thoughtfulness."

Aimee appeared from the kitchen and smiled when she saw my father. "Would you like some breakfast?"

"Just coffee for me, please, Aimee. I have a meeting to attend shortly." My father pulled out a seat at the table. Max and Raven sat down on either side of his chair, ears pricked and ready to move at the slightest command. They were very noble looking dogs. "What time is dinner planned for this evening, Harper?"

"Six thirty for pre-dinner drinks, and we should be eating at seven."

"Can I go and see what Cameron has brought in now?" I asked.

"Of course. Enjoy your private shopping experience. But do come down and show me what you've selected for tonight before I leave."

I tried not to run up the stairs, but it was hard to hide my excitement. Who wouldn't be excited by fabulous new clothes? Designer dresses from Rodeo Drive in Beverly Hills did not drop into my lap every day. My mother has always encouraged me to dress like a normal teenage girl, although I did try to put my own spin on the garments, removing a few inches from the length, or one sleeve, or accessorizing to fit my style. She wasn't always a fan of the changes I made, but she tolerated my alterations most of the time, unless I was showing too much skin. I opened my bedroom door and gasped. There were half a dozen beautifully wrapped large packages lined up on the bed, several shoe boxes and what looked like lingerie boxes stacked on the floor.

I pulled at the black ribbon securing the first oversized box and yanked off the lid. Nestled inside the layers of tissue paper was a long, figure-hugging dress of shimmering champagne-colored fabric. I pulled it out and held it against my body, smiling at my refection. The next package held a short, midnight-blue dress of embossed fabric, the third package a forest green knee-length dress with matching bolero. Another box contained a black cocktail dress, very smart but too sedate for this party. Yet another box contained a long, black skirt, and tops in three different styles and fabric patterns.

All the packages had excited me but, for some unknown reason it was the last package that beckoned me to open it. Tucked inside layers of white tissue lay a ruby-red dress. Tiny spaghetti straps held up a fitted bodice attached to a long skirt made of layers of chiffon. My heart beat faster. Was this dress the one? I eagerly stepped into it, adjusting the corseted bodice with built in support, and zipped up the side. It fitted beautifully, as if it was made for me.

"Please let there be shoes to fit me in one of these boxes!" I pulled off all the lids and found the perfect silver strappy heels, which miraculously were my size, and added even more inches to my impressive height. I twisted my ponytail into a bun and tucked in the ends. I stared at my refection. "Perfect. Simply perfect."

I hurried downstairs to show my father. They were discussing the menu for the party when I strode into the sunroom, head held high, shoulders back, chest out, like the runway models I had seen on the catwalk. My mother looked surprised, but my father wore that self-satisfied smile as if he knew that the red dress would be the one that I would love.

"Wow, Lucia, you look... different. So elegant," my mother said.

"It's wonderful. And it fits me."

"As if it was made for you," my father said. "Here's your birthday gift from your mother and me." He pulled a long, slim, black velvet box from his jacket pocket, came to stand before me, kissed my cheek and placed the box in my hand. "I'd like to give to you now, if that's alright."

I opened it to reveal a red, heart-shaped gemstone on a silver chain. He removed the necklace and fastened it around my neck. The gemstone nestled against my bosom and warmed my skin. Fine tentacles of heat radiated out from the stone, settled in my veins, and wrapped around my heart. Its power was tangible within my body, and comforting.

"Happy birthday, Lucia. I hope you like the necklace. It's a beautiful piece, but it is magical. Red sapphires help in self-awareness, and the realization of truth. It is said they will guide you toward your true path in life. If at any time you are unsure of your actions while wearing this necklace, close your eyes and allow the gemstone to help guide you. If your heart quickens painfully, perhaps reconsider your decision. The gemstone is already in sync with your heartbeat. I know you can feel it, as if it is now part of your body. You don't have to wear it all the time, to feel the power of this gem, but keep it close. When you're not wearing it, return it to the box which is lined with selenite to rest and cleanse the stone."

My father returned to his seat beside my mother, sat back and put his arm around her shoulders. He looked pleased with my choice of dress and his choice of gift.

"Thank you, I love it. And I love all the clothes. It wasn't an easy choice. This is the one I chose for the party."

"You look stunning. And I have just realized this new version of Lucia is the best of both of us. You are tall and dark like me, but you have your mother's beauty."

"Nonsense." My mother shook her head. "Lucia looks exactly like you. Tall and dark and elegant and is far more beautiful than I was or ever will be."

"Beauty is in the eye of the beholder, my darling." My father lifted my mother's hand, kissed her fingertips, and looked longingly into her eyes. "And you are the most beautiful woman in the world to me."

"Hey guys. I'm still in the room!"

"I'm appreciating how wonderful and sexually alluring your mother is," my father said, continuing to maintain eye contact with my mother, who was now returning a secret smile.

"No, no, no." I put up my hands to make a T. "Time out. Kids, no matter how old they are, don't want to hear about their parents' sexual attraction. Or hear anything sexual from their lips for that matter."

My father chuckled softly and patted my mother's hand. "Later," he said. He stood, bid us farewell and disappeared.

Lucia, you can keep all the dresses, shoes, and underwear if you like them, and they are the correct size. It's my gift to you on this special day. Give anything you don't want to Cameron, and he will return it to the store in question. I am aware you will need more casual clothes too. Your mother shouldn't have to worry about it. I've left a credit card in a purse in one of the boxes. Please be aware it has a limit, and I will be tracking your spending.

That is such a very generous offer, thank you father. I love my gifts. All of them. See you later.

3
HARPER

*I*t's going to take me a little time to get used to Lucia in this form. I wish I had been more prepared for such a dramatic change, before my little girl became this tall, imposing woman before me.

The stunning, red dress Luc bought suited her figure. With her hair piled up on her head, and her silver heels, she towers over me. She carried herself differently now, I'd noticed. It seemed that Luc and the sales assistant made the right clothing choices, and very little was being returned to the store.

For a brief period earlier today, when she tried everything on and modeled for me, I saw the young girl again in her eyes. Excitement bubbled from her, and I was happy that she'd been able to enjoy her eighteenth birthday, and her coming of age, before she's thrust into her new role as Luc's understudy. Unsure of what was going to happen, I am scared. Luc assured me he'd take good care of her, but I wasn't ready to lose my happy and carefree daughter to a life spent with the worst of society.

Oh, don't get me wrong, I know she's not an innocent, and she's very well versed in spotting the seven deadly sins and in the ways of seduction. Nevertheless, like any mother, I just don't want her to get hurt.

I decided I needed to clear the air before the party. I found Lucia in her room and sat down on the edge of her bed. "Lucia, come sit with me a minute. We haven't really talked about what happened, about what was said in the garden."

"What do you want to discuss? I made my pitch. I want to take over and give father a break and give you both time to be with each other. I think I'd be good at the job."

"I don't understand how you can say that. You have no idea what the job entails."

"I'm sure I'll find out soon enough. Have faith in me Mom. I've never felt as if I belonged or fitted in anywhere. Maybe that's because my role has yet to be discovered. Wouldn't it be wonderful if I could do it well and you could spend more time together? You can spend time with the new grandchild coming along in a few months, aren't you excited?"

"The new grandchild isn't going to take the place of my daughter."

"No, but she'll be a welcome addition and will bring more love and harmony to the family. Domenic and Sophie will make fabulous parents. I can't wait to meet her."

"Maybe we should forget about you leaving for a few hours and concentrate on having a lovely evening with the family."

"That idea gets my vote."

"I'd better go and see if Aimee needs any help."

"Mom, you know she'll say she's fine. Go and finish getting ready, they'll be here soon."

I chose a silver pantsuit, with a black silk open-neck shirt underneath, and black stiletto ankle boots. The highest ones I could find. This was the first time I hadn't been the tallest woman in the room, and the realization was a little new to me. Luc appeared in his traditional impeccable black suit and black shirt, but with a red tie. He snapped his fingers and the tie quickly changed to silver when he saw what I was wearing, which made me smile.

Domenic and Sophie arrived with Cameron, just as Luc began pouring the pre-dinner champagne. Sophie looked refreshed and happy after having a day to relax. She was glowing in a peach dress which showed off her little baby bump. Domenic was very attentive to his wife's needs and made sure she was able to have her feet raised, and a cushion at her back, which was very pleasing to witness. Lucia was correct, they were going to make lovely parents.

Dinner was magnificent. Lucia had insisted on decorating the table, with silver placemats, tall antique silver candlesticks, and glittering silver balloons she had repurposed from the New Year's celebration at Domenic's. The table looked very bright and sparkly, with Lucia, Domenic, and Sophie on one side and Cameron, Aimee, Luc, and me on the other. Aimee had produced a beautiful feast with many of Lucia and Domenic's favorite winter and festive dishes. We would be eating leftovers for days, but in the holiday season that was a blessing. I'm sure at the end of the evening, Aimee will pack up some food for Sophie to take home.

Aimee carried in the birthday cake (a triple layered chocolate creation, with piped buttercream frosting, and the required eighteen candles) on a raised cake stand and placed it in front of Lucia. Luc waved a hand in the cake's direction, and all the candles ignited simultaneously. We sang Happy Birthday. Lucia stood up to cut the cake, blow out the candles and make a wish, which no amount of teasing by Domenic could coax her to divulge. After cake and coffee had been served, we adjourned to the living room to open the birthday gifts. Cameron disappeared for a few minutes and reappeared with Max and Raven. Max carried a stick, which he dropped at Lucia's feet. It was well chewed, obviously a favorite of his. Lucia laughed and thanked him for his gift, rubbed his silky ears, and patted Raven's head too. The dogs strolled over to sit beside Luc's feet.

"I feel very spoiled. All your gifts are lovely," Lucia announced, pushing tissue paper to one side, and stacking up the boxes.

"But mine is the best, admit it. Although I did buy it before you... changed," Domenic said.

"A girl can never have enough bright pink purses. I love it." Lucia patted Domenic's cheek.

"But maybe a black Chanel purse would be a better and more elegant choice now?" Sophie offered. "I can exchange it for you."

"Please don't. I love your gift. I love all my gifts. A purse from my big brother and new sister. The gold earrings from dearest Aimee and Cameron, the two people I consider to be my protectors and are the closest to grandparents I will ever have. My beautiful new clothes from my father. My red sapphire heart necklace from my both parents. A chewed stick from Max, his favorite, I think. It's been a very special birthday spent with those I love the most in the world. I shall miss you all, you know that don't you."

"Cameron and I have loved you, from the moment you came into this world Lucia. You have been a whirlwind of laughter, mischief, and joy in this house, and we shall miss you terribly. But we're happy that wherever you are, here or in the underworld, we will be able to see you, spend time with you and help you in any way we can," Aimee said.

"I second that. Watching you grow up into a fine young lady has been such a pleasure. To have been able to watch over you and keep you safe when My Lord wasn't here has been a privilege, and one I do not take lightly. Aimee and I would give up our lives for you. For all of you. But to be thought of as your surrogate grandparents... well... that brings a happy tear to my eye." Cameron brushed away the moisture gathering at the corner of his eye. Aimee patted his hand.

I noticed everyone in the room had taken a few moments to let this sink in. Although to the outside world we come across as just another wealthy Hollywood family, who made their fortune through the movie industry, we all knew that there were forces and evil people out there who would harm us if they knew the truth. And Cameron and Aimee would indeed give their lives to save ours. Cameron has maintained this house and tended this estate, kept the gardens immaculate and driven me anywhere I wanted to go for over eighteen years. Aimee has been my constant companion since before Lucia was born and helped to bring her into this world. She has never complained or been anything other than kind and generous, both with her time, her advice, and the love she adds to all the beautiful meals she prepares for us.

"How long will you be gone, Lucia?" Sophie asked.

"I have no idea. But I will be back as often as I can, and I want to be here to greet my niece, of course. Can I come back then, father?"

"Yes, of course. We all want to be here to witness the new generation's arrival," Luc said.

All I could think of then was that this child will be the combination of devil and witch DNA. That's a lot of pressure for a tiny baby to have to handle.

4

LUC

I returned to my office to find Rourke waiting for me with a stack of new admission forms to sign. He didn't look happy, but that wasn't unusual given the extra workload around Hell at this time of year. The crazies came out of the woodwork during the festive season, and there were more murders and atrocious deeds performed than at any other moment. Which meant we got more inmates to attend to in Hell. Which in turn deepened the scowl on Rourke's face. He placed the forms on my desk and stood to attention.

"At ease. I've got some good news for you, Rourke." His left eyebrow quirked up half an inch but other than that he showed no signs that he'd heard me. "Lucia has shown an interest in joining the family business, and I want to start her probation in Hell this week. She could relieve you of some of your mundane admin tasks. I'm placing her in your care, and I would like you to assign a demon who will show her the ropes but also have her back."

"Lucia? Your daughter?" Rourke said incredulously, his face the most animated I had ever witnessed.

"Yes, my daughter."

"I thought that you had plans to teach Domenic?"

"Domenic has no desire to leave his mundane life on Earth, now or in the future, for something more rewarding in Hell. He wants to stay with his wife and soon-to-be-born daughter. Understandable, but not very convenient for us. However, Lucia has stepped up. She's excited by the prospect of taking over from me one day and wants to prove she's up to the task."

"I presume by your tone of voice that you don't believe she has what it takes."

"I've yet to be convinced. Our hellish work environment is no place for a woman. Never mind a young and inexperienced woman. But it has been pointed out to me that I shouldn't discriminate, and that she can, and will, prove herself to be worthy of my crown."

"I can't see the men agreeing to take commands from a girl."

"You haven't seen Lucia lately. She's changed quite considerably. Woman is more of an apt term now."

"She would have to come and go via the portal to Hell in the Gatehouse."

"No. Her wings have appeared."

"When did this happen?"

"On her eighteenth birthday. It was a complete surprise to me. I had no idea things were moving so fast. Up until then she has appeared to be like a normal human, with only a few tricks and abilities. But given the fact that she's half mine, I should've guessed that one day things would ramp up. It appears she's been keeping some of her talents a secret from me for a while now. Although the wings were a new addition, and they were a surprise to her too. They appeared just after midnight on the first of January."

"How is that possible? You're..."

"You don't need to rub it in, Rourke. I've obviously not been keeping such a close eye on her as I should have. But that will change from now on. And I will have you to help me in that task now that she'll be down here most of the time during her probation."

"Babysitting is not on my list of duties, My Lord."

"And that is why you will assign Lucia to someone more suited to the job. Perhaps someone younger than you, closer to her age when they came to reside in Hell. Do you have anyone in mind?"

"Drake is my most trusted demon. He's been an asset to me. He has spent some time with humans lately. You remember he stayed with Sophie and Lisa when the burglary occurred and was also responsible for managing the wedding ushers and the demon builders refurbishing Domenic's house."

"Excellent. Sounds like he would be perfect. Do what you need to do to get things moving. I will return with Lucia this week. An office at the far end of corridor would be best."

"You don't want her next door to you?"

"No. I don't want her living in my pocket. And I'm sure she doesn't want me living in her pocket either. She has her own elevator at that side of the tower, which works fine for me."

"As you wish, My Lord."

Lucia, I've arranged for you to start your probation this week.

That soon?

No time like the present. Hell has been especially busy, and Rourke could use the help.

I'll pack.

No need. Whatever you desire I can arrange for it to appear in Hell.

Clothes?

We have a uniform.

Personal things?

As I said I can arrange anything you desire to be there. You only need to ask.

Excellent.

"Rourke."

"Yes, My Lord."

"We will need a female guard's uniform."

"I'll get right onto it, My Lord."

5

LUCIA

I went in search of my mother to break the news. I had hoped to have a bit more time with her, to help her get used to the changes. But on the plus side, it looked like my father had taken my request seriously. Max and Raven were sitting on the patio, bathed in what little sunshine the winter's day provided, and my mother was walking back and forth in the yard, bundled up against the cold. The two Doberman heads followed her every move.

"Mom what are you doing?"

"I'm enjoying some fresh air and exercise."

"I am well aware that you pace when you are thinking or trying to work out a problem with a script. I think this time It's more to do with me, though. Isn't it?"

"I know your father wants to spend more time here, and he wants someone to cover for him. Don't get me wrong. I'm delighted by the idea of him being here more often. But the idea of losing my daughter so that we can have time together is stressing me out."

"Mom, for years you've tried to get me to look to the future and work out which career would fulfil me. I'm very competent in several languages, I have a quick mind, and I've proven myself to be a good actress. I've been told I'm attractive, beguiling and persuasive." I ticked them off on my fingers. "All of these attributes make me a good fit for the job, and I am sure we'll discover more along the way. Think about this. If I'd been born a boy, you would've known from the moment I was born that my father had this grand plan to teach me all he knows. It's the natural order of things. I'm going to prove to him that I'm just as good as any son would have been at stepping into his shoes, if not better."

I hugged my mother, put my arm around her shoulders and led her inside. Raven and Max followed, and as I stopped to close the door after the dogs, Max made eye contact with me. I had the distinct impression that he would be keeping a very close eye on my mother when I was gone. I would have loved to know what he's thinking. I cannot communicate telepathically with the dogs like Domenic and my father can. I guess that's something else I would have to learn.

"Mom, I came to find you to let you know that I'm leaving sooner than I thought. I don't want to make a fuss. I don't want another family dinner. I want to spend a few days here with you, as normal as possible. I want my room to be just as I've left it, because I'll be back as often as I can. I'm not allowed to take anything with me, and I imagine that when I return, I will be delighted to immerse myself in this world again."

"I guess there's no point in arguing with you, you've obviously made up your mind. I'll miss you terribly, but I'll have to accept it. Until you can prove to me that you're safe and happy with your decision I'll be worried about you down there."

"Father will take care of me. He won't let anything bad happen to me. You do understand that, don't you?"

"I know you need to do this to prove you're as capable as Domenic. But this was never a competition. Your father loves you both equally. His natural-born child and his adopted child. He thinks the world of both of you."

"I'm not doing this to prove I'm better than my brother. I think I've found my purpose, Mom. I think this was what I was born to do."

She reached for me then and hugged me tight. Then let me go, dashed tears from her cheeks, and took a step back.

"I'm exceptionally proud of the woman you have become. Let's go and find Aimee and make some hot chocolate. I'm sure she baked cookies this morning."

We walked arm and arm through the house. I made a mental note to remember this. Remember the hugs, remember the feel of my mother's arms around me and her reassuring words. I had a feeling I would need to draw on these memories while I was gone.

We were met by two large and powerful looking men when we touched down in Hell. I recognized Drake from Domenic's wedding. Tall and dark, with a perfectly handsome face and a bodybuilder's powerful physique, he was unforgettable. We were nearly the same height now. He didn't recognize me, of course. My father made the introductions and then he told me he would catch up with me later. He instructed Drake to take me to my office. and left with Rourke.

Drake turned to me, his eyes searching my face, but he showed no emotion in his. I presumed he was waiting for me to move, ladies first and all that, or maybe the boss's daughter first, but I waved him on. He led the way down the dark and dingy corridor.

Drake opened the door to my office and took a step back. It was a small room, dark walls, decorated in an early dungeon theme with a weak overhead light, and a cheap wooden desk and chair. I took a few steps inside.

"Well." I looked around. "This is less than charming."

Drake followed me and gestured to the cupboard door. "You'll find your uniforms in there."

I opened the door, scanned the contents, and pulled out a shapeless black coatdress, with a red collar. "What is this?"

"Your uniform. Demons wear a uniform to differentiate the guards from the inmates."

"I prefer yours."

"Mine!" Drake sounded shocked. His eyebrows rose. My goodness, the man was not a robot after all.

"Yes. Take me to the place where they made this."

"Now?"

"Yes, now."

We returned to the elevator and descended. After a few minutes the doors slid open, and the high-pitched hum of electric sewing machines greeted me. Suddenly several pairs of eyes swiveled in our direction. Demons, busy with their work, were surprised to see a woman down here. I walked between huge bolts of black and red fabric, reels of cotton and stacks of partially constructed uniforms piled up on tables. A rather officious-looking elderly grey-haired man, who couldn't have been much more than five feet tall, stood on a step ladder at the end of the room holding the front panel of a shirt up to an exceptionally large demon's chest. He wore a long leather apron over his standard black uniform and red shirt, and a tape measure hung around his neck. He paused when he saw us approach. He scowled in my direction.

"I'd like a uniform made."

"I've already sent uniforms to your office."

"Ah, you know who I am?"

"Everyone knows who you are. We were told to expect you."

"I don't want these shapeless sacks you have produced." I dropped the offending dress I had brought with me on the floor. "I want a uniform the same as Drake's."

"But he's a male."

"Yes. And I like his uniform. I'd like black fitted pants and shirt, a red leather waistcoat, and black leather knee high boots. And of course, the belt to hold my whip."

"I can't..."

"But you can. Rest assured you don't need to wait for my father's approval. You are going to be seeing a lot of me, and you don't want to get on my bad side. What's your name?"

"Preston."

"Okay, Preston. Measure me. And make sure it clings to every inch of my body. I need this to be as form-fitting as possible. I want both the demons and the inmates to be in no doubt I am a woman."

I turned my attention to the demon being measured. "Take a break."

He looked at Drake for approval and moved off to one side. I took my place on the small platform.

"Back to work," Preston growled at the workers. The machines began to hum again.

His hands shook as he took my measurements, trying very hard not to touch my body. I lowered my voice to a whisper. Only he could hear me.

"Preston. I know this is an unusual request. I know that you are having difficulty with the fact that I am indeed a woman, that I'm here in Hell to be a guard, in what was a man's domain, and that I'm requesting this from you. But be aware that I want these men to see I am a force to be reconned with. I am not a shy or incapable female. I am a strong woman and as such I am proud of my body. I'm Luc Nightingale's flesh and blood, remember, and was created by him. Believe me when I say I'm going to show everyone I mean business. And you, my new friend, are going to help me with that because I'm aware you know what it's like to be thought of as less capable than others, and to be dismissed because of your unimposing stature. You have a warrior's heart beating inside that diminutive body because of all the injustice you have had to tolerate. You're going to make me a uniform that will allow me to move with ease, to punish, to jump, to fight, to take charge of the inmates and demons in this hellish place. A dress has no place in my wardrobe down here. Do you understand?"

"Yes."

"Can I count on you?"

"Yes, Miss Nightingale."

"Good. We understand each other."

Drake and I returned to my office. As soon as I opened the door, my mood dropped dramatically.

"This won't do. We need to liven this up. I cannot possibly be expected to work within these walls every day. I need somewhere I can relax after all the bleak caverns and dirt and molten lava spewing from the walls down there. Who do I need to talk to about redecorating?"

"Redecorating?"

"Yes, making this a more enjoyable experience. We must have demons down here who have some decorating experience? Are there files of who did what on Earth? Someone with job experience in carpentry? There must be a whole list of people who are handy with a hammer and nails because I know demons were responsible for rebuilding Domenic's house. My father wouldn't have had anyone on our property who was from the outside world."

"I can summon some carpenters."

"And find me a decorator, too. There must be someone down here with flair. I'm not used to living like this. My father said I only have to ask for what I need."

6
LUC

I had been forced to return to Earth suddenly, to deal with a group of thugs who had been looting, carjacking, and stealing in their decrepit neighborhood. But their main form of entertainment was beating up and terrorizing another local gang. I brought a few of them back with me to Hell. I had also collected a dozen souls to add to my quota for the month, proving the trip wasn't a total waste of my time. When I returned to the underworld some days later Rourke was waiting outside my office with a group of demon guards. All of them had murderous intent written all over their faces.

"What in Hell's name does this welcome mean?" Rourke closed the door.

"It's Lucia. She's causing havoc. Your men aren't happy," said Rourke.

"They'd better come in then. Open the door."

They marched in and filled the space. There was a lot of muttering, but nothing made any sense to me.

"Tell me what happened."

Several of them tried to talk at once.

"One at a time. You!" I pointed at a face I recognized. "Your name's Sean, isn't it? You helped with Domenic's house."

"That's right."

"Out with it!"

"It's your daughter, My Lord. She's demanding changes and she's made a schedule for torture. She upset some of the long-term demons by allowing the younger men to have more privileges. And she's made us rebuild her office and she's redecorated her office with leopard skin pillows and cowhide rugs!" At this last comment, his face contorted in disgust.

Another man pushed forward and spoke. "She's getting all the men riled up. Sexually I mean. There is no doubt she's attractive. She's your daughter, after all My Lord, but does she have to shove it in our faces?"

I held up my hand. I got it. They didn't like change. They didn't like a woman in demon's uniform down here.

"It's going to take a bit of time for her to settle in. Of course, I can see your problem. Too many changes too soon I gather. I'll talk to her. Go back to work, gentlemen."

They grumbled, not satisfied, but they left. I presumed they wanted me to get rid of her, take her back to Earth. I asked Rourke to wait behind.

"Is this serious? Tell me she hasn't upset that many of them already?"

"She certainly has made an impact in the short time she's been here."

"I'll go talk to her."

Lucia's door was closed but I heard loud "heavy metal" music on the other side; recognized the lyrics of "Born To Be Wild". I pushed open the solid door, surprised to see oak wood paneling now lining the walls, the offending leopard skin pillows on the two visitor's chairs, the large modern oak desk and fancy office chair.

I stepped over the cowhide rug into the room and watched as Lucia attempted to hang a framed picture on the wall behind her desk.

Standing on a chair, her back to me, her high ponytail bounced and swung in the air and her hips moved in time to the beat. The black pants she wore looked like they were painted on above her leather knee-high boots and showed off her womanly curves. She turned her head, became aware of me, and stepped down. The red leather waist-coat she wore over a fitted black, open-neck shirt looked as if it was molded to her breasts. Her sleeves were rolled up to the elbows and she wore her leather cuffs with metal spikes attached. A whip hung from the belt at her waist. This costume left nothing to the imagination. She strode forward, kissed my cheek, and took a step backwards.

"You're back." She smiled.

"This was not the uniform I expected them to produce for you!"

"I made some changes. I wasn't going to wear that shapeless sack. Preston was persuaded to help me show off all my best attributes. I wanted them in no uncertain terms to know I was a woman."

"Oh, they know alright. And they are not happy."

"Well, that's too bad. They had better get used to it. I might be the only woman in charge down here, but I am not a shrinking violet cowering in the corner."

"I see you've also changed your office. The cowhide and leopard skins are a nice touch."

"I thought so too. The other décor didn't bring me joy."

"The men tell me you've constructed a schedule for torture. And the reason for that is?"

"We need to share the jobs around. You do realize that a lot of the older demons are hogging all the good torture methods. There are many young demons wanting to step up, earn their stripes too. Their talents are being wasted. But enough about that right now. I must go. I have a self-defense class to attend. Drake is teaching me how to take someone down in two easy steps today."

"Drake is teaching you self-defense?"

"You didn't know he was a martial arts expert as well as having other interesting hobbies in his previous life? You see what I mean. Wasted talents."

And with that she strode past me and disappeared around the

corner. I am beginning to realize that this version of Lucia is like no other I have encountered. And quite frankly I'm impressed by her self-assurance. I hadn't expected her to be trying as hard to make this work. In all honesty I thought she would be ready to go back to her comfortable life on Earth by now.

Boy, was I wrong.

7

DOMENIC

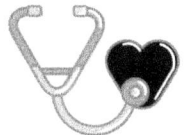

APRIL 2018

*O*ur baby was due any day. Amanda had rescheduled my private patients to later in the month and the hospital had been alerted to the fact that I might be called away at a moment's notice. I wanted to be there when our child came into the world. Sophie had been wonderful but she was tired and uncomfortable and well and truly over the pregnancy. The nursery had been decorated in soothing neutral tones, baby clothes bought, washed, folded, and dozens of toys had been purchased in readiness for every stage of our baby's development. The room looked like an upmarket toy store. I couldn't deny it was worth it, though, because the joy on my wife's face whenever she added another stuffed baby animal to the collection lit up the room. She was nesting in every sense of the word, and she had an ally in my mother.

I'd been pleasantly surprised by how close Sophie and my mother had become over the last few months. The proximity of our two houses was a godsend. I had anticipated my mother would miss Lucia, but Luc returned home often, and reassured her that Lucia was fine. Sometimes he only stayed with us for a few hours, sometimes for a day or two but that was enough for her to know he wanted to be here. Whenever he left, she didn't become a recluse like she used to. She'd just get back to her oil painting, or come over to help Sophie with the nursery.

❧

"Domenic, do you think Lucia will be back soon? I hope she can see the baby when she's born," Sophie placed the romance novel she'd been reading on the bedside table.

"I'm sure she'll want to come back then." I closed the laptop and slid it onto my side of the bed. It had become a ritual this past week, to join Sophie in bed while she read, rather than stay downstairs in the study if it was necessary to catch up on my email.

"I was thinking about asking Lisa and Andrew to come to dinner tomorrow night if they're free. We need to discuss them being our daughter's Godparents. Or do you think we should wait until after the birth to do that?"

"I don't see why we should wait. Let's see if they're open to it."

"I'll ask Aimee if we could borrow her for the evening. Make it a special meal. What do you think?"

"Whatever you want."

"I could pretty much ask for anything at the moment and you would agree, wouldn't you?" Sophie laughed.

"I guess I would. I want you to be happy."

"I'm happy. I would be happier if I could tie my own shoelaces or walk up the stairs without being totally out of breath, or sleep on my stomach, but all in all I'm happy."

"You'll be able to do all of those things soon. Don't worry."

"Oh, oh! She knew I was talking about her. She is moving about a bit now, pushing her little feet up under my ribs."

"Let me soothe her." I unbuttoned the bottom of Sophie's pajama top and laid my hand on her bulging stomach. The skin was taut over our child, and I could see where she was curled up. The head was engaged so her movements were limited to her arms and feet, and she used them whenever she wanted us to be reminded that she was listening to every word. I rubbed my hand gently over my wife and my daughter and received a sigh from Sophie.

"Shhhhh, little one. We know you want to be involved in the conversation. But take it easy on your mom's ribs, okay." I hummed a few bars of a nursery song that came to mind.

"She's behaving now. Thank you. Do you think she is going to be a daddy's girl? You always have the knack to soothe her."

"She knows my voice."

"She knows your touch too." Sophie reached up, placing her palm on my cheek. I leant down and kissed her lips.

Her response was immediate, her tongue flicking over mine. "Now that you've started to undress me, we may as well take advantage of the fact that she's gone to sleep."

"I thought you were tired?"

"I am tired, but I would really appreciate a bit of affection, and love making comes under that banner, too."

"As I said before, I want you to be happy." I captured her mouth once again and moved into a better position to make sure that Sophie wouldn't have my body weight on her. I moved to her feet, tugged her pajama bottoms off and placed a pillow under her bottom. "Okay?

"Okay," she said.

I kissed her thighs, lots of slow lingering kisses moving up towards her sex. She watched my every move, her face flushed and eager. I kept my body above her, moved the kisses up and over her stomach, unbuttoned her top all the way and took one of her nipples into my mouth, sucking hard. Her moan made me harder.

"Nice and slow. Okay," I whispered. I stayed on my knees, cupped my hands beneath her bottom and tilted up her hips. When I entered her, slowly, oh so slowly, she closed her eyes, and the flush in her cheeks became deeper. And this was how I made love to my very pregnant wife. With care and patience and watching her beautiful face as the orgasm overtook her, and her body clenched around me, aiding my release. I had all my married life ahead to go faster, deeper, and with passion-filled abandon. But now my beautiful wife needed slow and gentle love in every touch, in every stroke.

I was filled with a love I never thought I would experience. A closeness I thought was denied to me. Until my beautiful Sophie. She made me a better man and I would do whatever it takes to make her as happy as she has made me, every day that I can.

8

SOPHIE

*A*imee had made a delicious roast beef with all the trimmings and an Apple pie with cinnamon sugar topping and home-made vanilla ice cream for dessert. As Aimee cleared away the final dishes, I looked around the table and everyone appeared happy, and by the way they sat back in their chairs, they were sated. We all praised her for her beautiful meal and retired to the living room with coffee, and my English breakfast tea. I took up residence at the end of the couch and raised my feet on a footstool.

"The meal was delicious. You're very lucky to have Aimee to help. I'm jealous," Lisa said.

"Oh, don't I know it. She's been a godsend to us, especially in the last couple of months. My ankles are swollen by the end of the day, and the last thing I feel like doing is cooking. But Domenic deserves a hearty meal. Both my fridge and freezer are always stacked with Aimee's delicious healthy food. As well as some sweet treats. Also, Harper comes over occasionally in the evening and we all eat togeth-er," I said.

"It's nearly time for this little one to make an appearance. Do you have everything ready?" Lisa pointed to my swollen belly.

"I think so. All we need is the little angel to come out into the world. Gently, if you please." I patted my swollen belly. "As opposed to some of the stories I've heard recently. Isn't it always the way that people tell you the horror stories when you're nine months pregnant and can't change your mind?"

"You wouldn't want to change your mind, would you?"

"No. But I'm praying for an easy birth. And since we're talking about the birth, Domenic and I would like to ask if you and Andrew would care to be our baby's Godparents?"

"Really!" Lisa squealed and launched herself at me with her arms wide open, giving me a hug. "I think that would be wonderful. Andrew, what do you think?"

"We would be honored to be Godparents." Andrew got up and shook Domenic's hand. Then he leant down and kissed my cheek.

"It's settled then. I'm so pleased," I said.

"How are the wedding arrangements going? Only a couple of weeks now." Domenic asked.

"As well as to be expected," Andrew's smile appeared plastered on and did not reach his eyes.

"Both sets of parents came together to discuss the guest list. Andrew's list was small because he doesn't come from a large family. However, my family were not as understanding. I told my family that we were going to elope if they couldn't get the numbers down. I think they realized that I meant business. Italian families are huge. I don't need second cousins and uncles I've never met to be at our wedding." Lisa crossed her arms. "And as we're paying for most of this wedding, with a little help from the parents, our opinion counts a lot."

"You go, girl," I said.

"And I'm holding on to the hope you can still be my Matron of Honor."

"I promise I will try to have this baby business out of the way before the wedding."

"You'd better... otherwise you're going to be in the Guinness World Records for the longest gestation."

"I'm sure I will have had the baby. I mean I would like to look less like a baby elephant, and more like a gazelle in my bridesmaid's dress."

"I'm inviting Harper to the wedding, to look after the baby, since Domenic will be occupied as Best Man and you will be busy attending to my every whim," Lisa said.

"Every whim?" I laughed.

"Yes. As you've already noticed I'm Italian, and I'm sure I'll be a diva on the day. Or a bridezilla. Or..."

"A pain in the neck?" I smiled sweetly. "Those were the words you were searching for, weren't they?"

"You're going to look wonderful in that bright orange dress and shoes I ordered for you. The one covered in frills with the huge puffy sleeves." Lisa smiled and her eyes twinkled.

"Oh, oh. Baby is moving. Those feet are beating a drum solo on my ribs again."

"Can I feel her?" Lisa asked. I nodded and she laid her hand on my stomach. "She sure is a feisty little thing."

"I can't wait to meet her." Andrew said. He wasn't looking at me though, he was looking wistfully at Lisa. She smiled back.

"You want kids, don't you?" I asked him.

"Sure do. Lots," Andrew smiled.

"Lots? Hang on, I thought you said you wanted a couple?" Lisa said, her eyes as big as saucers.

"After seeing all your Italian relations, and cousins, and their kids the other day I thought it would be great to be a part of a big family," Andrew said.

"You've been talking to my mama, haven't you? She's got inside your head. She would love more grandchildren. More bambini to love, and spoil," Lisa said.

"Would that be a bad thing?" Andrew asked.

"No, if you were the one pushing them out, it would be fine," Lisa said.

"A big family is expensive," I offered.

"I have a few dollars put away. I'm sure we can manage," Andrew said, confidently.

"Can we stop this talk about babies and just get through the wedding. I'm stressed enough. Let's just take one thing at a time, okay?" Lisa put her hands together in prayer, pleading.

"Okay." Andrew grinned at Lisa. I had a feeling he would win her over. Eventually.

"Can we change the subject now?" Lisa leant a little closer to me. "Have you had any more visits from Maggie Mae lately?"

"No. I haven't seen her since the wedding. Although I have the feeling that she is watching over me. From time to time, I sense this presence."

"That was one of the strangest evenings in my life when she appeared in your mother's house, Domenic," Andrew said.

"It was a bit freaky," Lisa said. "But I've seen her twice, and it wasn't as much of a shock the second time."

"I took her advice though and bought my parents' house. Maggie Mae was right. My folks wanted to sell, get something smaller in town, and travel. After the wedding we'll look at renovating and moving there. If I can find suitable office space, I can relocate my business," Andrew said.

Lisa sat back on the couch and Andrew put his arm around her shoulders. "There's no rush. We're both working which means we can take our time." He smiled down at Lisa. There was a secret look which passed between them. It was lovely to see how wonderful they were together.

"Look at you two! You're adorable. Aren't they adorable Domenic? I'm so happy for the pair of you."

"Adorable," Domenic said in a high-pitched voice, mimicking me.

"You can both stop now. Before I throw up the lovely dinner Aimee made," Lisa said.

"Oh, come on. I get to tease you. After all I was the one who got you two together. If it hadn't been for me, you would be dating *losers*, instead of this handsome, intelligent, and very worthy *man*."

"In my defense, I was looking for Mister Right. I was just looking in all the wrong places."

Aimee appeared from the kitchen with Max and Raven walking behind her. Max cocked his head when he noticed Lisa.

"My goodness. Aren't they gorgeous? When did you get another dog, Domenic?" Lisa asked. "Come on Max."

Max strolled over to Lisa.

"Is your friend a boy or a girl Max?" Lisa held out her hands for him to sniff, before patting him.

Raven moved over to sit beside Domenic's chair. He put his hand on her sleek head.

"This is Raven. She is technically my mother's dog. They both are. But they patrol both properties," Domenic said.

"You're such a big teddy bear, aren't you, Max. You wouldn't hurt a fly, would you?" Lisa announced.

"Don't bet on it," Domenic said. "They are both very good watch dogs."

"I was just letting you know I'm leaving now," Aimee said. "The dishes are stacked in the dishwasher, and I've switched it on. I've packed away all the leftovers in the fridge for your lunch tomorrow. Max and Raven are walking me home."

"I'll drive you home, Aimee," Andrew said.

"No need. We'll be fine. But thank you for offering. It's only a short walk through the back gate," Aimee said.

"That's right, you have a gate in the wall of the two properties, don't you?" Lisa said.

"Yes. It's really handy. Cameron installed motion sensor lights along the path," I said.

"Goodnight, everyone. It was lovely to see you both again." Aimee nodded to Lisa and Andrew. "Come on." Aimee clicked her tongue, and the dogs followed her out. Max glanced back at the door, and Lisa waved to him. He did look as if he wanted to stay.

"I think you've found a very loyal friend in Max, Lisa. He clearly loves you," I said.

"Maybe they'll have puppies, and we could have one?" Lisa said.

"No, they're not going to have puppies. And you don't need a dog to complicate your life at the moment. Take it from me. A wedding, renovating, and then babies, means you are going to be very busy for the next few years," I said. "The last thing you need to be doing is looking after a dog as well. The vet bills, the grooming, the food. It all costs a lot." I knew these costs did not apply to me, but the bills would be real issue for Lisa if she decided to have a dog.

"I agree with Sophie. Let's concentrate on the wedding and then having the kids before we take on any animals," Andrew said. He placed a gentle kiss on her temple to soften the words.

"Looks like I'm outnumbered. But I'll be come over to visit my goddaughter often and I'll get a chance to have my doggie fix then. Hey, maybe we could have Max over to our house for a sleepover?"

"No, sorry. Max is a one family and one property guard dog, and I want him to stay that way. I don't want him to get too friendly. It defeats the purpose of a guard dog. I know he lets his guard down with you, and that's okay, because you are like family to us. But he has a job here to keep our family safe. He can't get soft," Domenic said.

"Domenic's right, Lisa. Max has a job to do," Andrew said.

"Okay I give up. No dogs, no sleepover dogs. It's time we went home and let you rest. You're looking tired honey," Lisa said, patting my knee.

"I am feeling tired. But it was lovely to have you both over. I'm delighted you agreed to be godparents." I tried to get up.

"Don't move. I'll see them out." Domenic rose, walked Lisa and Andrew to retrieve their coats from the hall closet, waved them off and returned to the living room.

"Time for bed?"

"Sound's wonderful," Domenic said.

"It was such a lovely meal. Lisa was thrilled to be asked to be godmother."

"Hopefully it will never come to them being needed to look after our daughter. But I am glad they want to do it." Domenic took my hand and helped me to my feet. We turned off the lights and made our way to our bedroom. I turned down the covers and got changed for bed.

"Have you thought any more about the names we picked out?" I asked.

"I haven't given it a lot of thought to be honest. Have you?"

"I'd like to throw another one into the mix. What about Daisy?"

"Where did that come from? I don't know anyone called Daisy."

"Yes, that's the point. I want an unusual name. Something pretty and feminine and a name none of our relatives have."

"Daisy Ericson. It has a nice ring to it. I'll think about it." Domenic gave me a peck on the lips and turned on his laptop.

9

SOPHIE

7th APRIL 2018

I'm restless. I can't get comfortable, can't settle on reading or watching a movie or doing a crossword. I know it's unreasonable, but whenever Domenic was called into the hospital at night for an emergency consult or an operation, I felt anxious. It was probably because the baby was due, but I couldn't shake the foreboding feeling that trouble was on the horizon.

Max and Raven lay at my feet. Domenic brought them inside to watch over me. As I got up and walked to the kitchen Max lifted his head, got up and followed me there.

"It's okay, Max. I'm only getting something to eat. Maybe Domenic was too literal when he said you must keep your eye on me. Perhaps some cake would make me feel better." But the plate I'd placed in the fridge after lunch was no longer there.

"Oh no, don't tell me Domenic ate it!" Now all I could think of was the taste of the delicious cake with creamy butter frosting that Aimee had made. Nothing else would do. That was the problem with cravings. There were other sweet treats in the pantry but now all I wanted was Aimee's vanilla layer cake with lashings of fluffy frosting on top. I picked up my shawl from the back of the chair and wrapped it around my shoulders.

"Come on, Max. Come, Raven. I'm sure there's more cake in Harper's fridge."

I opened the back door to allow the dogs to go first. I turned on the back porch light, grabbed the keys from the hook near the door, and locked the door behind us. I carefully descended the few steps to ground level and as I approached the garden, the solar motion sensor lights flickered on along the edge of the path. A long runway appeared toward the gate in the wall between the two properties. It was a cool night, and the moon was hidden behind clouds. A stiff wind suddenly sprung up and began to howl, blowing the trees and bushes along the high walls, whipping the branches, and dropping the air temperature dramatically. I pulled the shawl tighter over my shoulders, regretting I hadn't brought a coat.

My soft-soled shoes absorbed the freezing cold from the concrete path and my toes began to chill. I had almost made my mind up to turn around and abandon the trip next door when movement caught my eye. A dark shape appeared above the wall near the gate. It floated down to ground level. Both Max and Raven growled low and persistent. I had my hand on Max's collar, keeping him at my side. Raven, who was just ahead of me began to bark.

"Come here, girl. Raven heel."

She reluctantly backed up to my side never taking her eyes off the presence ahead.

We slowly backed up the path. Max's lips were drawn back, his razor-sharp canines showing now, and his growl became a snarl. My heart, pounding in my chest, had alerted my child, who kicked and moved about in my swollen belly. My anxiety was instrumental in Max becoming larger by the minute as he fed on my fear. The dark shape moved along the path, extinguishing the runway, one light at a time, absorbing each globe of light into its pitch-black heart. Max was not the only otherworldly being in the garden who was growing larger. The dark mass was the size of a tall man now, but still had no discernable features. Max surged forward, desperate to be set free of my hold on his collar, understanding that I was in command, and yet something told me to hold him fast. It was taking all my strength of will as well as physical strength to keep the dogs beside me. I feared for them if I let them go.

Suddenly a florescent glow appeared and floated in front of me, providing a barrier between the dark presence, and the dogs and me. I could see through this ghostly apparition and recognized Maggie Mae's features. She raised her arms to the heavens and an incantation of words and a language unknown to me floated out around us, over and over, and over again. The presence continued to advance inch by inch. Maggie Mae's words became louder, more forceful, and her arms made swooping circles in the air as if she was gathering up a ball of candy floss solidifying in her hands. An orange-sized ball of intense light sat in her ghostly palm, and she threw it in the direction of the presence.

The glowing ball made contact and a small burst of embers appeared in the center of the being, glowing, and burning through, like singeing a hole in black paper. Pieces around this hole detached and floated away in the wind, their edges still glowing. But still the presence kept coming. We had backed up slowly and were almost at the steps to the house now. The presence was nearly upon us. I could no longer hold the dogs, and Max launched himself snarling and snapping, but the presence kept moving forward.

Maggie Mae turned to face me, smiling, her lips moving, trying to tell me something. She placed her hands on my belly, and then with a flash of light she was gone. Calm descended upon me, and I knew we were going to be okay.

Suddenly Luc appeared beside me, pointed his finger at the presence and it exploded, dissolving into tiny black fragments which floated up into the night air and blew away. I staggered then as a pain gripped my stomach. Luc caught me and swept me up into his arms, and with a sweep of his hand the locked door flew open. He carried me inside, lowered me onto the sofa and sat down beside me.

"What was that? How did you know to come here, Luc?"

"It was a malevolent presence. I have no idea why it was here tonight, but I will make it my business to find out. Max alerted me, but even if he hadn't, your amethyst necklace made me aware of the changes in your body's chemistry and that you were afraid."

"Oh, the necklace." I gripped the amethyst stone hanging around my neck between my thumb and forefinger, rubbing gently. "I'd forgotten about that connection we have. Did you see Maggie Mae? She was here and she tried to help."

"No. I didn't see her. Are you alright?" Luc tipped up my chin to look into my eyes.

"I think I'll be alright when my heart stops beating so fast... oh, oooohhhhh." My stomach contracted again. "I think I'm in labor!" I gripped my stomach with both hands.

"Are you sure? It might be the excitement. What on earth were you doing outside?"

"Cravings. I was going to get some cake from Harper."

"Did you call? Why didn't Aimee bring it over?"

"No, I didn't call. Don't lecture me. It seemed like a good idea at the time. I know now it was foolish." I panted, trying to breathe through the pain.

"I'll let Domenic know to come home. I'll get you a drink of water."

Luc stood up and walked off to the kitchen to get the water. Raven followed him. Max stood guard over me, his eyes never leaving my face. He tilted his head, first to the left, and then the right, unsure of how to handle my obvious discomfort. I'm an unknown quantity to him. He sensed I was in pain but there was no opponent to tackle on my behalf. He moved forward and lay his large head on my lap, his ear against my stomach.

Am I imagining it? Or is he listening to what is going on inside my body.

I placed my hand gently on his large sleek head.

"Good boy, Max. Make sure when this little one arrives you take as good care of her, okay," I whisper.

Max turned his head and nudged my swollen belly with his nose. That was a good enough answer for me.

10

DOMENIC

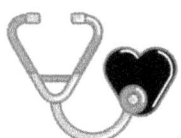

I was getting dressed out of my scrubs when Luc entered my thoughts.

Domenic?

Yes?

Are you nearly finished at the hospital?

Yes why?

Your wife is possibly in labor.

How do you know? Are you there with Sophie?

There was a bit of an incident here tonight and...

What kind of an incident? Is Sophie alright? I'm coming now!

Calm down, she's okay. Yes, I'm here with her. She's had a couple of contractions. It's too early to tell if the baby is coming tonight. I'll stay with her until you get here.

Tell Sophie I will be there as soon as I can. And I want to know about this incident.

I'll tell you later. Sophie wants you here. Drive your car home, it's not that urgent or I would come and get you. I know first stages of labor could take hours. First babies are not in such a hurry.

I'm on my way.

❧

The roads were empty which was a blessing. Once inside the gates of the property I pressed the remote of the garage door and was out of the car and into the house before the door fully descended. Max and Raven were laying at Sophie's feet. I saw Luc standing beside the sofa. We locked eyes, he nodded to acknowledge my arrival and disappeared.

"Are you okay, my love? Are you in a lot of pain? Have you timed the contractions?"

"No, the pain is manageable. I haven't timed them properly. But I'm sure this is it. We're going to be parents soon."

"Have you called the hospital?"

"Yes, they told me not to worry, to stay home unless my water breaks."

"I'll get your bag ready to put it in the car."

"It could take hours. And besides, I have a doctor on hand if things get tricky." Sophie patted my hand.

"I'd feel better if your OBGYN was in the driver's seat. I just want to be the one rubbing your back and feeding you ice chips."

Sophie was gripped by another contraction, and I held her hand and helped her to breathe through it. "What happened tonight? Luc said there was an incident."

"Maggie Mae was here tonight. She tried to help me."

"Help you?"

"I was in the garden..."

"Why did you leave the house at night?"

"I wanted some cake, I had cravings, and I was pretty sure Harper would have some."

"Why didn't you ask Aimee to bring some over?"

"You might have been brought up with servants, but I wasn't. I'm not used to asking someone to fetch me some cake."

"So... Maggie Mae brought you cake?"

"No. There was a dark presence in the garden, an evil presence, that chilled the air and sucked all the light from the pathway. Maggie

Mae appeared, placed herself between me and the... thing... whatever it was... and she tried to dispel it. But it would not leave. Max alerted Luc, and when he appeared he waved his hand, pointed at it, and it exploded into a million pieces. Then it floated off and disappeared."

Another contraction took Sophie's attention, and she closed her eyes and gripped my hand tightly.

"They *are* getting stronger *and* coming faster," she said.

"We should go to the hospital."

"The hospital said to wait until they are five minutes apart and lasting for one minute. Or my water breaks."

"I'll call Mom and Aimee. I'm sure they could offer some advice."

My mother and Aimee arrived, and they arranged the pillows on the couch to make Sophie more comfortable. I went in search of her bag and clothes to take to the hospital. I had nearly finished and was packing Sophie's favorite robe into the suitcase when I heard Sophie yell my name. I raced downstairs.

"What happened?"

"Pain. Strong pain," Sophie said through clenched teeth. Her face was covered in sweat. She was panting.

Aimee beckoned me to come into the hall. She held a stack of clean, white towels.

"There's been a sudden change. The contractions are coming very fast," Aimee said.

"We must get her to the hospital right away. I'll call her doctor." I pulled out my mobile phone.

"There's no time. This baby wants to be born now!" Aimee said, handing me the towels. "You're on. Go deliver your baby."

"You're sure?"

"She's nearly fully dilated, I've checked. This baby wants to come out."

"But her waters haven't broken."

"No matter. One way or another you are about to be a father." Aimee pushed me in the direction of the sofa. "Go help your wife."

My mom was kneeling by the sofa, holding onto Sophie's hand.

Sophie's eyes were tightly closed, and she was breathing through the contraction. Mom moved aside and I took over.

"Sophie darling, Aimee says there's no time to take you to the hospital. We don't want to risk the baby being born in the car on the side of the road. It appears I will be delivering our baby. Don't push. Keep panting."

"This pain. It's so intense. I thought the labor pains were supposed get stronger after hours. It's too quick. Something's wrong."

"Hush darling. It's going to be okay. I need to check to see how dilated you are."

"Here comes another one!"

I examined Sophie and she was indeed ready to deliver.

"Okay, it's time. Push Sophie. Push my love."

It wasn't long before I saw my daughter's head descending. With one massive push and in one swift motion she was delivered into my hands en caul. A unique and surprising event that enthralled me. I saw her features clearly through the thin membrane. Her little legs were pulled up to her chest, arms tucked in, her tiny body resembling a ball inside the unbroken membrane, with the umbilical cord still attached.

"Why isn't she crying?" Sophie asked, as she lay back on the pillow, completely drained from the intense pain of the quick delivery.

"Look darling. Our baby is en caul. She hasn't broken out of the sac."

"Is she okay?" Sophie looked as shocked as I felt. She reached down and touched the soft bubble of amniotic sac, in which our child still floated.

Aimee spread out a thick layer of towels. I snipped the sac with sterile scissors, allowed the fluid to drain onto the towels, and peeled it away from her body. I watched as she uncurled her limbs and let out a cry. I clamped then cut the cord with the sterile knife Aimee handed to me. I sponged and dried her tiny face, lifted our baby onto Sophie's breast and tucked a fresh towel around her. She stopped crying and seemed soothed by the feel of Sophie's skin.

"Hello, Daisy." Sophie cooed.

"She is beautiful. She looks like you." I was both humbled and in awe. I heard my mother and Aimee congratulating both of us and commenting on how beautiful Daisy was and then Luc joined in.

Congratulations, Domenic. Daisy is truly a special gift. She was born en caul. She is indeed a magical child, destined for greatness.

Thank you, Luc. I'm still in shock. I wasn't expecting to deliver her. I was totally unprepared for that emotional experience.

It was better to have happened here, given the circumstance of her birth. We can keep it under wraps. There aren't many en caul births, where the baby is delivered encased in her sac, and we don't want the media sticking their noses into our family business.

Yes. I believe they are very rare.

Indeed, they are. Maggie Mae was right. Daisy is special, even during her birth.

I had better go. My attention should be with my wife and new daughter.

Of course. By the way, I'm proud of you. Of all of you.

Lucia jumped into my head before I had a chance to turn back to Sophie.

Hey big brother. Father just told me. Congratulations. You are officially a father now, too! Who does Daisy look like? Does she have dark hair? Or blonde hair? Or red hair like her mother?

Thanks, Lucia. She is beautiful, like her mother, and she has red hair like Sophie.

I can't wait to see her.

When will that be?

Soon. I'll be back soon. Promise.

11

SOPHIE

*D*aisy was perfect. Ten tiny little fingers and ten tiny little toes. Bright red hair, and lots of it for a baby. Her skin was soft and smelled so good. I could drown in the depth of those big eyes when she looked at me. I didn't have much experience with newborn babies but to me she was the perfect child. She ate and slept and was content, loved a bath, hardly ever cried, and managed to bewitch everyone who set eyes on her.

Domenic was obsessed and didn't want to leave the house to go to work now that Daisy arrived. I'm thrilled to admit he's a hands-on father, taking her on walks around the house and garden, changing her diapers, reading his medical journals aloud to her. When I enquired about his choice of reading material, he said it wasn't important what he reads to her, only that he does, and she could hear his voice. He needed to read them to keep familiar with current practice, and therefore he was applying the two-birds-with-one-stone approach. Trust Domenic to be the practical parent.

As for Harper, I've never witnessed a more besotted grandmother. She even rivals my own mother, who is an old hand at being clucky, having had a few grandchildren already under her wing before Daisy. Oh, don't get me wrong I loved that I had many willing and caring babysitters as it allowed me to have naps during the day without stress. Aimee took over my household duties, and I presume this was also arranged by my kind mother-in-law. It seemed the only function allocated to me was to breastfeed Daisy.

"Have you heard from Lucia?"

"Yes, she wants to see Daisy as soon as Luc allows." Domenic put down his coffee cup and pushed his chair back from the breakfast table.

"It'll be lovely to see her. I know Harper will be thrilled to have her home. Even for a short while."

"Luc's impressed with her stamina. He said she's really putting everything into this role. I'm sure he'll let her visit soon."

"I wonder what it's like for her... down in Hell, I mean."

"Hot, dark, and claustrophobic, I should think."

"There must be some good points to working in Hell or Lucia wouldn't stay. I think you're surmising the conditions based on your own fears."

"It wasn't a fear. More like an absolute denial of it being the right avenue for me to take. I don't want to be immortal. I want to spend the time I have on this earth with you and Daisy, and our future children, and their children, and so forth."

"I'm constantly surprised by the way we can talk about Hell and all that entails, and the conversation flows as if we are talking about Italy or Greece or another international country. Your family must have bewitched me, because I would never have believed all that I have seen or heard was possible a couple of years ago."

"Darling, there's a whole underworld that we are not privy to. To be honest I'm happy not knowing, as long as it doesn't impact you or Daisy."

"I'd better get moving. I'm expected to be with Lisa today. This is the last chance to make any changes to the dresses before the wedding on Saturday. I hope I'll fit into mine."

"Is Mom coming over to look after Daisy?"

"Yes. I'm hoping I'll only be a couple of hours. But I've expressed enough for two feeds if I get caught up, and I'm taking my pump with me."

"I'm picking up my best man's suit after I finish at the hospital this afternoon."

"I'm looking forward to the wedding. It will be good to see Andrew and Lisa married and settled."

LISA'S WEDDING DAY – MAY 2018

"I can't do this!" Lisa said.

I pulled up the zipper on Lisa's dress. Her face was flushed. I asked Nicole the make-up artist to leave the room and give us a few minutes.

"Yes, you can. Sit down for a minute. Just breathe."

"I'll crush my dress."

No, you won't. Sit on the end of the bed with me. Tell me what's really going on."

"It's too soon. He's going to have second thoughts and he's going to realize he's made a mistake and divorce me before our first anniversary. And it's all my fault, cos I pushed the date forward." Tears welled in Lisa's eyes.

"Stop the waterworks, honey. You'll ruin your make-up." I took a tissue from the box on the dresser and gently dabbed at her tears. "It's not too son. Andrew loves you and he's not going to divorce you. But you have to be married before he can divorce you so let's concentrate on that."

"Everyone will be staring at me. I look fat in this dress." Lisa pressed both her hands flat against her stomach.

"No one will be thinking you look fat. You are stunning! Besides they will all be looking at me and wondering how you managed to score such a fabulous best friend and Matron of Honor. Even in this horrible dress you made me wear."

"You look beautiful in the dress I picked for you. It's the perfect shade of blue, the same color as your eyes."

"You would say that. You picked it."

I was secretly thrilled with the sleeveless empire line dress, with the scoop neckline. It had a fitted bodice, from which hung a long column of blue satin. Miraculously this hid the extra weight that remained on my tummy from Daisy's birth.

I collected the blue garter from the dresser, knelt, slid it onto her foot and pushed it up above her knee. I straighten her dress, pulled her to her feet and placed her cream satin heels where she could slip them on.

"And your diamond necklace is perfect with your dress Sophie. You wore that on your own wedding day," Lisa slid her feet into the shoes and immediately became taller.

"I did indeed. It brought me luck and I wanted to bring that luck to your special day." I tied the slender white satin ribbon her mother had given me, in a bow around her wrist and tucked it up under her sleeve.

"You have something old. The hair ribbon from your confirmation which your mother kept for you. You have something new, your dress, and something blue, your garter. Now we need something borrowed. And I have the perfect thing." I picked up my purse and found the scrap of lace handkerchief Maggie Mae had given to me at my wedding. I bent down and tucked it into her garter.

"I can't possibly take this. What if I drop it, and it gets lost."

"You won't drop it. And I'll retrieve it after the ceremony. Now let's call in Nicole and refresh your lipstick."

When Nicole was done, I turned Lisa toward the full-length mirror on the wall, and she finally saw the finished product. Her simple empire-line, cream, damask gown with long fitted sleeves, and vee neckline enhanced her figure and offset her dark hair, which was coiled on the back of her head, pinned, and dotted with pearls and tiny cream flowers. The tiara atop her head, which was also encrusted with pearls, held her short veil in place. Nicole had done a magnificent job with the makeup, she looked stunningly beautiful.

"I see what you did there. Distracting me." She cupped my cheek. "I love you, Sophie."

"I love you too." I handed her the bouquet of cream roses, dotted with lush green foliage, and brought her short veil from the back, down over her face, taking care to avoid her lipstick. "Now let's find your father and get you married."

The newly married couple took to the dancefloor for their first dance. I knew the butterflies in Lisa's stomach would be flapping around, just as mine had been, worried I might stand on Domenic's feet, or make a wrong step in the waltz when the spotlight was on us. Domenic came up behind me and put his arms around me, holding me tight, nuzzling my ear.

"Shall we dance?"

"Love to." I slid my hand into my husband's and walked to the middle of the dancefloor to join the happy couple. Then both sets of parents joined us before the MC invited everyone on to the floor.

"You look tired." Domenic looked into my eyes. "But you look happy."

"I am. It's been a long day, and nearly time to feed Daisy, then blissful bed. But I'm happy they're married, I'm happy the wedding ceremony went without a hitch, and that I talked Lisa down off the ledge."

"Really? She was having second thoughts?"

"It's normal. She wanted to get married for sure, but she was nervous. Jack up the percentage of nervousness to a million on your wedding day."

"Were you? Nervous I mean?"

"Terribly. I was worried I'd walk down the aisle and you wouldn't be there. I was fine when I saw your face smiling back at me."

"I couldn't have wiped the smile off my face if I'd tried. You were so beautiful, and I found it hard to believe how lucky I was to be standing there, holding your hand, looking into your eyes, and knowing without a shadow of a doubt that you were my soul mate."

"Awww, honey. What a lovely thing to say."

"I knew from the moment we first kissed that you were the only one for me. Although I did have a sneaky suspicion at the hospital that first day that there was something special about the way you looked at me. Come on, admit it. You were into me."

"Full of yourself, aren't you."

"Am I wrong? That first day there was something between us."

"Okay. I'll admit you had me curious. And I did ask around to see if anyone had some intel on you."

"It's just as well we were both interested then. Now look at us. An old married couple, with a baby and maybe another one on the way next year."

"Whoa. Hang on. Let me get used to being able to tie my own shoelaces, and not having a watermelon strapped to my stomach, for a little while longer."

"I guess I can wait. But just look at the beautiful baby we made together. It would be a sin not to give her a brother, or a sister. Or both."

"I'm changing the subject now. Your mom has been an angel today, taking care of Daisy, and making sure I had some privacy when feeding. She stood guard on the door and wouldn't let anyone in."

"I'm sure she loved being in charge."

"They are lucky. Jetting off to Italy tomorrow. Although Lisa's not as excited about visiting all the Italian relatives her family have arranged. I have a funny feeling that Lisa and Andrew will have a change in plans, mid honeymoon."

"Funny you should mention that. I know a secret that I can now share with you. As long as you promise not to tell Lisa."

"Cross my heart."

"They aren't going to Italy. Andrew has booked the Seychelles for their honeymoon. He knew she's always wanted to go there."

"She's going to be beside herself. I won't tell her. Promise." I was going to have to keep that secret later, when I helped her to get changed out of her wedding dress.

"Mom has arrived back at the table with Daisy."

"It's time to feed her. Maybe it would be nice to ask your mum to dance while I'm gone."

"Good idea. I'll do that."

§•

In the driveway of the hotel, we waved off the happy couple, and made our way back to our hotel room. I was glad Domenic had booked two rooms for the night and we were not rushing back home at this hour. Harper handed Domenic our sleeping baby and waved to us as she closed the door of her own room. We walked down the hall. As soon as I was inside our room, I thankfully kicked off my shoes and stretched out like a starfish on the king-sized bed. Domenic placed five-week-old Daisy, who was snug inside a blanket, into the cot the hotel had provided.

"The kindest thing would be to let you sleep in those clothes, but that's not going to happen. Let me help you get undressed." Domenic took my hands and pulled me into a sitting position. He tugged down the zip of my dress, sat behind me, slid the dress down and placed kisses along my shoulder blades. Tired as I was, my nipples hardened into peaks, and I knew I wanted him. His competent hands flicked off my bra and cupped my heavy breasts.

"Is that okay?" he asked, teasing my nipples with his fingertips.

"Yes."

"You looked stunning today it was hard to keep my hands to myself."

"You looked very handsome too, in your suit."

"I want you, Sophie. The doctor in me knows I should wait until you're at least six weeks postpartum. I know that's in a few more days. But I can't wait. Even though you're tired and even though you're probably thinking 'just let me sleep'. I miss you and I want to make love to you, slowly, tenderly, to worship your body, inch by inch, cover you with kisses and bring you to the most delicious orgasm..."

I stopped his speech and pulled his face around to kiss his lips. If I could have enveloped him inside my heart at that moment I would have. I loved him more and more each day, totally and deeply, and with that thought came the profound knowledge that I always would. But for now, I would be happy for him to make me swoon with his sweet and tender kisses, make love slowly, tenderly, as he said he would, and then we could happily fall asleep in each other's arms.

12
LUCIA

The stack of files on my desk was growing by the hour. Who knew there would be so many degenerates arriving on a Tuesday, of all days. Saturday was a big day, I knew, and Sunday was on a par, after the wild parties on Saturday nights. Monday's intake was smaller, and Tuesday was usually a quiet day for me, before the influx of new attendees ramped up again on a Wednesday. Tuesday was my day to tick off all the things I'd accomplished in the previous week, to kick back and take a breather. My day to stroll down to admitting and see if anyone took my fancy to tease or to torture with a walk by. I'm not sure which one I enjoyed more. My new body was a wonderful instrument of pleasure and pain. The inmates got a little crazy and lusted after me, I have no doubt about that. It seemed I exuded powerful pheromones when aroused. Walking amongst the new Hell dwellers gave me a buzz like no other. Of course, until they were processed, they were chained to the walls and couldn't get to me, but the older guards knew what I was doing, and they enjoyed watching the newbies fighting to be free to even touch my boots.

It was a shame I couldn't channel this sexual energy. There were some seriously handsome demons I would have loved to play with. It was frustrating but my father insisted I stayed celibate down here during my probation. *No fraternizing with the guards, Lucia,* he'd announced the first day I was here, much to my chagrin. It wasn't surprising I could take care of my own orgasms, thank you, but I did miss skin on skin contact. Perhaps I could remedy that when I was allowed to visit Domenic and Sophie. I couldn't wait to see Daisy. Something told me she was going to surpass me with her hidden talents. Her parents doted on her, that was natural. But I heard my parents were equally smitten.

"Mistress Lucia, you are wanted in My Lord's office," a demon announced from the doorway. He disappeared down the corridor as quick as his skinny little legs could carry him.

"Drake!" I yelled.

"Yes?" Drake appeared at my door looking less than impressed.

"I've been summoned. Do you know why?"

"Should I?"

"Let me rephrase that. Have I done something lately to annoy the population down here? Do you know?"

"Constantly. But I have no idea if that's why you've been summoned."

I brushed by him on the way out of the office, enjoying his swift intake of breath as my thigh touched his. It wasn't my fault he had muscular thighs. Drake hated me invading his personal space, which is why I did it as often as I could. I could almost hear the brain cells exploding in sheer frustration that he cannot keep me at arm's distance. Correction, if he had his way, I would be on the surface, and he would be happier down here without having to teach me. He saw it as babysitting. I saw it as pure unadulterated teasing pleasure.

Rourke greeted me outside my father's office and handed me a slip of paper. My father's voice boomed through the closed door and thick walls, reverberating in Rourke's small office space. I was glad he wasn't yelling at me.

"Your father has had to attend to other matters. He told me to give you this leave-pass. He thought you would like to visit your family and see Daisy."

"I wasn't expecting this. Thank you, Rourke. Please tell my father I'm very grateful. I'll leave within the hour."

I'm sorry Lucia, something unexpected came up. Rourke gave you the leave-pass?

Yes, thank you.

It has been brought to my notice that a demon working for me on earth has not been applying himself. I want you to take over his assignment.

Really?

He was the night manager at a cheap hotel, but he took advantage of his position and wasn't collecting souls as he should've been.

I'm flattered that you thought of me.

It's not a salubrious establishment I'm afraid. And you'll have to change into a body more suitable to the position.

I can do that.

Prove to me that you can handle this role and I will find something more exciting for your next assignment.

Thank you.

Enjoy your time Earthside.

I returned to my quarters, gathered up my personal belongings and stuffed them into an overnight bag. Devil knows when I would be returning, but I was excited about my first assignment. And I get to meet Daisy.

"Oh. My. Devil. She's gorgeous... aren't you little Daisy. She looks like you Sophie. Although she does have a certain je ne sais quoi, which gives me the impression that she'll grow to be more like you, Dom, when she's older."

"Thanks, Lucia. Coming from you, I'll take it as a compliment. Though I'm perfectly happy if she looks like her beautiful mother, and will continue to do so," Domenic said.

"I wanted to bring her a gift, but there are no gift shops in Hell."

"We have everything we need. It's lovely to see you, Lucia. Can you tell us how you are getting on down in... Hell?" Sophie asked.

"I'm quite surprised at how easily I've fit into the new job and accommodation. I know I drive the other demons crazy. But that's a perk of the job if you ask me. Father is pleased with my progress. Hence my visit to you. I'm to start collections. He's allocated me to a hotel on the other side of the city. I'm the new night manager. The hotel has a bad reputation and there should be many souls ready for the taking."

"I presume you're back in your old room at mom's until then?" Domenic asked.

"Yes, for a couple of days. I was planning on heading into town tonight. Cameron has offered to drive me. There's a party I'd hope to gatecrash. I heard that at least one of my ex-boyfriends will be there."

"But they won't know you in this body."

"Yes. And that's half the fun. Now, can I have a hold of my niece before I disappear for the rest of the day?"

Sophie placed Daisy gently in my arms. She opened her eyes wide and looked straight at me. There is no doubt in my mind that this child sees me for exactly who I am.

"Well little one. You have big shoes to fill. An ancestor of a famous Irish witch and a connection to the Devil makes me think there are interesting times ahead." Goosebumps appeared on my arms, and a shiver raced down my spine. I heard the words *"All in good time"* I'm certain that it's Daisy who is communicating with me.

The party was in full swing when Cameron dropped me off, cars lined up along the curb, and the house lights on in every room. I recognized a few old school mates on the front porch, who appeared to be swapping college football stories, and drinking what I assumed was beer in paper cups. As I climbed the front steps, they parted like the Red Sea to allow me to pass. One particularly tall jock I did not recognize, wearing a football jumper to prove to everyone that he's an excellent physical specimen, stepped in front of me and barred my way.

"This is an invitation only party."

"And you are?"

"Steve. The host. Who are you?"

"The entertainment," I said. I leant forward and whispered. "It's a surprise."

"I didn't pay for entertainment."

"Don't worry. This one's on me." I pulled aside the lapel of my black overcoat to expose a slice of lacy red bra and my ample cleavage. His eyebrows rose, but he stood aside to let me pass.

Although I had diminished my height to a more reasonable stature for a tall woman, there were a lot of curious looks, seeing a more mature woman in what was, essentially a teenage party, but no one else questioned me. In the kitchen I helped myself to one of the paper cups lined up on the bench and confirmed my suspicion of its contents. I sipped the beer as I wandered through the rooms looking for Paul, a particularly handsome ex-boyfriend who had a reputation for womanizing and had cheated on me with at least one other friend in our group. When I confronted him, he'd spread rumors about me being a dud in bed. I didn't waste another second in his company back then and kicked him to the curb in search of other boys to play with.

I found Paul dancing with a cute blonde in the living room. There was a DJ, music was pumping, and the bass of the sound system pulsed through the floor. I put down my empty cup and moved up behind him, my body touching his, swaying with the tempo. He turned, and his scowl changed into a smirk when he saw me. The cute blonde wasn't impressed however, she shot daggers in my direction.

"Aren't you too old for a freshman party?" she asked.

"Baby, it's cool," Paul said, turning around, and fully appraising me. He was clearly dumping cute blonde for, what was in his eyes, a more experienced woman.

"You want a piece of this?" he asked, arms spread wide. "I'm all yours." He wrapped his arms around me.

"Pig!" cute blonde yelled, punching him in the shoulder, and storming off.

Paul was tall, but now in my new body I was his height. His dancing left a lot to be desired, but the music slowed down and I started to enjoy the feeling of his arms around me. Until I had a tap on the shoulder.

"You're the entertainment. Entertain!" Steve stood behind me, arms crossed over his chest. He had his entourage from the front porch in tow. "Show us what's under that coat."

"You're a stripper?" Paul sounded amazed and yet delighted.

I positioned a dining room chair in the middle of the room and, with a flourish of my hand, and a slight bow, I invited Steve to sit on it. A crowd had formed, and they moved back, pushing furniture away to create an open space. He took up a relaxed position in the chair, legs akimbo, smirking at me. The crowd appeared curious, and the music changed again to one with a throbbing beat, building anticipation.

I danced, unbuttoning my overcoat slowly, one button at a time. Flipping it off one shoulder, then back. Then the other shoulder and back. I held the front lapels, and let it slide a little down my back. Then lowered my arms and allowed it to fall to the floor. I kicked it away. I laughed at the sharp intake of breath of those around me. In a red lacy bra and tiny red thong, there was more of me on show that covered up. I pulled out the two red silk scarves I had tucked into the top of my black leather stiletto knee high boots, took both of Steve's hands and tied them behind his back and then to the chair. He tried to cop a feel, but I dodged it.

"No touching allowed," I whispered in his ear. I flicked his earlobe with the tip of my tongue and was rewarded with a slight moan.

"Aww come on!" he protested.

I moved around him, gyrating my hips, offering my cupped lace covered breasts for his appreciation. I could see the effect this performance was having on him. He looked to be well endowed within the confines of his jeans. The other guys in the room were also enjoying this dance. However, Paul looked annoyed.

I brought over another chair and positioned it opposite to Steve and offered it to Paul. The crowd moved back. He couldn't sit in it quick enough.

"I don't have any more scarves. How about you remove your belt for me."

I fastened his hands to the chair behind his back with his belt and made sure it was extra tight. I shimmed between the two chairs. I bent down toward my toes, running my hands up one leather covered calf and gave Steve a good look at my breasts, while also giving Paul a very close and personal look at my derriere. I heard more than one moan in the room. I flicked off one bra strap. Then the next. I took my time in releasing the clasp, and allowing the bra to dangle, clinging to the swell of my beasts. One little shimmy and the bra was gone. I heard more than one exclamation around the room. I couldn't blame them. My new She-Devil breasts are now magnificent. Luscious, if I do say so myself. High and full and firm with protruding dark nipples. Every man's fantasy.

I shimmied and gyrated between the two chairs, coming closer, but never close enough. I could see the sweat on the faces of them both. It was time to end this in a way that would give me the most satisfaction. I straddled Paul's lap, rubbed my breast on Paul's cheek, allowing the nipple to slide close to his mouth then pulled away. I looked him in the eye and said, "Tell me your heart's desire?" His expression was one of sheer terror. I held up my hand, palm toward the DJ and the music stopped.

"I want to suck Steve's cock so badly." The words were said between clenched teeth, as he tried in vain to stop them from being announced. But you could have heard a pin drop. All eyes were on Paul. I stood up, flicked the belt restraining him with my fingertips, and it fell to the floor.

"Go on then, Paul. He's all yours." I immobilized the crowd around the three of us with a flourish of my hand. They could see but they could do nothing to stop it. Paul fell to his knees between Steve's legs, unable to stop his desire from being fulfilled, and proceeded to undo the fly of his jeans. Steve fought to get away from him, hurling abuse, the chair tipped, and they both ended up on the floor. Paul was grappling to open Steve's jeans, tugging them down off his hips. Steve's erection was evident for the world to see.

"I think he doth protest too much," I said. Obviously, this idea was turning Steve on more than he wanted to admit, but his teammates were there for the show.

I picked up my coat and pulled it on, stuffed my bra into my pocket, made my way to the door, and unfroze the crowd. I left them to either watch the tug of war or stop it. I think Paul was going to have some explaining to do to the Captain of the Football team, and a reputation he was going to have to either confirm or deny. I wanted to teach him it wasn't fun to spread rumors, and after tonight, there would be plenty going around about him.

Either way, I had a fun night.

13

LUCIA

JUNE 2018

*I*t sure felt strange to be back in my old room again. Mom was trying hard to make me welcome back home, and Aimee had outdone herself with meals and treats for me, but I realized that not only had I evolved on the outside, I also evolved internally. It was as if I had the wisdom of the ages running through me. Facts and figures, details I couldn't have read about or heard from the media kept running through my brain. My skills had intensified. My ability to see through people was becoming stronger every day, to see their essence, to judge their hearts. Sometimes I just brushed by a person and captured their whole history, good and bad, from the time they were born. It all happened in a flash, and sometimes it appeared with a video reel of a particularly bad episode of their depravity.

Was this how Domenic had lived his life? I knew he was averse to touching because of the download of medical information. What a burden this must have been for a child to carry. It gave me a new appreciation of my brother and made me even happier I took on this role and saved him from more stress. His family needed him now. He needed to be a solid presence in his daughter's life. I was curious about Daisy though. There was more to that baby than met the eye. What secrets did that child hold within her?

"Good morning, Mom. Aimee, I'll just have coffee to take to my room while I get dressed and be on my way."

"And good morning to you too Lucia. You can't be in that much of a hurry? Aimee has made breakfast for you. Your favorite cheese, onion, and red pepper omelet, with extra chili."

My mother was dressed in a soft lemon kimono, her hair pulled up on top of her head in a messy bun. She appeared relaxed and happy. She never ceased to amaze me with how chic she looked, even early in the morning. She took a sip of her coffee.

"I'm going downtown to check out my new workplace," I said.

"Sit. Please. Eat your beautifully prepared breakfast. Indulge me for a few minutes." Resigned to my fate, I accepted the plate of food placed Infront of me with a smile.

"Thank you, Aimee. it looks and smells delicious."

"I realize you're leaving here tomorrow to fulfil your next assignment, but will you promise to come back from time to time. Your room's always ready for you."

"Of course. Unfortunately, I can't tell you when that will be. I'm afraid you might have to get used to me dropping by now and again unannounced."

"I can handle that. I miss you, Lucia. I want you to know that."

"I miss you too Mom. But I'm excited by what's happening to me. I wish I could explain what I'm feeling inside."

"Oh, I understand. I was young once."

"No Mom. It's not the same. I'm sure I'm experiencing things through my father's DNA. It's as if I have a tutor inside my brain, constantly feeding me information, like he's teaching me about this world and beyond. My brain is growing. Yes, I know people could say 'she's always been big headed'... and now I *feel* big headed. Sometimes the weight of it all appears too heavy for me to contain. Does that make any sense?'

"I understand. I think," Aimee said. "When Cameron and I passed over and did our time in the Underworld, we absorbed a lot of information over time. When your father chose us both to come back here to protect the family he loved, he gave us extra powers and all the facts and figures about this modern world. We had worked for intelligence in the Army. He thought that adjusting would be easy for Cameron and me. We both had to absorb a million details quickly, and I was sure I was going insane with all the information bombarding me. Cameron was better equipped to handle it, but we both struggled."

"Maybe I should talk to your father if this is too much for you Lucia."

"No! I need to prove I'm up for the task. I'm getting stronger. I'm getting better. I need to do this. If this is a test, I need to show him I'm capable. Please. Not a word."

"Alright. If you say so. I'd better go and get dressed. I'm babysitting Daisy today."

"Good luck with that. Give my best to Sophie and Domenic."

The building looked run down, I could see that in its heyday it would have been a nice establishment, somewhere you'd be happy to stay for a few days, seeing the sights and wandering around Hollywood's landmarks. Or maybe a couple's special weekend treat, having dinner and taking in a movie. Looking at it now, I couldn't imagine why anyone would want to stay here, for even an hour. Although I heard certain rooms were being rented out 'by the hour' to the local street walkers. Those rooms were positioned at the back of the building, convenient to the car park and near to an emergency exit. Handy if the clientele didn't want to be recognized. Most of the businesses nearby were either dingy shop fronts, fast food premises or boarded up and tagged so badly no one would want to venture near them.

My father had demonstrated the numerous advantages in tailoring my visual appearance to fit into the surroundings, and I've become more adapt at morphing my body's shape and features. I was wearing a crisp white business shirt, black fitted skirt, and low black pumps. I've adapted my body to what I consider appropriate for this lowly paid position. Medium height, average weight, dark blonde hair sitting on my shoulders, glasses with dark frames and a face most people would consider semi-attractive. But not too attractive. I want to blend in, be unmemorable if guests are questioned later. My father had given me instructions, and I intended to follow them to the letter. My mission was to gather as many reprobate souls as possible, and get them to sign on the dotted line. I didn't think it was going to be too hard, judging by my surroundings.

I approached the receptionist and asked to speak to the Manager, Ray Walsh.

The woman's name tag said "Peta". She looked me up and down, picked up the handset of the phone on the desk and pressed a few buttons. After a brief conversation, Ray appeared from a corridor to my left. I had dressed in what I thought was appropriate attire to meet my employer. However, I was expecting a more salubrious hotel when dressing at home, and the bemused expressions on both their faces confirmed my rookie mistake.

"What can I do for you? Whatever it is you're selling we ain't buyin', honey," Ray said.

"I came to introduce myself. I'm Lee Edwards. Your new night manager. The employment agency said they would give you all the details."

"You sure aren't what I was expecting."

"What were you expecting?"

"A man, to start with. Someone older, someone with some hotel experience."

"I have experience. But what I don't have in years I have in ability to learn quickly. I can help you grow your business."

"A babe in the woods like you? I doubt if you are going to have what it takes to manage the night shift. We get some unsavory characters in here. The night manager sometimes needs to get physical. I don't think you could..."

I took his hand, turned his palm skyward, flexed his wrist back and pushed it down hard. With a couple of quick moves Drake had shown me, Ray was on his knees, his face showing his surprise, and I was towering above him. It was a simple example. My glasses had slipped down my nose. I let go of his hand to push them back again. I could have demonstrated how I could also hurt him, but then I didn't think I'd be employed at the end of the day. I held out my hand to help him up. He ignored it and got to his feet.

"Okay. You can handle yourself. Let's talk about the job requirements in my office." Ray placed his hand in the small of my back and guided me toward the corridor to his office.

As I brushed by her, Peta gave me "side eye". I didn't blame her. Ray's hand was moving dangerously close to the swell of my buttocks, and she had no idea that I would rather have cut off my arm than have touched him. But needs must when you had to prove a point. My newly devilish intuition told me their affair had been going on for years, and the only reason she stayed working for him was her need to care for her disabled mother and very elderly father.

I learned quickly which regulars came to the hotel with the working girls. I selected those most corruptible and composed a secret file with names, ages, credit card details, in addition to their home addresses, which I acquired from a particularly friendly cop who had soft spot for my Lee Edwards persona. He was a regular drop-by, arranged by Ray to make sure things were running smoothly, and I wasn't getting into trouble. The regulars, most of whom were married or partnered, would not want their private sexual exploits to be broadcast to the world, and they often registered under other names.

To my amazement the hotel did a roaring trade in the middle of the night. I wondered what their excuse would have been to leave their home and travel downtown for some highly questionable anonymous sex. I also wondered why they just didn't leave the marriage and find a more suitable bed partner, rather than pay for it. Peta explained that the monetary and psychological cost involved in a messy divorce would put them off. Peta had become my friend once she realized I was no threat to her relationship with Ray.

To get her off my back, I told her I preferred women.

14

LUC

JULY 2018

*O*n the odd occasion when I observed Lucia behind the Veil, I was surprised and delighted by how well she was managing her first assignment. I'd been keeping an eye on her because Harper was concerned, and I promised I'd make sure no harm came to her. But I was impressed by her tenacity, her ability to blend in, and the connections she'd made all by herself, without any help from me.

If I had to be totally honest, I hadn't expected her to last this long in the unattractive hotel with its unsavory clientele. Rourke told me that the demons have calmed down in Hell and the status quo has been restored since Lucia has been earthside. I wasn't not sure if that was a good or a bad thing. It was time to shake them up a bit, and Lucia did put some things in place which Rourke admitted had been useful. Some of the younger demons had shown a desire to take on more responsibility. They demonstrated the talents they had when living on earth. Made improvements. And that was down to Lucia's influence. Yes, she ticked people off. They didn't like a woman telling them what to do or voicing her opinions of the antiquated system. But she had also brought a breath of fresh air to the stale, unfiltered, rank smelling, sulfur-infused caverns of Hell.

15
SOPHIE

OCTOBER 2018

*D*aisy was growing fast. I missed the tiny baby who was so dependent on me. She was sitting up now, rocking back and forth on her knees, and very soon she'd be crawling and getting into mischief. She lit up my life, and everyone who saw her commented on her bright and happy demeanor. Of course, Domenic was besotted with her. Daisy had twisted her father around her little finger, there was nothing he wouldn't do to keep her happy.

"Where's my big girl? I'm so happy to see you." Domenic reached down into the playpen on the floor and swept Daisy up into his arms. He nuzzled her neck. She giggled and grabbed handfuls of his dark hair in her tiny fists.

"Don't get her too excited. It's nearly time for bed."

Domenic reluctantly placed Daisy back down on the blanket in the playpen.

"I hate coming home late. I would rather be here for dinner and her bedtime routine, but the operation went on longer than anyone anticipated."

"Complications?" I walked into the kitchen to get a glass of water. Domenic followed me.

"Yes. And I'm not sure that this will be his last operation. My patient's in a pretty bad way."

"I'm so grateful my dad hasn't needed any more heart ops. Although my folks are getting older, and I imagine there may be health issues to face in the future."

"Both of your parents are healthy for their age. Never fear. There's nothing in their physical body to cause any concern for the time being."

"I sometimes forget that you continue to get their medical download when my parents visit us."

"Unless I'm holding your hand, or you're touching me at the same time, this happens routinely when your mother kisses my cheek, or your father shakes my hand. This is the way I've lived my life."

"I wonder if Daisy has inherited any of your family quirks?"

"Quirks? That's an interesting way to put it."

"Well then, magical abilities."

"Since Maggie Mae was a witch, it's also possible she would inherit magical abilities from your side of the family.

I returned to the living room and noticed Daisy had rolled over, was on her knees and was rocking back and forth, intent on crawling to reach a toy elephant in the corner of the playpen. I turned my head away for a second and when I turned back Daisy was sitting in the same spot but holding the grey plush toy in her chubby little hands. I looked around for Domenic. He was still in the kitchen. Did I imagine that? Or did she somehow crawl to the toy and then back again?

"Domenic. I think Daisy's crawling."

"What do you mean you "think"?"

"I didn't see her crawl, but she's holding a toy that wasn't near her."

"You missed seeing our daughter crawl for the first time?"

"Apparently."

Domenic went over and took the stuffed toy from Daisy and placed it a few feet away.

"Go get it, honey."

Daisy looked at me, then at Domenic. She didn't move.

"Maybe it was nearer than you thought, and she reached out for it?" Domenic returned to sit on the sofa beside me.

"I know what I saw. She would've had to crawl to get it... Domenic. Look!"

We both turned around and Daisy was sitting in the same spot, now holding the toy elephant.

"Wait a minute." Domenic took the toy and placed it outside the playpen on the carpet. He returned to sit on the couch. We watched. Nothing happened.

"Is your father here playing tricks on us perhaps?"

"No, Sophie. This is something else. Turn away."

We both looked away, then turned back around at the same time. The toy was back inside the playpen, in Daisy's chubby little hands. She was making baby noises, mumbling something at the elephant, shaking it around.

"That answers your question. Our daughter is moving the toy by herself."

"I don't believe it."

"I've seen this before."

"When?"

"When Lucia was a baby. She would move things around. Bring things to her. Conjure up fruit, transported it from the bowl in the kitchen."

"This was not how I saw the baby years. I was worried about her falling and bumping into things. Scraping her knees. Losing a tooth. Not conjuring up miscellaneous items into the playpen. What if she brings something that could harm her. I'm going to have to watch her every moment!"

"Let's talk to my mother. She might have some advice. After all, she's been through it with Lucia."

"Good Idea. Get her on the phone. Better still. Ask her to come over, please?

My anxiety is at dangerous levels."

Domenic took his mobile phone out of his jacket pocket and walked off to have a conversation with Harper. I sat staring at my child and wondering what other tricks she had up her sleeve. This was a dangerous world, where my baby could magically move things at will. Could she move people as well? No, no, no. This wouldn't do.

"Mom's coming over. I'm sure once you talk to her, you'll feel calmer."

❧

"Let me get this straight. You're telling me there is nothing I can do except watch her like a hawk?"

"Sophie, I know it sounds terrifying that your child is capable of things you cannot control, but you do get used to it, and you can teach her to be careful. Just as you'll teach her how to walk and how to talk." Harper laid a reassuring hand on my arm.

"You had Aimee to help you watch Lucia. I don't have that luxury."

"I'm sure Aimee would be happy to spend more time here with you and Daisy. If that would make you feel better?"

"I can't do that. You need Aimee."

"I'm rattling around in that big empty house. No one is making it untidy. Aimee would be happy to help during the day. Then in the evenings Domenic is home, and there are two parents to watch over her."

"That's a good solution for the time being, Mom." Domenic held Daisy on his knee. She clutched the elephant to her chest.

"Time for Daisy to go to bed," I said.

Domenic gave her a final hug. I picked her up and Harper said goodnight and kissed her cheek. I carried her upstairs to the nursery where I breastfed her, and changed her diaper before laying her in the cot and turning on the camera. I left the elephant in the cot beside her, hoping that was the only thing she wanted to play with tonight. When

I returned to the living room Luc was also there talking to Harper and enjoying a glass of wine. Domenic appeared from the kitchen with a mug of herbal tea on a tray.

"I thought you might need this." Domenic placed the tray on the table by my chair.

"I'd like something stronger, but tea will do for now. Hello Luc. Who summoned you? Domenic or Harper?"

"Harper. It just so happens I was planning to visit. Domenic has explained what happened earlier. I find it unusual to say the least because telekinesis wasn't one of Domenic traits when he was a child. Only Lucia. I don't think this talent is coming from our side of the family through Domenic."

"I don't remember ever being able to move things through the air. I don't think it's my side of the family."

"Really? You have witches in your side of the family tree. And you're a direct descendant. Maybe it's Maggie Mae moving the toys, and not Daisy. Have you seen any evidence of her lately?"

"No. I haven't seen any evidence of Maggie Mae since the night in the garden. The night Daisy was born."

"Interesting. Can I have a word with Maggie Mae, Sophie? Do you mind?"

"I don't understand?"

"Relax. Remember Maggie Mae tagged along inside you for many years. I want her to come out and talk to me. Maggie Mae. Are you here with us?"

I felt nothing. Everyone was staring at me waiting for something to happen.

"Looks Like Maggie Mae has moved on." Luc stood and finished his wine. "Time to leave. Keep me updated." He disappeared.

16

LUC

I had a feeling that Maggie Mae had found a new home. I visited the nursery and watched through the Veil. Daisy was sound asleep, the elephant tucked in by her side. I didn't want to wake her. Plenty of time to see if my assumption was true. Aimee would spend more time here and report back to me with what she sees. I remembered some interesting times with Lucia when she was a baby. It looked like Domenic and Sophie would have to be extra vigilant with Daisy over the next few months.

I returned to Hell.

17

LUCIA

*I*t had been a long night. The hotel was unusually busy for a Thursday, and I'd hardly any time to think about how tired I was until now. Weariness sucked at my body, and I was glad to be heading to the tiny one-bedroom apartment I'd found near the hotel just after I took on the position as Lee Edwards. I welcomed a few hours' sleep. It took quite a bit of effort to maintain my altered human form for an extended period. I was getting better at it, and I imagined that in time it will become second nature.

While making my way through the parking lot, I dropped my keys beside a car, and bent down to pick them up. When I stood up, I bumped into a tall woman, with shoulder length blonde hair, wearing a tan trench-coat, and coming from the opposite direction. She grabbed onto my arm to steady herself. Immediately I had a surge of information download, flowing through her touch. A wave of sadness, fear and utter desperation hit me like a ton of bricks. I saw flashes of this poor woman's life and experienced her pain. She let go of my arm, and I was brought swiftly back to the present. I could see she was upset and had been crying.

"Oh, I'm sorry, I didn't see you down there." She brushed by me and carried on walking through the rows of cars.

"Wait! Are you alright?" I called out to her. She turned back around to face me.

"What? I'm sorry?"

"You're upset. Are you hurt? Has someone hurt you?"

"That would be an understatement!" She half-laughed, half-sobbed. Fresh tears welled up in her eyes.

I looked around the parking lot for the perpetrator. We were the only two souls.

"I must go. I'll be late for my shift at the diner." She turned and headed in the direction of the street.

Something about this woman had me following her at a distance, through the parking lot and into a modest diner tucked away on a nearby side street. Contrary to this neighborhood, the interior appeared clean, bright and well maintained. The vinyl booths and laminated tabletops, although old, sparkled under the strip lighting. The 1960's pastel color scheme was restful and inviting. Only a few tables were occupied with people enjoying coffee and donuts or plates loaded with breakfast food. I chose an empty booth away from the other diners, tucked into the corner. The woman was nowhere to be seen. Delicious aromas wafting from the kitchen made my stomach grumble. I picked up a menu and scanned the printed contents. I glanced up to scan a chalkboard mounted on the wall behind the counter, with advertised specials and the pancake of the day. Today's special was "Fire & Brimstone Friday". *Appropriate.*

The woman from the parking lot pushed the kitchen door open and entered the diner, tucking a small notepad and pen into the pocket of her pink checkered apron. When she saw me, she stopped and looked startled. I beckoned her over. She scowled but approached the booth.

"Are you following me? Did he send you to follow me? Is this his new way of punishment?"

"I have no idea what you're talking about. I came to eat."

She looked skeptical but pulled out her pad and pen and waited.

"I'll have the Fire and Brimstone special please. And coffee." I put down the menu. She jotted down my order and turned to walk away.

"Thanks Rachel." She spun around to face me, eyes narrowing suspiciously.

"Your name is written on your name tag," I said.

The delicious breakfast of fluffy scrambled eggs, spicey fried potatoes with extra chili, maple bacon, sausage and tomatoes with a side serve of toast was so good and so filling. I sipped my coffee and waited for Rachel to return to clear away my plates. She began wiping the table of the booth near mine.

"Rachel, can you sit with me for a minute? I want to ask you something."

She reluctantly came to stand beside the booth.

"I don't know what you want from me. I can't sit, I don't want to get fired. I need my job." Rachel glanced over her shoulder to check if she was being monitored.

"Let me ask you a question then." I needed her to look me in the eye. She turned back, looked at me and waited.

"Tell me," I locked eyes with her and asked. "What is your heart's desire?"

"I want him to pay for what he's done to me. I want him to suffer. I want him dead!" Rachel's eyes were wide open, like two saucers. She slapped a hand across her mouth, and backed away from me, terror written all over her face, and disappeared into the kitchen.

I paid the bill, left a generous tip for Rachel, and vacated the restaurant through the front door. I went around the back of the building, and sure enough Rachel was sitting on the outside steps with her head in her hands. When I laid my hand on her shoulder she flinched.

"Rachel, let me introduce myself. My name is Lee Edwards. I work in the hotel down the street. You don't need to be afraid of what you said in there. I'm the one person you can tell, who can help you reach your goal without fear of retribution. And before you say anything let me tell you that this conversation is between the two of us, and only the two of us. I will help you. However, I do seek something in return.

It's not money. It won't cost you anything, not in this lifetime. You can live your life free of this person with no repercussions to you or your children..."

"My children?" Rachel squeaked.

"Yes, you do have children, don't you?" I'd seen two young girls in her video download.

"Yes." She nodded.

"I must leave now, but I want you to think about my proposal and I'll come back tomorrow morning. I can help you to get rid of this man. All you need to do is promise me your soul when you die."

"Isn't that what the Devil asks? I thought the Devil was a man."

"Things are changing, Rachel. Don't you think a woman can do the job just as well, or even better than a man?"

"If I believed you, if I thought I could get away with it and would be free of him, you could have anything you want." She sat up straight and folded her arms over her chest.

"Let me demonstrate." I glanced around to make sure we were alone. I pointed at the dumpster in the alley and it rose about six feet in the air. Her eyes grew wide. I lowered it to the ground again.

"Oh my god. How did you do that? You really are... the Devil?"

"Let's say, just for the sake of it, I'm the Devil's protégé."

Rachel took a few minutes to let this sink in. I could almost see the wheels turning inside her head.

"If I agree to your proposal, you say you can help me without me being involved?"

"Yes."

"I don't need to wait till tomorrow. I agree. What do I have to do."

"I'll need your signature." I extracted a printed contract from my purse. I noted Rachel's left eyebrow rising. "I never leave home without one. Needs must when the Devil drives, as they say. You don't know who you'll meet."

Rachel took the document I offered, removed a pen from her apron pocket and signed away her soul with a flourish of her hand.

"I'll be back tomorrow to make sure you're sticking to your guns. I want you to give some thought about how you would like Mr... What's his name?"

"Let's just call him Aamon for now."

"Okay. How you'd like Aamon to suffer. I'm not squeamish. Don't hold back. You can jot down some bullet points. Don't worry, we'll burn the note once you show me."

"You'll be back here tomorrow? Early?"

"Same time. I work night shift. Now, I must leave you to plot your revenge and go home and get some sleep."

"Of course, I should've guessed the Devil would work night shift. That's why we don't see him during the day."

"Devil's protégé remember. Not the actual Devil, Rachel. The Devil is my father."

"I must be having a bad dream. I'll wake up soon. This can't be real. The Devil's daughter?"

"Why does that surprise you?"

"I've just never imagined a female could be the Devil, although I've met some pretty nasty bitches in my life."

I peeled off Lee Edwards outer garments, walked into the bathroom and turned on the shower. I dropped the bra and panties in the laundry hamper and gratefully stepped under the warm spray. All the night's stress and troubles flowed down the drain with the soapy water. I enjoyed the way I could walk into the shower as Lee and emerge as Lucia. I returned to the bedroom, wrapped in a towel, and sat on the bed with my laptop to update my file. It had been a productive shift at the hotel. I had collected two more souls from men who should have known better than to play hard and fast with other people's money in their company's trust fund.

Meeting Rachel and having her sign on the dotted line this morning had been an unexpected bonus. I had yet to find out all the details, and hear the story in her own words, but the taste of her pain had made me want to bring this man to justice. Even without the promise of her soul, there was something so sinister about Aamon, the female part of me wanted to see him suffer. Too many men are getting away with hurting women who are probably too frightened of the repercussions to report their atrocious behavior. The way the courts crucify women on the witness stand, making them justify their rights to safety, it's no wonder they're gun shy.

I hung up my wet towel, pulled my dark hair free of the hair tie and slid my naked body beneath the cool, cotton sheets. All other thoughts would have to wait until later. It was time to rest.

The next morning, I returned to the diner as promised, although a little later than yesterday, and reclaimed my booth from the previous day, tucked into the corner. The diner was nearly empty, as the break-fast rush had passed. Rachel came out of the kitchen and smiled when she saw me.

"I thought I'd actually dreamt meeting you, and our deal, when you didn't come earlier." Rachel handed me a menu. She looked a lot less haggard than the day before. There was even a twinkle in her eye.

"You look happy to see me. Does that mean you've worked out a plan?"

"I haven't worked out a plan, but I want you to read this first and then we can talk. I need you to understand what Aamon did. What started this downward spiral for me. After I wrote that letter last night I felt better. For the first time in a long time, I feel I can breathe." She handed me an envelope. I tucked it into my pocket without looking at it.

"Sure, I'll read it. We work opposite ends of the day. Can you come to the hotel after ten tonight? I need a photograph and we'll work out when you want me to do, to take extra special care of Aamon." I handed her a business card with the hotel's address.

"I'll have to get a sitter. But I'll break my neck to get there."

"Honey, we don't want you dead before Aamon's demise, do we?

Do the best you can. There's no time limit on this deal. You've already signed on the dotted line. Remember?"

"But it's all I can think about now. I want to do this and finally rid myself of this monster. My girls and I need to be able to live our lives in peace, and without constant fear of another court case. I'm working two jobs to make ends meet cos it's taking nearly every dollar I make to pay my expenses and my legal fees."

"Have you ever thought of doing something else? A job that makes you more money."

"I might look like I have nothing, but I have a degree. He made sure I lost all the well-paid jobs I managed to get. Waitressing and making cakes on the side was what I've had to do to survive. I made those cakes on the counter. That was how I got this job to begin with. I'd better take your order." She glanced back over her shoulder.

"I meant no disrespect. I'll try a piece of the chocolate cake and coffee, please."

"None taken. I wanted to set the record straight. I'm not a dumb blonde."

Rachel delivered my order and I noticed she had piped a little chocolate heart on the plate beside the generous wedge of chocolate cake. I dug my fork into the soft, fudgy treat and raised it to my lips. Delight danced along my tastebuds. Rich chocolate flavor with a hint of coffee hit me, and light whipped ganache in between the layers and on the top melted on my tongue. I was in heaven. I closed my eyes around the second mouthful and moaned.

"That good?" a customer at another table said. "I'll have what she's having."

We both laughed at the movie reference. I know it was made before my time, but my mom made me watch it once or twice when I was growing up.

I gave Rachel me a thumbs up. She certainly was a fabulous baker. I pulled out the letter to read while I sipped my coffee.

Dear Lee,

I feel I need to explain what led to my circumstance and homelessness a couple of years ago. Hence this letter.

I had taken my two girls under ten years old to visit my father who had been unwell. He lives a couple of hours drive outside the city. While I was driving back home, I received a call from Aamon (my husband). He said he would be in the driveway and would take the girls out for some fun when I returned. That was so unlike him I sensed something was wrong. When I pulled up in the drive and tried to open the garage door with the remote it wouldn't work. He approached the car with his hand raised to stop me. I lowered the car window. He told me to get out of the car and that my remote wasn't going to work. He said "You know we've been having problems. I'm leaving you and I'm taking the children. All your stuff is in the garage. I've cut you off the credit card, and I've changed the locks."

He told the girls who were visibly upset, to get into his car. They were afraid of their father but did as they were told. I was in shock. He drove off with my children and I suddenly realized that if I couldn't get into the house, I had only the clothes I was wearing, the car I arrived in and an antiquated mobile phone I was holding which didn't even have internet access.

Our marriage hadn't been great, but I had no idea this was coming. I was in denial. I thought it must be a terrible joke, but when I tried to open the door to the house, it wouldn't open. I started shaking, I couldn't believe this was real. I went back to the car and called my father, who called my lawyer, and my brothers. My lawyer instructed me to get a locksmith, break in and get new locks for the house. My two brothers arrived and called a locksmith.

When we got inside, the locksmith changed the locks and left. None of us could process what we were looking at. There was debris all over the floor. All the furniture had been moved out and only a few tiny pieces that were unattractive or broken had been left. All the bedrooms were empty. All my personal files, my information, my laptop, and my passport contained in my filing cabinet were gone. I didn't even have any paperwork to authenticate who I was to open a new bank account.

Every room had signs of desperation. Every room looked like some madman had gone through it scooping up the best and leaving the worst for someone else to manage. The pantry was completely bare. No food, no drinks, nothing edible in the house. Nearly all the dishes and cutlery were gone. No towels, sheets, or blankets. Looking around me was an assault on the senses, the dirt on the floor where the refrigeration no longer stood, the dust and assorted debris under where the beds had been. The house looked exactly how I felt. Torn apart. Bruised. Violated.

We went into the garage, and some of my clothes and shoes etc had been stuffed into boxes. The old, damaged fridge was wedged into a corner, along with a very old mattress that had been in the garage for some time. My bother wanted me to come home with him, but I needed to go through what was left and see if these boxes contained anything important. I was afraid if I left, I wouldn't get back in. My brothers dragged the old mattress inside. I found a comforter in a packing box. When my brothers left, I wrapped myself in the comforter to sleep that night. But sleep evaded me. Instead, I started to dry retch and felt so sick. He had taken my kids. I was very worried for them, and what they would be feeling. I was so shocked that I couldn't even cry. The dry retching lasted for months. I was told by a professional that I had gone into a post traumatic state. It lasted for at least 12 months. I was scared that he was going to come back and kill me. He had guns, and I was also fearful for my children.

The next day I had to work out what I was going to do. I didn't know where to access paperwork I needed. I was a stay-at-home mom. I had no recent credit history as he was responsible for paying the bills. He was very much a control freak.

I'd owned my own house when I met Aamon. Early in our relationship he coerced me to transfer that property into his name. I couldn't even claim that it was mine to get the tenant to vacate and move in, as it was in his name now.

I spent the first two nights hiding out, scared for my life. I did not put the lights on at night as I was scared that he would realize I was in the house. Two days later he called.

"I know you're back in the house, I've been around there this morning and I see you've gotten in and you've changed the locks," he said.

I listened and said nothing.

"You can stay for the next 2 weeks. Then you'll have to leave. I need to clean the house to vacate the lease," he said.

I felt as if I was doing a deal with the devil. I knew I had fourteen days grace to find somewhere to live.

That was the beginning of a very long road I've had to travel. With my *father's help I found a place to live, and bit by bit I managed to furnish it with things people did not want or from thrift shops. After a long legal battle, we now share custody of the children, one week with their father and one week with me. He has taken me to court if I don't follow the court orders to the letter, even if the reasons are valid. I've lost many well-paid jobs because I've had to take leave for multiple court appearances over trivial things relating to the children. It has taken a lot of money to hire a lawyer and barrister. I have been grateful to receive financial help from my family. He is intent on bankrupting me. Lawyers cost a fortune.*

Now I work in a diner and make cakes at home for birthdays and special occasions. That small side business is making the money I need for the kids' clothing and education. I'm grateful my cakes are very popular, and word of mouth is increasing.

I'm locked into this until the children are older. He takes every opportunity to disparage me to them. I see no way out of the hell I deal with every time he comes near me. I'm still afraid that he will kill me, or something might trigger him to hurt the children.

I wanted you to understand why I want to make sure he gets the 'gift" he deserves.

Rachel

I folded the letter and returned it to the envelope. I looked up to see Rachel behind the counter, watching me. I smiled. She smiled. I nodded. We understood each other.

I was excited to think that Aamon was finally going to get what he deserves.

18

LUCIA

OCTOBER 2018

*L*ucia?

Yes father.

Daisy has been showing signs of telekinesis and since this was something you also had a talent for, I thought it would be good if you would visit your brother and sister-in-law and calm Sophie down.

Interesting. Sure, I'll stop by tomorrow. I have some time off owing to me.

Thanks. I'm sure your mother would also appreciate it.

Apart from moving stuff around has she shown any other interesting habits?

Not that I'm aware of. But you'll need to check with Domenic. As I said Sophie's having a hard time coming to terms with the fact that her adorable baby can move heavy objects. She's worried she might cause herself harm.

I'll let you know how my visit goes.

Excellent.

. . .

I was looking forward to returning to the family home. I knew Mom would be happy to see me and the thought of being in my own body for a whole day and night was liberating. I drove the car up to the gate and called Cameron on the intercom. The solid metal gates slid open, and a beaming Cameron waited on the other side to welcome me home with a wave and an official salute. Aimee stood on the front doorsteps, excitement written all over her face, waiting to give me a tight hug. It was almost worth being away for months to have such a warm welcome home.

"Lucia. It's lovely to see you. Your mother will be beside herself that you're here. How long can you stay? Your room is just as you left it. What would you like for dinner? You are staying for dinner, aren't you?" Aimee's questions tumbled over one another.

"Aimee. It's good to see you too." I laughed. "Yes. I'm staying for dinner. But will probably only be here until tomorrow, or possibly the next day. Where's Mom?"

"In her studio beside the sunroom, painting. I'll make tea. And I have some of those little tarts you like. Go on then, go see your mother." Aimee waved me down the hall and hurried off in the direction of the kitchen.

I made my way to my mother's studio. It always amazed me that I never encountered my mother looking less than put together. She wore a long black skirt and top, with a white paint spattered smock covering it, and the sleeves rolled up to her elbows. Her hair was piled on top of her head with a multicolored scarf, tied securely, to keep it in place. Large gold hoop earrings dangled from her lobes and caught the light reflected through the floor to ceiling windows. She wore dark-framed glasses. They were a new addition and suited her very well.

"Mom you always look like you belong in a studio in Paris when you paint. Was that the aim?"

"Lucia! Darling, it's lovely to see you, and so unexpected. Come over here and let me give you a hug."

"An air kiss might be better. This jacket cost a fortune."

"Get prepared for a hug later when I take off this smock and wash my hands."

"I love the glasses by the way. Very chic."

"My eyesight's not what it used to be. I reneged and ordered some expensive Dior frames. To what do we owe the pleasure of your company?"

"Father asked me to come. He told me that Daisy has started moving things about the place and it makes Sophie very nervous."

"Ah, I see. That's why you're here. I mistakenly presumed it was because you missed us."

"Of course, I miss you. I do. But I'm doing well, getting my numbers up, and making a difference. I want to impress father. This wasn't a planned visit, it was his idea, but I'm glad father gave me the opportunity to come home for the weekend."

"I'm sure you will impress him, Lucia. Ah, here's Aimee with some tea. I see you brought us lemon tarts, Aimee, Lucia's favorite."

"She could do with a bit of spoiling, I'll bet. It's so good to have our girl home, even for a short spell." Aimee dashed away a tear.

"I saw that! No tears. Tell me all about the new little girl in the family. I bet you love having Daisy to spoil, Aimee?"

"I do indeed. She is the most beautiful child. Such a pleasant nature. And those eyes! My goodness. You can lose yourself in those eyes, bottomless pits of blue water, they are!"

"And how are you enjoying being a grandmother, Mom?"

"It's a wonderful thing. You love your children of course, but when they have children of their own, you have a very different love for your grandchildren. Everything they do delights you, even the smallest achievement. But when she started to move things, I must admit I was also concerned. I remembered what it was like when you wanted something badly enough and you literally brought it into your cot or your high chair."

"I don't remember that you were worried, specifically. But I do remember being told on numerous occasions not to share my special talents with anyone outside the family," I took a bite of the flaky pastry and sighed as the lemon filling melted on my tongue. "Delicious, Aimee." I licked my lips. Aimee beamed at me.

"I was lucky because I had Aimee to help me, and we made sure there was always one of us watching you. Until you were old enough to understand of course. You were a very bright child. It didn't take long."

"I'm going to pop over to see Sophie soon." I drank the last of my cup of tea.

"Give me ten minutes to clean up and hang up my painting smock, and I'll come with you."

"We can all go over together. I've a container of chicken soup I wanted to take to Sophie for their meal tonight. And I planned to dig up some potatoes and collect some vegetables from the garden to keep us going for the next couple of days. I'd better bring back some extra now you're here Lucia." Aimee collected the empty cups and stacked plates onto the tray and carried them off to the kitchen.

"It's lovely to see you. You're looking well, Sophie. Although I hear that our little Daisy is keeping you on your toes these days."

"That's a nice way to put it."

"Father thought I could be of some assistance. Although I have my doubts. But I'm here nevertheless to see what I can do. I presume Daisy's sleeping?"

"Yes, she's due to wake up soon. We put a baby monitor in her room. I can hear her and see her when she wakes." Sophie turned the little screen to show me Daisy sleeping peacefully in the nursery.

"Have you noticed anything else?"

"No, nothing unusual. But she's been trying to talk. She's been quite vocal lately. But I image that's normal for a baby her age."

"Is it okay if I go to the nursery and see her before you bring her down?"

"Sure. But she's not used to you, and she might cry."

"I'd like to try something. Don't worry I won't do anything that would upset her. I have a toy I think she might like, and I want to see if she moves it while I'm here. I believe that no one has seen the items move through the air. Is that correct?"

"That's right. One minute they are in one spot and when we turn around, then turn back they've moved."

"Nothing caught on camera?"

"No."

I opened the door to the nursery very quietly and tiptoed over to the cot. Aimee was right. At seven months Daisy was a beautiful baby, and I could see why people would fall in love with her, even with her eyes closed. Her red hair had grown a lot since I last saw her, and tight curls were forming. Her skin was pale and flawless, her eyelashes fanned out over her chubby cheeks, and her cupid's bow mouth pouted a little in her sleep. Rapid eye movement behind her lids indicated she was having a dream.

I placed the soft toy at the end of the cot. It was a white unicorn, with a multicolored mane. I tiptoed out of the room and closed the door quietly. When I returned to the others, they were watching the baby monitor.

"Is she still asleep?" I asked.

"She's stirring. Any minute now I imagine she'll wake up," Sophie said.

We watched the screen and sure enough Daisy stretched her little arms above her head, yawned and opened her eyes. When she saw the unicorn, she kicked her chubby legs until the cot blanket moved out of the way. She raised her hands, and the unicorn quickly flew into her grasp. Her baby giggles were a sure sign she loved the toy.

"That clinches it. She's moving the toy, not crawling to get it." I moved away from the screen, to sit on a chair.

"Now what happens?" Sophie asked.

"Nothing happens. You will need to keep an eye on her, and when she understands, you will have to explain to her she can only do this at home, with family," Harper said.

"Not all family Harper. My family won't understand," Sophie said.

"If genetics are anything to go on, she will comprehend very quickly, and work out what she can and cannot do. I can tell you from experience that I was very cautious growing up and trusted no one outside of my home. Family business was family business and stayed within the walls of our property," I said.

"The good thing is that you have cameras operating to watch and learn. I'll go and pick her up, now that she's awake, okay?" Harper left the room.

I could see that Sophie was no more relaxed now that we had witnessed Daisy moving the toy.

"How's the O'Connor family these days? Your father's heart?"

"They're fine, thank you for asking. Dad hasn't had any more heart issues, and my mum is looking forward to a big family Christmas lunch with everyone at her house this year. I'm not thrilled about it, especially now we've found out Daisy has abilities no other child will have at the lunch."

"Here comes the girl in question. Hi Daisy, do you remember Aunt Lucia? Probably not as you were so small when I saw you last." I held out my hands for her.

"Do you like your new toy? Aunt Lucia brought it for you." Harper said. She carried Daisy on her hip, and Daisy had the unicorn under her left arm. Daisy put her right hand out to me. Harper placed her on my lap.

"Hello, beautiful. Look at those eyes!" Daisy looked up at me, and took everything in. A new sense of peace flooded me, happiness bubbled up and filled me with joy. I remembered how Domenic could do this when he was a child.

"Mom, I think Daisy has another family trait. Like Dom when he was small. He would lay his hand on you, and you would instantly feel calm. Daisy has it too. I'm sure of it."

"It's true everyone loves her, and everyone feels happy when she's around. I didn't realize she was causing it to happen," Sophie said.

"I don't know if she's doing it deliberately or if it's happening just because she is who she is. The child who has a witch for an ancestor and the Devil's DNA running through her. But whatever the reason, Maggie Mae's prediction is coming true. She will make a difference she said, remember."

Thank you.

No one in the room had spoken, yet I heard those words. I am sure it's Daisy who is communicating with me again.

19

LUCIA

The face in the mirror was Lee Edwards' face. Her hair combed and neat, the dark suit brushed and pressed. The white shirt with only the top button undone, showing a modest amount of skin but no cleavage. This image was so far from how I knew myself to be, that I grinned at the reflection. Prim and proper Miss Edwards, who was probably thought of as a virgin by everyone she encountered, was ready for another night behind the reception desk. I walked out of the hotel bathroom, turned left sharply, and bumped into a tall, well-built man in a dark suit coming the other way. He mumbled an apology and hurried past me. I didn't get a good look at his face, but I caught a waft of his delicious cologne. Bergamot and Sandalwood and something more alluring. The fragrance aroused me, and tingles run up and down my arm from the slight contact. I wanted to follow him and bury my face in his neck. *Interesting.*

"Hi Peta. What's the latest news? Anyone famous in tonight?"

"Nope. Same old, same old. A couple of new girls working the streets, so I've been told. But I've not had the pleasure of booking rooms for them in here yet. That big spender... aka Mr. Jones, who brought in three working girls, last weekend. He's back tonight with three other girls. Don't be surprised if guests on his floor complain about the noise."

"Thanks. Noted. Have a good evening."

"I hope your night's quiet."

"Me too."

I watched her exit by the front door, placed my purse in a drawer under the desk, locked it and slipped the key into my jacket pocket. Not that there was anything of great value in that purse, except my car keys, but not trusting anyone is in my nature.

I settled into the chair and opened the computer to check bookings. It was going to be a busy night.

I turned around to the printer to collect the list I'd printed out, and when I turned back, I was staring at the midsection of a tall man in a navy business suit, standing at the reception desk. I looked up and his shoulders blocked out the light behind him. He was wearing dark framed glasses and I immediately thought of Clark Kent from Superman, which was a totally stupid association. He was surprisingly light on his feet because I didn't hear him approach the desk. He unbuttoned his jacket and his cologne wafted toward me. My olfactory senses sat up and paid attention. *He's the man I'd bumped into earlier.* This man was affecting my libido without my consent.

"My aircon isn't working."

"Room number, Sir?"

"106."

"I'll report it to maintenance."

"Can someone look at it now?"

"I'm not sure. It's ten o'clock, sir. They've probably gone home."

"It's as hot as Hell in there."

"Maybe we could move you to another room. Let me have a look."

"No!"

"But if I can't get someone to look tonight..."

"Whenever. I'll manage. Ring my room if you can get someone from maintenance." He turned and hurried off toward the stairs. Not the elevator. Strange.

I went through the internal directory and called the number for maintenance, but it went straight to a recorded message. I guess he'd have to manage until morning.

An hour later he was back. He'd removed his suit jacket and undone a few buttons of his blue business shirt. He looked hot. Not just hot from the broken aircon... but *hot*. The fragrance of his cologne was so much stronger now too. His carefully buttoned-down look from earlier had gone. His tousled hair and flushed face had my imagination working over-time. The glasses were gone. I couldn't take my eyes off that glimpse of firm chest with a smattering of dark hair. The fitted cotton shirt highlighted a trim waist. As he talked to me, he rolled up his sleeves... I didn't hear a word. I'm a sucker for strong hands and tanned corded forearms, and his were perfect.

"Miss? Hello?" He snapped his fingers in the air, and I returned to earth. A slight scowl had formed on his attractive face, his forehead puckered, his eyebrows had drawn together.

"Sorry, what?"

"I've changed my mind. I want to move. I tried to fix it and I've made it worse."

"Move?"

"Rooms. Move rooms. You suggested it. Remember?" He folded his arms across his chest. His biceps bulged. I reluctantly tore my eyes away from him and back to the computer.

"Right. Let me have a look. The room next door is vacant."

"Can you come up so we can check that room's aircon is working?"

"Sure." I removed my suit jacket and hung it over the back of the chair. *Was it hot down here too? Maybe all the air cons had gone on the fritz?*

I placed a sign on the reception desk to say I'd be back in five minutes. He headed for the stairwell. I followed. It wasn't far to climb to the first floor. He stopped at the heavy fire escape door, and I slammed into the back of him. In such a confined space I experienced the tingling sensation in my arms again. But more interesting, my whole torso had also begun tingling deliciously, my nipples peaked, my neither region perked up as if it had awakened from a deep sleep and was now taking serious notice!! And that fragrance. Pungent, and alluring. What the hell is going on? This man has charisma in spades if he can awaken the virginal body of Lee Edwards. I had that libido locked down hard and fast from the word go.

I took a step back and he glanced back at me, his eyes lowering to the peaks in the front of my shirt. He yanked the heavy door open, and we made our way to the new room. The aircon was working. He cranked it up to maximum.

"Can you help me get my things?"

"Um. I should be back at the desk."

"It would be quicker if you could help."

"Okay let's go."

The door opened and I totally understood why he wanted to move. The cooling aircon function was broken and it seems the heating was blasting from the unit instead. It was like a furnace. Normally it wouldn't have bothered me. But humans had a problem with it. Specifically Lee Edwards' body had a problem with it. My white shirt quickly became plastered to my chest, my bare inner thighs were damp. I began to gather up the toiletries from the bathroom and stuffed them into his case. He pulled the clothes from the closet hangers, and as he turned to throw them on the bed, we collided in our haste. My hand shot out, I grabbed his arm to stop myself falling, and I was plunged into his video of a life of sexual addiction. All my senses were overwhelmed with his fragrance, his heat, his allure. My body literally melted into his.

Before I knew it my mouth was being devoured, the suits and shirts littered the floor around us, and he was pulling up my skirt and yanking aside the crotch of my cotton panties. I heard it tear, the fabric fell away, his fingers exploring my folds were now slick, searching, probing. I heard his zip being pulled down and then he was plunging inside me! All the breath left my body, and I could not get enough of him. I wanted him so far inside me and standing up wasn't doing it for me. I pulled him back, down onto the bed and wrapped my legs around his hips, encouraging him deeper inside.

It had been so long since I'd had a man inside me, I was so close far too quickly, but I didn't want this to end. I reluctantly pulled my lips away and pushed him over onto his back. This way I had all the control. I rode him hard, then pulled back the excitement a little so I could enjoy the buzz but not hasten the climax. I played the game of getting so close then pulling back, reveling in the drawn-out anticipation. He appeared as if he was also enjoying the ride. His hands cupped my breasts, which were still encased in the bra and sweat soaked cotton shirt. That was the tipping point. His fingers squeezed my nipples and I roared into the first orgasm I'd had in Lee Edwards body. It was blissful. I clenched around him not wanting this buzz to end, and we reached a climax together.

My breath slowed down and my heart stopped hammering in my chest. I pushed my hair back off my face and looked down at the disheveled mess I had become, and suddenly became aware of my surroundings. *What the hell just happened here? How was it possible for this man to look so innocent yet have such a voracious sexual appeal. Where was my self-control? Pull yourself together and get the hell out of this man's room!*

"I'm sorry. I don't know what came over me. I must go."

I gathered up what little dignity remained, rearranged my shirt, and skirt as best I could, and headed for the stairs. Thankfully no one was waiting at reception. I found a reasonably small size tee shirt, with the hotel logo on it, ditched my sweat-soaked shirt, and covered up the tee with my suit jacket. It would have to do. I had no choice but to go commando, but so long as I didn't fall over no one was going to notice.

The rest of the night was uneventful, and the smile never left my face. When I clocked on the next night both rooms were empty. Just as well. Now I know what Lee Edwards' body is capable of I'd better be more careful.

20

LUCIA

*R*achel had given me a photograph of Aamon. He has the
smug look of a man who appeared satisfied with his place
in life. I wanted to wipe that smug expression off his upper-class face
forever.

She told me where he liked to go for coffee in the morning. I took
particular care today with my wardrobe because I wanted to look
appealing, but not too flashy. A black fitted skirt finishing at my
knees, with a split up the back. Enough to show off a small slice of
inner thigh. High black heels of course. I planned to have a car
malfunction. He needed to feel obliged to help me, but I didn't want it
to look too obvious. Yes, I knew I could've broken into his house and
killed him on the spot, but where was the fun in that?

I arranged Lee Edwards features to be a bit more appealing,
including adding two or three cup sizes in my bra. I intended to open
a few buttons on my white shirt to show off what was normally
hidden beneath. No need, because due to the extra inches, the buttons
popped open of their own accord!

I drove my car to the coffee shop, parked at the curb and opened
the hood. I looked confused, tried poking at a few engine parts. When
Aamon exited the coffee shop he turned right and glanced at me as he

passed by. I swore loudly using several German profanities which I knew would trigger something in him as he loved the German language. He looked back, stopped walking, turned around and approached the car.

"Can I help you? I'm not a mechanic but I might be able to help?"

"I'd appreciate it. I don't know what I'm doing. Thank you."

"What happened."

"The car slowed down and then just stopped. I got it started again and managed to pull over."

"Gas?"

"No. I filled up the other day."

"Let's check the water."

"I did that too."

Aamon wiggled a few things, checked, tightened a few engine parts, and stood back. "Try it now. Turn it on".

I climbed in and turned on the ignition. The car started. As it should, because nothing was wrong with it. He beamed at me like he was the biggest hero. I got out of the car.

"Oh, thank you. You obviously have that special touch." I tried hard to sound sincere and managed to keep the sarcasm out of my voice.

I found a couple of clean paper napkins in pocket of the car door, and handed them to him. He wiped his hands, rolled the paper into a ball, tossed it up and over, into the trash can beside the curb, like a cocky basketball player. He stepped up onto the sidewalk, turned, raised his hand in a salute and began to walk away.

"Can I give you a ride to your office, or home?"

"No, it's fine. I'm only a few blocks away," he said.

"It's the least I can do. Honestly. You saved me from calling a mechanic." I smiled sweetly and pushed my chest out further.

He tried not to look, kept his eyes on my face, but I was aware his peripheral vision had enjoyed the expanse of plump, creamy, flawless flesh pushing its way up and out of the lacy bra cups. He licked his lips. *Naughty boy Aamon, that's a dead give-away.* I tried not to laugh. He shrugged, walked back and opened the door, and climbed into the passenger's seat.

"You know a bit about cars. I guess you know a bit about a lot of things?" I slid into the driver seat and placed my hand on his forearm and smiled sweetly.

"I try to keep up with what's going on in the world." He smiled, and nodded his head a little, confirming that he thought he was indeed knowledgeable.

"I should introduce myself. I'm Lee." I held out my hand.

"Aamon. Nice to meet you."

"You've been so sweet." I kept hold of his hand a little longer than necessary.

"I don't like to see a lady in distress."

"Lots of men wouldn't have stopped. God bless you."

"Just doin' my duty and being a helpful citizen."

"You know, I've been having problems with my roller blinds in my bedroom. It's stuck open and I think the man in the building opposite is copping an eyeful when I'm getting undressed. I wonder, could you help? I'm sure you could fix it in a flash. The building manager is a bit of a creep, so I wouldn't invite him into my bedroom. But you look like someone I could trust. I've only started moving my stuff in. I'm new to this part of town."

"I don't know, I have a lot on today."

"Please?" I placed my hand on his thigh, twisted around in the driver's seat to face him, which made my tight short skirt ride higher. I leant closer and gave him a good look at my cleavage. "I'm just around the corner. I'd be so *very* grateful."

I could tell he was debating with himself whether he could spare the time, and what he could gain if he helped me.

"Okay. I'll take a quick look. But if I can't fix it in ten minutes, you'll have to call someone."

"Great. I really appreciate it."

I drove around the block to the small apartment building I had prepared. I pressed the remote and drove into an empty garage under the building. We took the elevator to the top floor and walked to the apartment at the end of the corridor. There were a few packing boxes in the living area, but the bedroom was set up with a queen-sized bed and a few personal items. The bed was rumpled, top sheet thrown back, sexy black lingerie on the pillow, and a set of fur handcuffs attached on either side of the metal railing of the headboard. The top drawer of the bedside table was half open and an assortment of toys, lube, and a vibrator was visible.

"Sorry I didn't make my bed before I left. I wasn't expecting visitors." I giggled nervously, stuffed the lingerie under the pillow, pulled up the sheets and nudged the drawer partly closed. "I'll go find my stepladder."

I saw him take it all in, so I left him to enjoy the fantasy going on in his head. When I returned with the stepladder, he had moved from the end of the bed to stand beside the bedside table. I noticed the drawer was open wider than when I left.

I position the ladder, climbed up to the top step to show him where the cogs had become entangled, and explained what I had been trying to do to free the blind. He stood behind me and watched me climb. I knew he was enjoying the view all the way up my thighs. I grabbed the chain and tugged it hard. It suddenly gave way, the blind descended to the windowsill. I turned, lost my balance, and fell off the ladder into Aamon's arms. He held me tightly, then slackened his grip allowing me to slide down his body until my feet touched the floor. We were face to face, his breath was my breath, his chest was pressed against mine. His heart was thudding in his ribcage, his erection so obvious and pushing against my stomach. Our eyes connected, and he read what he saw as acquiescence in mine. It took only a few seconds, then he lent in to kiss me.

When he felt confident that I wasn't going to push him away, he deepened the kiss and began to touch me. I silently allowed his exploration, which made him bolder. He pushed me back onto the bed, laying on top of me, his hand roughly forcing my skirt higher, his fingers sliding between my thighs, testing how wet I was. Satisfied by what he thought was arousal on my part he unzipped his jeans.

"Woah. Slow down. Let me get undressed. I'm sure it would be better for us both if we were naked."

He pushed off me, stood up, and quickly undressed, dropping his clothes on the floor.

"You know what I like? What really gets me off."

"Tell me," he said.

"Toys." I pulled a set of nipple clamps from my drawer. "And I like to be on top. I like to ride hard." I pulled out a tube of strawberry flavored lube. I laughed and he laughed too, and I could see he was getting excited by the prospect of getting laid before lunch by someone who liked kinky games in bed. "Why don't you sit back against the headboard and let me get my lips around that magnificent cock for a while." His cock bobbed and lengthened with the mention of oral. He climbed onto the bed and did as he was told.

He watched me undress down to my bra and panties. When I slipped off the lacy bra, he licked his lips. I attached the nipple clamp on one prominent nipple, and he all but salivated. I slipped off my panties, straddled his legs on the mattress and bent down to hold his cock, pumping it a little, getting it harder, and more erect. I lowered my head, opened my mouth, and stopped just before my lips made contact.

"You know what would turn me on even more. Let's use the hand-cuffs." Still straddling him I reached up rubbing my breasts over his face, allowing the unencumbered nipple to slide between his lips, as I cuffed his right hand to the rails of the headboard. His cock nudged my thigh, impatient, waiting for his treat. While he was engrossed in sucking my nipple, I also handcuffed his left hand to the rail of the headboard. I pulled my nipple out of his mouth, and he looked annoyed. I grabbed my panties off the bed and held them under his nose with one hand and grabbed his cock with the other.

"What do think. Do you like the smell of my pussy?"

Aamon nodded his head. His cock swelled in my hand.

"Do you want to taste my pussy?" I pumped his cock harder.

"Yes." I could hear his heart thumping in his chest.

I moved up his body, my crotch only a few inches from his face. "Open your mouth."

I offered him the soaked crotch of my panties and he opened his lips. I stuffed the whole garment into his mouth and got off the bed. He frowned wondering why I wasn't getting down to business giving him a head job. I pulled a roll of electrical tape from the back of the drawer, and it began to dawn on him that things were not turning out as he'd hoped.

He struggled against the handcuffs, shook his head trying to spit the panties out. I wrapped the tape around and around his head securing the gag. He tried kicking at me, but I was faster and got out of the way. I was imagining he was calling me every bad word he could think of, although it sounded like squealing, with tears streaming down his face. He watched me get dressed and pick up my purse. He was now writhing on the bed yanking at the metal head-board. But I had no doubt of the strength of the metal, or the strength of the real handcuffs which, thanks to my DIY craft project, had leopard skin superglued to them. The bed was secured to the floor and the wall, he was never going to be able to get free. I made sure of that.

"Goodbye Aamon. No one will hear you. This building is condemned, they're building something bigger and better soon. You're going to get a chance to think about all the terrible things you've done in your life to innocent people. Make good your time here and admit your sins. And when you go to Hell, because that is where you are headed, just know that the punishment will continue down there."

I pointed to the windows, and metal shutters descended. It suddenly dawned on him that he was going to die, and who he was dealing with.

"Adieu Aamon. Rachel sends her love by the way. I'll see you in Hell."

I drove the car out of the building, secured all the doors, windows and garage doors so they would not open for anyone but me, and left the area.

I want him to suffer, so I'll give him a few days without food and water and no chance of escape. He will die alone, in pain, and with the realization that the person he hurt most was indirectly responsible.

I returned ten days later, made sure he was well and truly dead, removed the handcuffs, destroyed all the evidence, and set the building alight. They found an incinerated body in the rubble. Squatters were blamed for the fire.

I called Rachel.

"It's done."

"It's done! I'm free?"

"You're free."

"Thank you."

21

LUCIA

"Rachel, I have an idea and a business proposition I want to put to you." I pushed away the empty plate, raised the paper napkin to my mouth and dabbed away the chocolate evidence. I lifted the coffee cup and took a sip, watching Rachel's expression turn from questioning to wary.

"Oh yeah. What?" Rachel took a step back from the table and crossed her arms.

"Hey, don't get defensive. I'm constantly amazed and thrilled by the delicious cakes you manage to whip up in your tiny kitchen. As evidenced by the fact I have eaten here so often. I wonder what you could do if you had your own bakery."

"That's a question I can't answer. I have no money for that kind of expense."

"But I do. Well, my family does. And I know I can persuade them to come on board with a loan until you can get on your feet. With a cut of the profits of course. What do you say?"

"You're not serious?"

"Totally. I have a strange compulsion to see you succeed. It's like a little voice inside my head saying, 'Help Rachel, help Rachel.' Now that other matters have been delt with, you can finally move on with your life and create something of your own. Your money can go into the business instead of paying legal bills."

"What do you get out of this?" Rachel lowered her voice. "You have my soul. I though the Devil …sorry… the Devil's protégé … got off on torture. Not helping people," she whispered.

"I've had a chance lately to consider that myself. I enjoyed helping you. Maybe helping women who've been wronged by men is my thing. Sure, torture is one part of the job, but this way I get your soul when you die, which will make my father proud, and I get to help you when you're still living, which will make my mother proud. Plus, cakes of course. Lots of cakes. It's a win/win/win for me." I patted my satisfied stomach. "What do you say? Will you consider it?"

"It would be a dream to have my own bakery. I'm finding all this hard to believe. I'm waiting for the other shoe to fall. For someone to walk in that door and tell me it's all a big joke. That you-know-who is still alive and he's coming at me for something else he thinks I haven't done for the kids. I don't understand where all this good fortune is coming from."

"To tell you the truth, I'm a little surprised by how much pleasure helping you is giving me."

"If I say yes, what happens next?"

"I go see my parents and sell this business proposition to them."

"Hell, what do I have to lose? I've always dreamt of getting up at 5am and baking bread and making cakes and working in a shop till I'm exhausted and everyone else goes home for dinner and eats my creations. Then I pour my profits back into my business so it thrives, and I make a few million dollars, and can retire on the Cote d'Azur."

"That's settled then. Let the games begin. I'll go talk to my father. But before that I want my family to try your cakes. Box up that chocolate cake in the glass cabinet, and the deep-dish apple pie. Better throw in a few of the raspberry and white chocolate cupcakes. And a couple of eclairs? What do you think?"

☙

I paid my bill and left with the boxed-up cakes and drove straight to my family home in the Hollywood hills. The gates slid open, and Cameron waved me through. I plucked a cupcake from the box on the passenger seat and passed it through the open window. His eyes lit up. He saluted with his free hand, then hit the lever and closed the heavy metal gates. As I watched him through the rear-view mirror, he took a big bite and licked the frosting off his fingertips.

I parked at the front door where Aimee was waiting. Either she has a sixth sense about my arrival or Cameron alerted her. They were becoming used to seeing me as Lee Edwards now and have accepted I may arrive in Lee's body or in my own.

"Hello there. What have you brought? Morning tea?" Aimee reached out to take the boxes.

"Hi Aimee, take these cakes into the kitchen and cut them up into samples please. I want to share them with Mom, with you and Cameron too. I want your unbiased opinion."

I headed for the back of the house where I found my mother sitting at the table in the sunny breakfast room, drinking tea, and reading a book. I leant down and kissed her cheek.

"Darling! I wasn't expecting you. What a lovely surprise."

"I hadn't intended to come today, but I had an idea and wanted to put it to you before I approach father."

"Do tell."

"Ah here comes Aimee with the sweet treats. And some fresh tea. Good idea Aimee. Mom, can you please taste these cakes and tell me what you think. You, too, Aimee. You're the baker, and your opinion is most important to me."

I waited patiently while they selected a sample of each one. I made myself useful by pouring two cups of tea into the pretty bone-china cups Aimee had provided and placing them within reach on the table. I sat down and waited, watching their expression as they ate. My mother finished her tasing plate first. Aimee had selected a second small piece of the chocolate cake. I took that as a good sign.

"Mom?"

"They are all delicious. Fresh and light and very moreish. The chocolate cake was rich and intense, the frosting velvety smooth, and the cake was moist. I could taste the cinnamon and lemon in the deep-dish apple pie, but I imagine it would be even more delicious warm from the oven with cream. The pastry crust was flaky and buttery. The cupcakes were so light, and the frosting was delicious. The punch of raspberry in the frosting was a nice touch. The eclairs were my favorite. I had a bite of each flavor. Vanilla bean, and chocolate cream. The chou pastry was superb. I won't have room for dinner Aimee, I've eaten my weight in calories already today."

"Great. How about you, Aimee? What's your appraisal."

"I second everything your mother said. I will add that I could taste a hint of rum in the chocolate cake. Delicious. And honey and cloves in the apple pie. The flavors and balance of each were slightly different to the norm. Whoever made these has a gift."

"That's what I wanted to hear. Thank you both. I knew I could count on you. Anything negative you could add to that?"

"I have nothing," my mother said.

"Nope. They were delicious," Aimee said.

Cameron arrived, strolling through from the kitchen. "Could there be another cupcake waiting to be sampled? The last one was superb. Not better than yours of course, my love." He winked at Aimee.

"Help yourself to whatever you like, Cameron, there's plenty here. I need to talk to father. Do you happen to know where he is today?"

Cameron shook his head, lifted another cupcake from the table, and left the room through the kitchen door.

"Need to talk to father about what?" My father strode down the hallway and into the room, accompanied by Max and Raven. "No one informed me we were having a party. What are we celebrating, Lucia?"

"I'm so glad you're here. You can sample some of the cakes, too."

"Have you taken up baking?"

"No. These were made by a talented friend of mine."

"You haven't answered my original question. Need to talk to me about what?"

"My friend could really do well in her own bakery. She has no funds to start this project. However, she does have plenty of talent. I would like to go into partnership with her. I want to put it to you, to help her get started and bankroll her business venture. In exchange for a share of the profits and ..."

"And?"

"And you'll be helping me, help her. I'm really drawn to helping her."

"I see. And just how long do you think it will take to make a profit on this venture Lucia?"

"That depends on where we open the business, the marketing, and getting regular clientele. And how much you're willing to put into this bakery to get it off the ground."

"If I decide to help you. If. There will have to be contracts signed, a financial check..."

"She has no money. She has nothing of any value. He took it all from her."

"Her husband?"

"Yes."

"The recent case I'm familiar with?"

"Yes."

"To put this into context. You only met this woman recently, you've helped her get rid of a nasty problem in her life, and now you want to bankroll a business with someone who has nothing to back it up. No money, no assets, nothing to prove she can financially succeed."

"She has talent. Don't underestimate the fact that she *wants* to succeed. As do I."

"Hmmm. What do you say, Harper? Are the cakes any good, Aimee?"

My father took a seat on the empty side of the table. Max and Raven came to sit at each side of his chair and watched him select a cupcake. They were probably hoping he would share. He peeled off the paper wrapper, slid his fork into the soft sponge, scooping up some raspberry frosting, and popped it into his mouth. Then he selected a piece of chocolate cake and repeated the process. We all watched his face for signs of enjoyment. He gave nothing away. My mother spoke first.

"I'm inclined to believe Lucia has a good idea here, my love. Her enthusiasm is enough of an indication to me that she will see this through and make it work. Her friend is talented."

"My Lord, the cakes are delicious and would easily sell in any five-star restaurant and believe me people pay handsomely for well-made desserts," Aimee said.

My father put down his fork and pushed away his plate. "If I decide to do this, you will have to locate suitable premises downtown. I will pay to renovate and to set up the business. You will be responsible for negotiating with builders and painters and suppliers to get the best deal. I will provide start-up costs, but on a budget. I'm not going to make this easy for you, Lucia. I want to see what you are capable of. Your friend has talent. But as we all know talent only gets you so far. Money makes the world go around. Show me this venture has made money, and I will invest more."

"Thank you. You won't regret this. I will make sure it succeeds."

"And don't forget, you have a job. You can't ignore that in favor of this little pastime."

"It's not a pastime! You'll see. You'll be proud of us this time next year."

"I'll hold you to that."

"I'm leaving now. Got to get some sleep. Enjoy the cakes." I kissed my mom's cheek, and hugged Aimee. "Thanks again, Father." He stood up and I threw my arms around him, sinking into the solid expanse of his chest and his strong arms, enjoying the wave of love I knew he had for me. He held me for a few seconds longer than I did. *He misses me too.*

At times like this, when I returned home with my new sense of self and my new independence, I appreciated my family and what they meant to me so much more. I missed them all terribly, but most days I could push that thought to the back of my mind and get on with my job. It was my time to show father what I could accomplish, to prove to him that I was up to any task he set for me. The fact that I found another purpose, and another means to show what I was capable of, thrilled me. The future of this venture excited me. I'd prove to him that I have all that it takes to get this bakery off the ground.

And the little voice in my head, encouraging me, became louder.

22

LUCIA

I was waiting by the diner the next morning when Rachel arrived. Her smile was tentative.

"Hi," Rachel said.

"Hi. Do you want the good news, or the bad news?"

"I knew it! I knew it was too good to be true. They said no, didn't they? I shouldn't have got my hopes up that my life was turning around." Rachel walked past me toward the door.

"He said yes."

Rachel stopped and turned around.

"What? But you just said there was bad news."

"The bad news is you'll have to give notice here, and I know you *love* your job." I laughed. "Running a business means long hours."

"I'm really going to open a bakery. Be my own boss?"

"If we do this, we'll be partners Rachel. I'm not going to tell you how to bake, but I will have a say in running the business. This is new for me too, but I have something to prove to my father."

"Okay, sure. I'm fine with that."

"The first thing I want to put to you is the name of the bakery. Are you opposed to Sweet Devil Bakery? Because I think it has a nice ring to it."

"It sounds good to me. Hell, anything sounds good to me at this moment. But I must get to work. My shift starts in ten minutes. Can we discuss all this later?

"Yeah. Come see me at the hotel tonight."

Rachel threw her arms around me, hugged me tight, pulled open the door and disappeared inside the diner. I went home to bed and dreamt of spreadsheets and lemon meringue pie shaped like clouds and cakes with devil horns sticking out of them.

I'd met with realtors and selected a location. I had a meeting with a designer named Sarah Wall, to design and complete the fit out. I had selected Sarah from a list of designers used to dealing with the fit-out and remodeling of vacant retail spaces. I liked Sarah from the moment she stepped out of her car to greet me. She had a glow, a vibrancy that bridged the gap of the few feet separating us. Her wide smile was contagious and resulted in an equally wide smile from me.

The information about the building and her knowledge of which materials would be needed, convinced me to have a second meeting with Sarah and her sub-contracted fitters and installers, brothers Jason and Michael Goss, who measured everything with exacting precision. Then it was time to bring Rachel to have a look and see what she thinks. We could lease half of the ground floor, as another business took up the other half. If she didn't like this building, I would find another, but I was really hoping I'd found a winner. We'd agreed to meet downtown after her shift, so that she could get home to cook dinner for her kids. I would have to catch up on lost sleep tomorrow.

"What do you think?" I watched her turn full circle in the wide vacant space. My voice bounced off the brick walls, high ceilings and wooden floorboards.

"It's a great location. The room back there could be the kitchen but needs a huge renovation to take the commercial ovens. It's light and open out here with the big windows. There seems to be parking available across the street."

"So, what are you saying? Yes, or no?"

"Do you think that we can fit out the existing space to accommodate commercial ovens large enough, and a pantry storage area?" Rachel addressed Sarah, who was standing a few feet away at the window overlooking the street.

"I have no doubt we can turn this space into a functioning bakery and still have enough room for a small café near these windows," Sarah said.

"A café?"

"Yes. Didn't we discuss opening a small café?" I asked.

"Later down the track, when the business was turning a profit," Rachel said.

"If we have the space for it why not now?"

"Money. Do we have enough?"

"I'll deal with that. This building ticks all the boxes Rachel. Location, size, parking, permits, office buildings nearby with plenty of scope to encourage walk-ins. Coffee-to-go and a pastry on the side when walking to work. Who has time to make breakfast these days? Or lunch for that matter. A pie, a baguette filled with ham, cheese and salad, and your special sauce…"

"What special sauce?" Rachel asked.

"Come on. There must be a special sauce in your brain you can whip up …"

"I'm a baker, not a chef. I have no special sauce in my brain. I have cakes and pastries, and bread."

"No need to get annoyed I'm trying to get you to see the bigger picture..."

"Ladies, we're getting ahead of ourselves here," Sarah said, bringing us back to the present.

Sarah extracted a floor plan from her satchel, and tentative sketches of the cafe to show Rachel. I was counting on this being the only floor plan we had to make. Sarah wasn't cheap.

"I've drawn these sketches to show you what we could do in here, to maximize the square feet. Every inch is valuable real estate. I want to utilize walls as room dividers but also functioning with a few small standing tables attached, between the café and the shop. I have added sockets to recharge phones, small wooden seats that can be unfolded from the wall, or retracted if it's busy and you need more standing room. I need to discuss what your requirements would be for the kitchen, apart from the ovens and countertops."

Rachel took the sketches and walked over to the window to get a better look. I took the opportunity to talk to Sarah.

"I like the sketches. I'm keeping everything crossed that Rachel does too. I want to thank you for putting in the time, considering I haven't officially hired you. Yet."

"It's in my nature to go the extra mile and give the customer a comprehensive vision of what I could do with the space. It's up to the customer then to work with me to make that happen, and to make it better. I'm confident that I'll be toasting your success on your first-year anniversary of opening day. I'm so certain of that, if I get this contract, I'll bring the bubbles."

"I'll hold you to that," I said.

Rachel returned. She was smiling.

"Let's do it," she said.

"Yes!" I grinned and hugged Rachel.

I held out my hand to Sarah. "You're hired. When can we start?"

23

LUC

I'd been keeping my eye on Lucia's new business venture and what they had accomplished so far impressed me immensely. Early stages yet but it appeared to be working. She did her calculations, as I had asked, contracted the workmen and the designer and tried to adhere to the budget. I allowed her some grace with the fittings, knowing that she wanted this space to be quirky and memorable. Not just any café. Something that drew attention, and had the media interested in covering the opening day. Lucia planned on a grand opening with free cupcakes and a local singer and their acoustic guitar serenading the morning foot traffic.

The fact that she was getting a kick out of this, and still managing to work her night shift at the Hotel, while managing to collect souls from the many unscrupulous people staying there, was a credit to her. She was knocking this probation period out of the park. I was surprised but delighted, of course.

24

LUCIA

Sweet Devil Bakery was off and running! Our first day was epic. We sold more cupcakes by the dozen than we'd expected and boxed more layer cakes and tarts than planned. Thankfully Rachel had thought ahead, and had frozen extra cakes for future orders, as well stacking undecorated cakes in the cool room for tomorrows refrigerated window display. There had been a mad dash to frost and decorate several chocolate mud cakes, and she even roped me into getting creative and piping meringue peaks onto the lemon meringue pies. I guessed I'd be helping in the kitchen when we closed the doors, because Rachel needed to be working overtime again tonight!

There was one last customer to serve, waiting by the counter. She paid for a dozen carrot cake muffins, topped with swirls of lemon cream cheese frosting, and a chocolate chiffon pie. She had a bakery box in each hand, so Rachel came out from behind the counter and held open the door to let her out.

"We did it." Rachel closed and locked the door and did a little jig on the spot.

"We sure did."

"I'm blown away. Today was wonderful, I'm so happy." Rachel

pushed the bolt home at the top and bottom of the front doors and pulled down the blinds on all the windows of the shopfront. "We sold so much of the stock I had prepared for tomorrow I'd better get back into the kitchen and start baking again."

"Paula is stacking the dishwasher and making sure the napkins and coffee cups are ready for the morning trade. I'll wipe down the tables out here and sweep the floor, then I'll help you in the kitchen for a couple of hours. I must leave by nine to get to my other job."

"I really appreciate all your help. I couldn't have managed without you."

"I can't do it every day, though. We need to hire extra help. I'll put a "Hiring" poster in the front window."

"I think I know someone who could do with a job. Her name is Rose."

"Great, get her to come in tomorrow for an interview."

"She came into the diner a few months ago, to see if there was any food that was being thrown away. She was homeless too for a while, but I bumped into her the other day and she's living at the shelter a block away from the diner now. I know what it's like and I want to help her. She's due for a break."

"Can you get in touch with her?"

"I'll stop by the shelter on my way home. She's a kind and gentle soul. You'll like her, I'm sure."

"If you think she's capable to help you in the kitchen and can work casual odd hours, I'm sure I will."

"You've never been homeless, so you won't understand. But you lose your identity, you're dragged so far down that you feel useless. Even when you're capable and intelligent, the loss of your home means you don't belong anywhere, despair and loneliness can have a catastrophic effect. It takes just one person to reach out a hand and help you up."

"I understand."

"I don't think you do. You see, *you* did that for me. You held out your hand, and I will be eternally grateful."

"It was fate, I think. We were meant to bump into each other that morning. Something made me follow you. Now look at what we have created." I raised my arms. "And it's only the beginning."

ཞ

Rose was exactly as Rachel had described. Tiny in stature, quiet and reserved, with salt and pepper hair tied back in a bun at the nape of her neck. Her clothes were drab and ill fitting, probably due to fact that she was malnourished, and her shoes were worn and old. She clutched her battered purse on her knees. But her eyes shone with kindness, and when she shook my hand I witnessed a slice of her tragic life in rapid video form, and knew I had to help her.

"Rachel tells me you're currently at the shelter."

"Yes. They took me in recently. They are very kind, and I was lucky to find them."

"We need help in the kitchen for a few hours a day. I can't guarantee how many hours a week, but we will pay cash. Cleaning, helping Rachel prepare, washing up. You'd be on your feet all day. Is that something you'd be able to do?"

"That would be wonderful. I'll work as many hours as you can give me. It's been a long time since I've had any money of my own. I may look frail, but I can manage."

"Good. Then you could start tomorrow at seven o'clock to help Rachel set up for the day, stack the shelves, prepare the refrigerated window display. There are a few new uniforms in this bag. Rachel guessed your size." I pushed the canvas bag to her side of the table. "One or two of them will surely fit you, you can bring back the others. Once I know your size, I'll make sure you have a steady supply in your locker in the staff change room. I insist on a clean uniform every day. Wear your own clothes to and from work. Leave the dirty ones in the hamper at the end of the day, we have a laundry service that picks up our towels, aprons and uniforms every couple of days. Here's some cash. Go buy yourself some comfortable plain white sneakers today."

"Thank you. I'll be here bright and early."

"Rachel will be here, but I won't see you until later in the day. Some days not at all."

"You won't regret this. I promise you."

"I believe you. Now come with me to the kitchen and take some pies back to the shelter for your meal later today. On the house."

"Bless you. You're doing God's work."

"I doubt that. But I appreciate the sentiment."

Rose left with a bakery box filled with nourishing meat pies and a couple of treats.

"You did a good thing." Rachel patted my shoulder after Rose left.

"She's painfully thin. Make sure she leaves with something to eat at the end of her shift. And give her any leftover food we can't use next day. Make sure nothing goes into the dumpster if it's edible. I'm sure the shelter could use it."

"Are you positive you're the Devil's daughter? Cos you seem more like an angel to me. And I bet that Rose feels the same."

"I'm sure I'm the Devil's daughter." I laughed. "And on that note, I'm heading home for some sleep."

25

LUCIA

APRIL 2019 – SIX MONTHS LATER

*T*he long hours were catching up with me. Sleep no longer came easily and I found it hard to maintain Lee Edwards' body for more than a dozen hours at a time. After working a couple of extra hours at the bakery this morning, I yawned, and my face morphed back to my own. I altered it as soon as I realized. It wouldn't have been a problem, but I was in my car, waiting for a traffic light to change and the elderly lady in the car alongside mine looked horrified by what she'd witnessed.

Father, I need a break.
Why?
Because it's becoming harder to retain Lee Edwards body.
It should be getting easier for you, not harder.
Well then, I must be ill.
Devils don't get ill.

I am only half Devil, remember. Maybe the human part of me needs a rest.

Would a few days in Paris help?

Yes!

Then apply for leave. I'll have a travel agent friend arrange a hotel and plane tickets, I want you to travel normally, Lucia. No wings, understand.

Can I travel first class at least?

So long as you promise to behave. No international incidents.

I'll need new passport photographs. I've changed a lot since the last ones were taken, in fact, I think I might need a new passport.

It will all be taken care of. Someone will be in touch.

Thank you, father.

You are welcome. Don't make me regret it, Lucia.

Paris, the city of love. I was happy to be here, to be seen in my own body, to be able to acclimatize myself once again to my normal height and size. Perhaps that was the problem back in the States. It took a supreme effort to be Lee Edwards every day.

Everywhere I went there were couples holding hands and kissing, sharing cheese and bottles of wine, and eating ice creams. *Have I stepped into the pages of a Romance Novel?*

Maybe it would have been a better idea to have headed to Greece, or a tiny island in the middle of the ocean. Sunbathing, swimming in a blue ocean, eating delicious fresh seafood and drinking cocktails under an umbrella. Anywhere would be more appealing than being solo in Paris.

My father had given me the name of a friend of his who owned a boutique on Rue du Four. Perhaps a new dress or two would help brighten my day.

The taxi stopped beside a narrow, cobbled street, in front of a tall, impressive old building with a pale pink façade. There was a quant vintage bicycle, with a wicker basket attached to the front, chained to an ornate cast iron lamppost outside the premises. Flowers in a profusion of colors burst from window boxes under two tall glass display windows on either side of the door, and vines trailed down the trellis underneath. Dresses draped over mannequins in the windows featured the same jewel colors from the floral display. The sun suddenly broke through a cloud, illuminating the building, bringing the scene to life. My mood lightened. It was the right decision to come here today.

When I turned the brass doorknob and opened the door, a tall slender woman in a black fitted dress walked toward me, holding a silver tray with a glass of bubbles. Her hair was captured in a coil at the base of her neck. Elegance oozed from her. The silver Directrices' badge on her chest announced she was the Manager of the boutique.

"Bonjour mademoiselle."

"Bonjour. Merci." I accepted the proffered glass and take a sip.

A happy sigh escaped my lips. There were several women browsing the racks along the walls, all holding a similar glass.

"Vou est englais? American?"

"Oui. American."

"Then I shall speak in English, oui?"

"Je parle francais."

"But it helps with my English, no?"

"Sure, if you want to."

"What can we assist you with today?"

"My father gave me this card to give to Claude, the owner." I handed over the card with the gold embossed lettering.

"One moment, mademoiselle."

She disappeared through a curtained archway. I sipped my bubbles and turned to look around the elegant salon. The curtain rustled and I turned back around.

"Good morning, Miss Nightingale, I am Claude Durand." Claude held up the embossed card. "It is my pleasure to welcome you to Paris.

Your father contacted me and altered me you would be visiting my premises. I see you have a glass of our finest champagne. Tres Bon."

I knew I was staring. I had a sudden realization that my mouth was open, so I brought the glass to my lips and took a sip. I am guessing Claude is in his forties but could have graced the cover of any of the Billionaire romance books I had seen in the airport bookstore. Handsome seemed an inadequate description. His eyes were one of his best features. They held you, captured you within their hazel depths. He smiled at me, but I noticed his smile was cheeky, intimate, as if he knew something I didn't know. His teeth – perfect in every way – shone, dazzling me. Easily six and a half feet tall, he wore an immaculately cut double breasted navy suit, pale pink shirt, darker pink silk tie with matching handkerchief peeping out of his breast pocket. A large gold signet ring on long slender fingers holding up the card, and an expensive Cartier watch peeping out of his sleeve when he raised his hand completed the image. A subtle intoxicating fragrance wafted my way. This man knew how to dress to impress.

His short dark blond hair had been styled with a little flick of hair over his forehead. My hands itched to tuck it back, to experience the texture. *Get a hold of yourself. You're acting like you've never see a handsome man before.*

"I'm enjoying the champagne thank you. I've been admiring the beautiful, elegant dresses in the window."

"Your father has requested I select a surprise for you, as his gift. Now that I see you in the flesh, I feel I've made an error. I was expecting a young girl, but I see you are very much a woman."

There was that enigmatic smile again.

"I love a surprise."

"Angelique, s'il vous plait, accompagnez la jeune femme jusqu'au vestiaire."

"Thank you." I handed the empty glass to Angelique and followed her to the dressing room.

"I will select some pieces for your consideration. Please come out to show me." Claude disappeared behind the curtain.

Within a few minutes Angelique returned with an armful of

dresses which she hung on the door. The rich fabrics caught the light, tempting me to touch. I selected a light green knee length dress to try on first. I stripped down to bra and panties. Angelique positioned herself behind me, slipped the dress over my head and pulled the zipper up at the back. The vee neckline was very flattering. The dress fitted like a second skin, hugging every curve, showcasing my breasts and small waist. I looked at the vision in the mirror and witnessed the knowing look in my eye. Yes, I could easily seduce Claude in this dress. Time to test my theory. I slid into the high heels Angelique gave me, pulled open the dressing room door, and walked slowly into the salon. Claude was sitting in a chair, holding a glass of bubbles, waiting for me to appear. I had the pleasure of seeing his hazel eyes darken when he saw me.

"Good choice. I knew this color would look magnificent with your dark hair."

"This one jumped right out at me, but there are many more to try."

"Please do. I'm patiently waiting here for the show."

Claude lifted the glass of champagne to his lips and took a sip. His tongue swept the bubbles from his top lip. I wanted to take care of that for him. My skin warmed and I knew my cheeks were flushed. My nipples hardened and pressed against the firm bodice of the dress. I didn't look down, no need, I knew they would be visible. Claude's eyes connected with mine. *He knows what he's doing to me. Perhaps I'm the one who is being seduced.*

I selected four dresses, because in the end I couldn't pick just one. They were all different, cleverly designed, and highlighted my assets better than any dress I had purchased since my body has changed.

"I am very impressed Claude. There's something very special about your designs."

"Merci. It was always my dream to create beautiful garments, for beautiful women."

"I will wear the burgundy one to dinner tonight."

"Ah yes. A perfect choice. However, I wonder if you would do me the honor of accompanying me to a cocktail party at a friend's house. There will be other Americans attending and you could help me if my English becomes a little rusty."

"I'd be delighted Claude. It would be nice to see inside a Parisian home. What time shall I be ready?"

"I shall pick you up at seven o'clock."

I wrote down the name and address of the hotel, and my phone number on the back of a business card and handed it to him. His fingers wrapped around mine and he gently pulled me toward him and kissed both of my cheeks. I saw his video then, flashing through my brain, and realized he had a generous, sensual soul, and he lived a life full of art and music, fabrics and color, design and surrounded by lots of very attractive men and women. Food and wine and sex also played a big part in his video. He would be the perfect host for the evening.

"Au revoir a plus tard."

"Au revoir Claude. Je serai pret."

I had a feeling tonight was going to be memorable.

There were already a dozen people at the cocktail party when we arrived, talking, and laughing, and obviously enjoying themselves. Claude made his way through the apartment, greeting friends, introducing me, until we found Remy, the host, in the kitchen cutting up lemons for cocktails. Claude kissed Remy. I noticed he lingered a little longer on that skin-to-skin contact, than with other friends he had encountered in the living room. Remy kissed my cheeks, and in the instant of that touch, the video I had of his life was of sexually explicit scenes. Interesting. These two men could not have been more different. Claude was tall, slim, and blond with eyes in which you could drown. Remy was muscular, shorter perhaps just over six feet, and dark, with eyes like coal. Unreadable. The yin and the yang.

The current of sexual energy in the room changed when Remy

joined the party. Claude took every opportunity to touch me. Either on the arm, or the hand, the lower back and at one stage he put his arm around my shoulder to lean in and tell me a funny story. And all the while I could feel Remy's eyes on us. Remy was the perfect host. The delicious French cheeses and dips were plentiful, and the cocktails flowed freely. I was enjoying myself, speaking both French and English depending on the subject matter. I stayed away from politics, it was not my forte, but became very enthusiastic when discussing art. The time flew by, and guest after guest made their way out the door, until there were only three of us left.

As soon as the last guest had waved goodbye, and the door firmly closed and locked behind them, both men became very attentive. Claude changed the music to something softer, turned off the overhead lights, leaving a multitude of candles burning around the room, and poured three glasses of very fine French champagne. We all sat down on the green velvet couch, a man on either side of me. I was grateful to get off my feet and had been waiting for the chance to sit. I slipped off my shoes and relaxed into the cushions.

"It was a lovely party, Remy. Thank you for inviting me, Claude.'

"It was my pleasure." Claude took my hand and kissed my fingertips.

"Our pleasure," Remy said. He moved closer on the couch and leant in and kissed my neck.

"Is it okay?" Claude asked.

"Yes," I said. I was surprised that the word was almost a whisper, and I wasn't totally sure what I was agreeing to.

Claude on my left and Remy on my right. Both men apparently wanting much more than polite conversation. Having multiple partners was new to me, but I was about to find out if the pleasure could be doubled. Claude leant in and kissed me on the lips, and it was sweet, sexy, and thrilling and my body responded to his touch. He pulled back and ran his fingertip lightly down my neck and over my collar bone. My pulse fluttered.

Remy took me by the shoulders, turned my body around to him and kissed me with such force, my head spun. His hands explored my breasts, knowingly, competently, over my clothes. I felt my zip being pulled down by Claude who was sitting behind me. He pushed the fabric off my shoulders, along with the straps of my bra, down to my waist and exposed my breasts. Claude's hands appeared under my ribcage, cupping my breasts, offering them up to Remy, who took one nipple in his mouth, sucking hard, his teeth grazing the tender flesh. A bolt of electricity shot to my core. My sex sat up and took notice.

Claude turned me back toward him and both men took a nipple in their mouths sucking and licking and tugging at the puckered flesh until I heard someone moan and realized it was me. I closed my eyes and enjoyed the different sensations each man was giving me. Claude was gentle and teasing, Remy was a man on a mission and boy did he have something to prove with that nipple. He tugged and sucked, biting, and pulling at it with his teeth, but instead of hurting me, the rough play was turning me on, and making me so wet and ready for whatever they had planned.

My hands wanted to explore. I ran them along the muscled shoulders of Remy on my right admiring his build, and cupped the cheek of Claude who was being so gentle with my left nipple. Remy stood up and tugged the dress down, until it was off, discarding it on the floor along with the bra. The only thing remaining on my body was a thong, a scrap of French lace for which a boutique had charged a fortune. Remy grabbed both sides and it ripped very easily. It flew over his shoulders onto the floor.

Up until this point I had been a pliant and willing participant, allowing their exploration, judging my body's reactions to see if I wanted to be with these two men at the same time. I had pretty much kept my hands to myself. But the lack of care for my expensive underwear tipped me over the edge. I wanted to touch, I wanted to explore. I began to unbutton Claude's shirt who was still kneeling at my feet. I ran the palms of my hands over his hairless chest and hard nipples and pushed the shirt off his shoulders. His mouth came back to mine, his tongue searching, probing and his hands returned to my breasts, skimming over the skin, bringing my nipples to peaks.

Remy was back kneeling at my feet. He nudged Claude aside,

pushed my legs apart and dove straight in between my thighs. Heat surged through me as his tongue slid between my folds. *This man has no finesse, but oh my god his tongue is magic.*

I wanted to slow it down and I tried to wriggle away from him, but his hands clamped onto my thighs and pulled me toward him for better access. His tongue was doing a wonderful job, and I was in two minds of wanting more control but not wanting him to stop. Ever!

Pleasure flooded my senses. He captured my clit between his lips and sucked so hard I flew over the edge into a shuddering orgasm.

When my breath returned, and my heart slowed down, Remy sat back on his haunches, grinning. Both men were on their knees at my feet, watching me expectantly.

"We would like to take you to our bed. We would both like to make love to you. Is that something you would enjoy?" Claude asked.

"Don't you think that you should've asked me that before you both kissed me?"

"So far this has only been foreplay. We have not entered your body. Do you want to make love with us both?" Claude asked.

"Make love is a very old-fashioned term. We call it fucking these days."

"No Lucia. We will make love to you. We will bring you great joy, great passion, and you will leave our bed a changed woman," Claude said.

Remy stood and swiftly removed all his clothes, casting them aside. The man had the physique of a bodybuilder, muscles rippling on muscles, dark hair covering his chest and trailing down to his groin. But it was his cock that held my attention and from which I could not look away. It was massive, standing to attention, straining to be noticed, the head dark purple, engorged, and ready for fun. Remy placed his hands on his hips, legs akimbo, awaiting my decision. I was hesitating, even although the naughty girl inside me wanted so badly to say yes, because to be honest I wasn't sure if I could fit it all in.

"If I say yes. If. Can I change my mind if I cannot go through with it?"

"Of course. This is your decision. We want you, but only if you want both of us," Claude said.

"Can I have more champagne?"

"Of course. We have more in the bedroom. Come."

Claude took my hand and I stood. As we passed by, I touched the head of Remy's cock and it bobbed and straightened, becoming even bigger. I was amazed by his ability to stay hard for so long without touch.

In the bedroom Claude led me to the super king-sized bed, poured me a glass of champagne from the bottle in the ice bucket, and undressed. His body was hairless, waxed to perfection, smooth, beautiful, and lightly tanned. He placed his clothes neatly on the chair, and I admired the perfectly round, high, tight cheeks of his derrière. Apart from the large erect cock jutting from his body, everything about him had a more feminine edge than I had been anticipating.

Now I had two naked men climbing into the bed, both rampant and ready to go, and I was dying to find out how they would choreograph this dance. Who does what and with whom? Instead of analyzing this new-to-me experience, I decided to put down my empty glass, close my eyes and let my body enjoy the intimate attention of two lovers.

And the rest they say, is history.

26

LUCIA

$\mathcal{M}$y brief respite is over and I'm sorry to leave Paris, but I know I must return to help Rachel with the business and get back to my night job at the Hotel. However, I'm leaving the city with experiences my new body will never forget, an extra suitcase full of beautiful new clothes and memories that I will treasure forever.

Good evening, Lucia, I presume the trip was successful and you're refreshed.

Yes father, I'm a new woman. I'm heading to the airport now.

Good to hear. When you've returned to American soil and have a moment, I'd like you to join me in Hell. We have something to discuss.

That sounds ominous.

No. Not necessarily so. It's time we had a talk. Father to daughter.

No. Not ominous at all, father. You like to hold the cards close to your chest, don't you?

Always. Goodnight, Lucia.

Goodnight father.

What could he want to discuss? *Lucia, why did you decide that sharing a bed with two men instead of one was a good idea?* That couldn't be the topic because it would be like calling the kettle black. My father has enjoyed multiple partners in the past, before my mother. And of course, he's the Devil, and so - devilish by name, devilish by nature. Orgies are part of his DNA.

No, that surely couldn't be the topic. Maybe he wanted to know how the bakery was running. I had all the invoices, spreadsheets, and paperwork to show we were doing well. It would be a while before we made enough to pay him back for his investment, but he knew that going in. I have collected my quota in souls from my night manager's job. Surely that couldn't be the reason for the talk. No point in worrying about it, I'd find out soon enough.

There was a queue at airport security screening. I placed my purse in the tray, removed my jacket and heels to place in another tray. An elderly couple were ahead of me, holding up the progress, but no one in line appeared annoyed. The woman was leaning heavily on a walking stick. She hobbled to the body scanning machine. They told her to put her walking stick in the tray. It was obvious to me she wouldn't be able to negotiate very well without the stick. They were adamant. She placed the stick on the rollers to be screened and stepped carefully, gingerly, into the body scanning machine. The screens lit up, and she explains she has two titanium hips. The female security guard roughly frisks her, causing the elderly lady to wince and close her eyes. The stick appeared through the scanning machine, and she hobbled to retrieve it. The security guard didn't move or help her in any way. I detected a smirk on the guard's face. It was my turn in the machine, and I'm cleared to walk through. The same security guard called me over, did not ask if she could frisk me in public and then placed her hands on my shoulders. Her video is of pain and torture, heartlessness, and cruelty. All of which was at her hands.

This woman needed a wake-up call if she thought that being unkind to an elderly disabled woman was amusing. I sent a bolt of pain through her system, her hands slipped from my shoulders, she clutched her chest and sank to the floor, unconscious. Several Airport security staff rushed over. I haven't moved but to anyone watching, or the overhead cameras, I look as shocked as they all seemed to be. To all intent and purposes, it appeared she's had a heart attack. Another security guard moved us all along and they closed off that section, while they attended to her on the floor. She would come to in a few minutes with a new appreciation of what excruciating pain really felt like, and possibly a new awareness of how to treat the elderly.

§

Being back in Hell, albeit briefly, gave me a new appreciation for life on Earth. I was aware I'd grown as a person and as an apprentice devil and I'd learned many important lessons in the last few months. I'd become better at reading people, to tailor the punishment to fit the crime, and I was more tolerant when my targeted soul collection did not go exactly to plan. I knew I could make up the numbers eventually, and things would even out.

Rourke was waiting to greet me outside my father's office door.

"Your father is expecting you. Go on in," he said gruffly.

"Nice to see you too, Rourke. Maybe one day you'll break out a smile when you see me."

"Smiling's not in my job description."

"And yet I know if you did smile, it would make such a difference to your day."

"Not going to happen."

"Challenge accepted."

"Lucia." My father called me into his office.

"Close the door, please," he said.

I did as I was asked.

"Must you rattle Rourke? You know he has a lot on his shoulders."

"He's always so stony-faced. Has he ever had any fun? Does he even know what fun is?"

"He had a hard life before he came to Hell. It hasn't got any easier. Give him a break."

"You wanted to see me? Correction you wanted to talk to me."

"Yes. Your progress hasn't gone unnoticed. I've been pleased by your dedication, and to your credit, our quota of souls has increased our population. I feel you're ready for a new facet to your abilities. I want to show you The Veil."

"What's the Veil?"

"The Veil is a corridor of space where, when entered, I am neither on Earth or in Hell. Some talented demons can pass through The Veil going between the two, but most of the time we use portals. Like the one in the Gatehouse. If I want to observe activity on Earth, but don't want to be seen, I can observe behind The Veil."

"I would be invisible?"

"Yes."

"Cool"

"Whilst in The Veil you would only be an observer. Unable to change anything or talk to anyone."

"Sounds like a handy little trick to have up my devilish sleeve."

"Use it judiciously."

"Got it."

"Please take this seriously."

"I promise. Cross my heart and all that."

My father raised one eyebrow, stood, and crossed to the back wall of his office. He turned to face me.

"And your mother would like you to come to dinner. Domenic, Sophie, and Daisy will be there too. You missed Daisy's birthday, so this is a special celebration just for you."

"I'd like that. When?"

"Tonight. As soon as I've shown you The Veil, you can return to Earth."

"What a shame. I was so looking forward to visiting the new admissions and torturing them…"

"Should I tell your mother that you won't be at dinner?"

"It was a joke. Of course, I'll be there. I haven't seen them all for ages. I'm sure Daisy is crawling by now."

"Daisy is walking."

"Really. I've missed a lot of her milestones. What can I get her as a birthday gift?"

'The child wants for nothing. Your mother makes sure of that. Talk to Domenic."

"What did you give her."

"A car."

"A car?"

"A child's toy car, she can sit in and drive around the yard."

"Maybe a rocking horse?'

"She has one. Ask your brother."

"I'll ask Sophie. I'll probably get a better response."

"Come." My father placed his hand on the brick wall, and it glowed like a furnace, as if lit from within, He stepped forward into the heart of it and disappeared. His hand and arm appeared once more in the room, beckoning me to join him.

"Here goes nothing!" I stepped into what appeared to be glowing embers. He waited for me in The Veil. Within this space the surrounding atmosphere had no parameters, it was dark with tiny pinpoints of light around us. It reminded me of those movies of outer space, astronauts floating between the spaceship, tethered by an umbilical cord providing oxygen. Except we did not have an umbilical cord and we could walk, not float.

"Pick a location and think about where you would like to be. Be clear on the country, town, street. Be as precise as possible. Or pick a person you would like to see. This is happening in real time, so depending on where you chose it will be night or day."

"Can I visit Daisy? Perhaps see her walking?"

"Of course. This is only a short-term thing. You can't stay within The Veil for too long. Other demons can only pass through from Earth to Hell or back."

"Are you the only one who can stay in The Veil?"

"I was. And now you can too."

"And do I have to enter through your office?"

"No. I'll show you how you can achieve this. But you must keep this to yourself. I sometimes observe your mother to make sure she's okay without me."

"Oh, that's so cute."

"I do worry about being away from her for such long periods of time."

"I won't give the game away. Your secret's safe with me." This insight into my father's thinking made me smile.

I thought of the exact location. One of the pinpoints of light became bigger, rushing toward us, and there it was. My brother's living room, as clear as day, shown to me as if on a huge TV screen. Daisy was standing beside her toy box, Sophie knelt on the carpet behind her, a few feet away. Daisy turned, clutching what looked like an old book to her chest, and took a few steps into her mother arms. The vision of this happy family scene was so clear I wanted to reach out and touch them.

Then the image faded, moved off into the distance to a tiny pinprick once again and I was enveloped in black.

"You can only hold it for a short time. It will get better the more you practice. But there is a problem with coming into The Veil too often. It weakens your other abilities. Please use this with care." My father turned to the glowing embers which had appeared behind him, grasped my hand, and pulled me with him back into his office.

"You have outdone yourself again, Aimee. Dinner was wonderful."

"You say that every time. But I bet my meal doesn't stack up to that gourmet food you had in Paris."

"Aimee I can say with my hand on my heart, that your meals mean the most to me, because they are cooked with love, just for me."

"You are right Lucia. Aimee takes great care to make sure you have all your favorite dishes when you visit. Although in saying that, she does the same for all the family." Mom reached out and put her hand over Aimee's hand on the table. "Love goes into every bite."

"Goodness me. You know I'm happy to cook for those I love. It's so nice to have you back Lucia."

"I can't believe how big Daisy is getting, Sophie," I said.

"Neither can I. She is walking and trying to talk. She loves books, carries one everywhere she goes."

"That's nice. I loved books too when I was small. Nursery rhymes and colorful characters were my favorite."

"Most of Daisy's children's books don't get played with now. Her favorite is a book she picked up at my parent's house the other day. It's very old and came over with them from Ireland. I was worried she might damage it, but my mum told me to take it, as she has no use for it. Daisy is very careful with it though and turns the pages slowly. If I didn't know any better, I'd think she was reading it." Sophie laughed.

I wondered if that was what I had witnessed Daisy holding when I was in The Veil.

"It must hold some significance for her."

Sophie got up and brought the book back to the table.

"I don't know why she likes it. The cover is dark with yellowed pages inside. Some pictures, a few hand drawings but mostly scrawly writing inside." Sophie handed me the book.

The cover was indeed dark. Blood red – old blood to be precise – with faded gold lettering on the front and spine, entitled Irish Spells & Potions. *I didn't expect this.*

I flipped through the pages, which were yellowed with age and use, and noticed some tiny writing scattered down the edges of most of the pages, where someone had made their own comments. I couldn't believe what I was reading. This book was basically a recipe book. Food and preserves and potions for all manner of ailments. Love potions featured heavily. And spells to use on people who were making your life miserable. Common plants, herbs and spices and some ingredients I have never heard of were included.

"Would it be okay if I took this home and had a look through it. I promised to give it back tomorrow."

"Of course. I'm sure she won't miss it for one night," Sophie said.

"Why are you so interested, Lucia?" Domenic asked.

"I've always been fascinated by old books. Besides, this might give me a better appreciation of your wife's family history."

I noticed my father, who was sitting across the table, raising an eyebrow. I walked over to place the book near my purse. As I passed Daisy in the highchair she reached for the book.

"No sweetie, you have mashed pumpkin on your fingers. You'll get it dirty. I promise I will give it back soon." Daisy started at me with such concentration.

Promise

Again, I was sure it was Daisy communicating with me.

27

LUCIA

When I arrived at Sweet Devil Bakery after a long and tiring night at the hotel, Rachel was already crumb-coating all the celebration cakes she had baked that morning, ready to go back into the cool room to set. The shop was busy, and several people were enjoying coffee and cakes in the café.

"I need to let you know I've hired another baker to help me in the kitchen. It was very busy when you were overseas, and we missed out on a few commercial orders. There weren't enough hours in the day. I made an executive decision. I didn't want to bother you when you were in Paris. Her name is Stella Harris, and she works the afternoon shift."

"That's great if the orders are coming in. I'm happy we're getting busier."

"Stella's at Uni but her passion project is baking and she's a bit of a whiz with flavors. She's a Batchelor of Applied Science and has a degree in Biochemistry. We've added some new cupcakes flavors to the menu."

"Really?"

"There's a pineapple shimmer donut too, which has tiny pearls of pineapple jelly in the icing."

"Sounds interesting."

"Red Devil cupcakes with a new ganache. The raspberry flavor is so intense!"

"Now I need to taste these fabulous cupcakes."

"There are some in the cool room. The ones with the tiny chocolate horns on top."

As soon as I tasted the Red Devil cupcake, I knew that we had a winner. If the color red had a flavor, this ganache would fit the bill perfectly. I ate two cupcakes, in quick succession and pulled another one from the rack. I couldn't get enough. Surprisingly along with the party in my mouth, my mood lifted significantly. Considering how bone tired I had felt a few moments ago, this was amazing. I recognized this feeling. I was high! But was I high on sugar alone or was there something more in these sweet flavor bombs?

"Rachel, I need to meet Stella."

"She'll be here around noon."

"Do you have her address. I've got to get some sleep. It's been a busy night, and I can't hang around here until noon."

"Give me a minute and I'll get it for you."

I selected a dozen red velvet cupcakes and placed them in a bakery box. Rachel handed me a slip of paper with Stella's address, and I headed home to sleep.

That night I took the box of baked treats to work with me, cut them in half and placed them on a plate under a glass dome on the reception desk with a sign offering free samples. Very few people ignored them. I observed the reaction of the hotel guests as they consumed the cupcakes, noting a marked difference in their faces when they'd finished and licked their fingers clean. Their smiles were broader, they eyes were sparkling. Even Mr Henry, one of our grumpiest regulars had a smile on his face when he'd sampled the cupcake.

In a quiet moment after six in the morning, I called Rachel on her cell. She picked up on the third ring. "Sorry to call so early Rachel, but

I figured you'd already be at work. Have you noticed an increase in cupcake sales in the last couple of weeks?"

"Yes. I told you it's been busy."

"I'm interested specifically in the cupcake sales."

"I'm probably making triple the quantities of the red velvet. So yes. I guess that line has increased."

"Since Stella changed the flavor?"

"Let me think. Yeah, probably since then. Why?"

"They taste fabulous."

"I did tell you that yesterday morning."

"You did."

"What's going on? You didn't call me at six in the morning to tell me you enjoyed the cupcakes."

"There's something in those cupcakes that's making people happy."

"Duh... they're cupcakes... people love cupcakes."

"No, there's an added little something in those cupcakes."

"You've lost me."

"Possibly something illegal."

"No way."

"I'm not one hundred percent, but I'm leaning toward that answer."

"How can we find out for sure?"

"I'm going to pay Stella a visit."

"Buy why would Stella put something in the cupcakes?"

"That's what we need to find out."

"They'll close us down! Should I get rid of the batch I made today?"

"No. Calm down. Let me get my facts straight first. I'll call you later."

When my nightshift finished, I headed to the address on the slip of paper Rachel gave me. The area was full of commercial buildings, some of which had been turned into loft apartments. I rang the doorbell for number five.

"Hello." The voice sounded young.

"Stella?"

"Yes."

"I'm Lee Edwards. I own Sweet Devil Bakery along with Rachel.

She gave me your address. I know it's early, but I'd like to talk with you if you have a minute."

"Okay. I'll buzz you in."

The door buzzed, I walked into the foyer, and took the elevator to the top floor. Stella was holding her door open, waiting for me. I estimated she was about twenty-five, short and petite, with a pixie face and dark shoulder length hair tied back with a red ribbon. She wore a navy apron, dusted with flour, over jeans and a white tee shirt. Her feet were bare.

"Come in. But excuse the mess I wasn't expecting a visitor."

The loft apartment was open and spacious, filled with light from floor to ceiling windows along one wall. The caramel leather furniture, both modern and functional, took up most of the space in the living area, and there was an oriental rug in green tones between the couch and the stone fireplace. A long wooden dining table, with benches on either side, lay between the living and kitchen space. The sun streamed in, glinting off the stainless-steel kitchen and metal appliances.

It was obvious money wasn't short when furnishing this apartment. Mixing bowls, wooden spoons, and measuring jugs filled the sink, and assorted baking items cluttered one end of the long bench. The tantalizing aroma from the two trays of freshly baked croissants wafted under my nose. My stomach rumbled. A lump of dough sat in the middle of the flour covered marble benchtop, waiting to be shaped into bread or rolls.

"You have a lovely apartment."

"Thank you. My family owns it. I'm lucky I get to live here rent free while I'm studying." Stella walked around to the kitchen side of the bench, pulled the butler's pantry door closed, and resumed kneading the dough. I slid a kitchen stool out from under the bench and took a seat.

"Rachel tells me you have a couple of science degrees."

"Yes. I'm currently studying for a degree in Molecular Biology."

"You're a smart girl. Let's cut the small talk and get right down to the reason I'm here. What did you put in the cupcakes?"

"What?"

"Please don't play coy with me."

"I don't know what you mean."

"You added a certain little 'extra' to the cupcakes. I want to know what it is and why you felt you could tamper with Rachel's work."

"Rachel approved of the new flavors. There is nothing *extra* in the cupcakes."

I was hoping she would tell me of her own accord, but I didn't have time to waste. I waited until she looked at me, and locked eyes with her across the top of the bench. She couldn't look away, and she had to tell me the truth.

"What did you put in the cupcakes?"

"I've been experimenting with high levels of synthetic dopamine."

"Is it legal?"

"It's my methodology on a proven formula. All components are legal."

"Why would you want to do this, and how on earth did you think you could get away with it without anyone noticing?"

"I needed test subjects. I didn't think anyone else was paying attention."

"Stella, tell me, what is your heart's desire?"

"I want to make my mark in the culinary world. If people keep coming back for the cupcakes, I'll know my experiment worked. I'm studying mood enhancers."

"So instead of lab rats you're using human guineapigs."

"Yes. But I'm not hurting anyone."

"That depends on if this dopamine is addictive."

"It's not."

"How do you know for sure?"

"I've tested it on myself, and on other students at the university. It's an accelerated short-term lift in mood."

"Is it traceable in the bloodstream?"

"It only lasts for a short while, then it disappears. My molecular gastronomy recipe isn't traceable."

"Molecular gastronomy sounds ominous."

"No, it's a cross between cooking and science, using scientific experimentation to deconstruct food to its simplest elements, then to reconstruct it in new and unexpected ways."

"Have you added any other extra things I should know about to the baked goods?"

"Only the dopamine so far."

"So far! What else have you manufactured?"

"I have a truth serum and..."

"A truth serum!"

"I haven't tested that one yet on anyone outside of a small group of friends. But I have high hopes with the formula. It would be interesting to try it out on a large group."

I turned away from Stella, and she snapped out of the "eye lock" I had on her. She shook her head.

"What just happened?"

"I have my own way of getting to the truth, Stella."

"Did you just hypnotize me?"

"Yes. That's it." I'm not about to tell her anything different or expose my identity.

"What's in the butler's pantry?"

"Food and supplies."

I got up and walked over to the pantry door, but she rushed to stand in my way, her arms flung wide over the doorway.

"This is private property. You've no business going in there."

"Do you honestly think you could stop me?"

I picked her up under the arms and moved her to one side. She weighed hardly anything at all. The door opened into a mini science laboratory. It was full of bottles and jars, beakers, and racks of test tubes.

"Stella, Stella, Stella. I'm lost for words, and that's unusual for me."

"What are you going to do?"

"I'm going to talk to Rachel about this. I think this could be beneficial for the three of us."

"You're going to tell Rachel?'

"Of course. We're business partners."

"Do I still have a job?"

"Sure, for the time being. But no more experiments. Understand."

"Not even the cupcakes?"

"Well okay, only the red velvet cupcakes. They're selling like hot cakes." I smiled at Stella, who relaxed a little.

"Okay." Stella smiled back.

I headed straight to the bakery. Instead of being horrified by what I had just witnessed, I was very interested in learning more about Stella, and her "recipes". The more I thought about it, the more I rationalized the added little extra in our cupcakes was beneficial for our business. Marketing gurus had been doing this since forever, getting us hooked on products, adding more sweetness to foods, for that sugar high. We were just taking it a little further that's all. We were in fact just omitting more sugar and adding the "high".

Rachel took a bit of convincing, but my devilish brain was devising methods to utilize all of Stella's talents. Her truth serum really piqued my interest. She said it wasn't tested yet, but if it worked, I could see the potential in all sorts of scenarios. Pages of the cookbook that Daisy had discovered suddenly came to mind. In fact, people had been concocting potions since the beginning of time. Potions to make you sleep, to help with hair loss, gout, or constipation. Love potions had always been popular. Who was to say that in this modern day and age that home-made concoctions couldn't be put to good use. Stella had impressive credentials and I can understand wanting to make your mark in the world. But I needed to make sure that what she was doing wasn't going to backfire on us.

28
LUCIA

I'd become familiar with a few of the hotel regulars, not exactly friends, but enough for them to call me by name, sometimes bring me little gifts, or stop to chat when checking in or out. I wasn't interested in their souls. They were the genuine upstanding citizens just travelling through for work. The souls I was interested in acquiring were degenerates of the lowest order. The men, and sometimes women, who frequented the hotel for nefarious reasons, who were cruel, unkind, and lacking any moral integrity. Last night one such despicable regular signed in under the name of Mr Jones, obviously not his real name. As per usual he was accompanied by two young attractive women. He always requested the room near the fire escape door, near to the car park, and I'd never been aware of the women leaving until tonight.

As I walked from the staff kitchen, I heard loud cursing on the other side of the fire escape door. I'd gone to get a cup of coffee to ward off the constant yawning that usually occurs at the tail end of my shift. I pushed open the heavy door and saw a young woman with long black hair wearing a skimpy blue dress, in high heels and slumped on the ground, with her back against the building.

She was sobbing and cursing, rummaging in her purse, searching for her keys, or her phone, or a tissue perhaps to stem the blood dripping from her nose and lip which was soaking into the front of her dress. I wedged my mug of coffee in the door to stop it closing all the way and bent down to help her to her feet.

"Can you stand? What happened?"

"I'm okay. I fell and dropped my purse." She pulled a set of house keys from the purse, closed her eyes, and made the sign of the cross on her chest.

"I'm Lee, the night Manager." I bent down to pick up a small notebook. "Is this yours?

"Thank you, Lee."

"Do you have a car? Or do you want to come inside, and I'll call you a cab."

"I'm not going back into that place! He might see me." She glanced at the door.

"Don't worry, I'll make sure that doesn't happen." I took her arm and guided her back into the room behind reception. I called a cab and gave her a glass of water.

"Thank you. I'm Veronica. I'm sorry for all the trouble."

"No need to be sorry. What did the man do to you, Veronica? I'm presuming it was a hotel guest."

She wouldn't look at me. "You don't want to know," she said quietly.

"Oh, I can assure you I do." I tilted up her chin to lock eyes with me. "Tell me what he did."

"He can't get it up unless he's watching women fucking each other or he's hurting someone. He gets off on causing pain and humiliation. Tonight, he tried to strangle Julia while he was fucking her, and she was gasping for air, desperately trying to push his hands away. I was scared for her. I pulled him off and he punched me in the stomach and kept on punching me. I think he broke my ribs cos it's hard to breathe. Julia tried to help, and he turned back on her. I grabbed my purse and clothes and ran out. I'm a terrible friend, but I thought he was going to kill me. I got dressed in the stairwell. When I checked my purse outside, I thought I'd dropped my keys back in the room. I was afraid I'd have to go back."

"Is it worth it? The money I mean?"

"He pays well. This is the first time he's punched me with a closed fist, though."

"I think you should try working another neighborhood."

"He thinks he's slumming it down here, and no one knows him. But I know who he is. I have the dirt on him. He's the CEO of a corporation in that renovated building downtown near the Wells Fargo Bank. Everyone hates him. I talked to one guy who works for him. He paid me a ton of money to spill the beans about Mr-so-called-Jones."

The cab arrived and I helped her into the back seat.

"Get that rib checked."

"There is nothin' you can do for broken ribs. They heal themselves."

"Take it easy then, and I hope I don't see you back here with him."

"Don't worry, that's not going to happen."

I shut the door and tapped on the roof. The cab took off. I returned to my desk and logged into my computer. I was determined to find out more about Mr Jones and to think of a way in which I could repay him for his bad behavior.

A plan was hatching in my brain. I called Stella and left a message. She called me right back.

"You know that truth serum you're working on. I think I have a test subject."

I hit the fire alarm and watched the guests stumbling into the parking lot. I spotted Mr Jones wearing a bathrobe to cover his naked body, coming down the fire escape. The young woman accompanying him was scantily dressed but had her purse over her shoulder, and I could see she had fresh bruises coming up on her face and neck. In the dash to get out the door, Mr Jones surged forward. I grabbed the woman's arm and pulled her into the room where I'd concealed Veronica.

"Julia, I spoke to Veronica, and I know what happened. You need to stay here until the guests go back to their rooms. I presume you're happy to go home?"

"Yes. Thank you. I'm worried about Veronica?"

"She's okay. Like you, she's bruised, but thankful she's still alive. Don't open this door for anyone, okay." I pulled the door closed and locked it behind me.

When it was apparent it was a false alarm, the guests were allowed to return to their rooms. Mr Jones searched the crowd, but had to admit defeat, and return to his room when he couldn't find his bought-and-paid-for punching bag. Then I called a cab and made sure Julia had safe passage out of the hotel.

Mr Jones was going to get his comeuppance. I would make sure of that.

JUDY SLEDGE

CUSTER INDUSTRIAL CHEMICAL COMPANY

*A*t 10am Monday morning, Judy Sledge, executive assistant to Jeff Hollis, the CEO at CICC, signed for and took delivery of a large package in reception. It was secured with red tape covered in black arrows, and marked "Fragile, this way up". The courier took the clipboard from her outstretched hand and turned to wait for the elevator.

She placed the delivery on the reception desk, and carefully cut the tape to open the package. The aroma wafting up to her nostrils from inside the cardboard box triggered memories of learning to bake in her grandmother's kitchen and flooded her body with happiness. A flyer tucked inside the box announced Sweet Devil Bakery had recently moved into the area and were dropping off samples to local offices.

Cocooned inside were one dozen red velvet cupcakes, nestled together in a shiny white cardboard baker's box with a clear lid. A red heart shaped sticker held it closed. Each generous swirl of fluffy red frosting piped on top, had a tiny chocolate trident inserted at a jaunty angle near the peak.

The smell of freshly baked goods and sugar made Judy's mouth water. She hurried down the corridor, placed the open box beside the coffee machine and began to make the coffee for the senior managers' board meeting. Twelve cupcakes meant she had one for each manager around the table. She figured she was bound to get extra points for this. No need to mention they were free samples.

This meeting had been called to decide who would take over now that Jeff Hollis was due to retire within the next twelve months. A CEO everyone hated, but everyone sucked up to. Truth be told his senior staff couldn't wait until he was gone, but they did what was necessary in this business to keep their well-paid jobs, and all the fabulous perks that went along with their titles. Trips overseas, flashy company cars, charge cards for all the best restaurants, Christmas bonuses and cases of wine and champagne at New Year.

Too many pluses to ever challenge the status quo and jeopardize their working relationship with the man himself. Yet he was known to have treated his staff badly. It was common knowledge he had slept with at least three of the senior manager's wives which had resulted in divorce, and even dated a couple of their daughters. His morals were questionable, he had never married, and he had lived his entire life with little thought for anyone but himself.

Judy placed the twelve coffee mugs on coasters and lined them up at right angles to the twelve folders of paperwork in front of each chair at the table. It was her custom to place an insulated pot of freshly brewed coffee, creamer, and a bowl of sugar within reach of every chair. Then Judy placed a small plate containing a cupcake and fork beside each coffee mug. She placed the biggest cupcake with the biggest chocolate trident at the head of the table for Jeff. He would expect no less.

She prided herself on her attention to detail and stood back to make sure everything was perfect. Judy was thrilled there were twelve cupcakes, so that each manager could have their own delicious treat.

They were fiercely competitive and she knew that her head would be on the block if one manager missed out.

They filed into the room and took their seats. Satisfied her work was done she closed the door, returned to her desk outside Jeff Hollis' office, and picked up the phone.

"They're waiting in the board room for you sir." Judy turned and watched her boss exiting his office.

"Come on. I want you to take notes today. There's a lot to discuss and I don't want to miss anything. I don't trust Rajeev's secretary to record every detail."

"Oh! Yes, sir." Judy ejected her laptop from the base, tucked it under her arm, and hurried along the corridor to catch up with him. He was a fit man for his age and showed no signs of slowing down to wait for her.

In the boardroom Jeff took his seat at the head of the long table, which could accommodate at least twenty people. Judy closed the door. The managers were filing their coffee mugs and pulling the delicious looking cupcakes closer. The sweet smell of sugar and chocolate permeated the room and made Judy's stomach rumble.

Judy took the spare seat to the left of Jeff and set up her laptop. She wished she'd had some warning and time to grab her own coffee before the meeting started. As he poured himself a black coffee, all eyes turned to Jeff and all conversation died down.

The managers tucked into the cup cakes. Jeff was holding the floor, waffling on, outlining the extensive list of attributes he would be looking for in his replacement and reminding them all to be supportive of his choice.

"I'm also relying on you all to maintain the reputation of the company I've built from scratch," Jeff said.

"You're a fine one to talk about maintaining the reputation of the company, you whoremongering bastard!" Peter the Finance Manager said, shoveling a large piece of red velvet cake into his mouth. All eyes turned toward him. His face was scarlet, his eyes were bulging from his head, and he looked like he was choking.

"I'm surprised your dick hasn't been cut off by someone's husband by now. I wish I'd had the courage to do it when you fucked my wife ten years ago," Joe, the Country Marketing Manager, said. As he spoke, red crumbs of cake fell out of his mouth onto the table. He wiped his mouth with the back of his hand and held it there, eyes also wide open, but suddenly speechless.

"His dick isn't all it's meant to be. Did you know he has to take little blue pills to keep it up. And even then, his performance is lackluster. He's all talk and no action. I got more pleasure from my vibrator and believe me I had to use it as soon as he left my apartment. Those fake squeals of pleasure and "Ohhh baby, you're so big" should have earned me an Oscar. And to think I had to continue fucking him just to keep my well-paid job," Annette, the Marketing Manager for Southern division, said. Her eyes were as big as saucers. She clamped a hand over her mouth.

"If we're talking Oscars, I should get one for keeping a straight face when he lies about his college days. I know he was a loser at college. No girl would look at him or fuck him. And I want to throw up every time I listen to him tell me the same old stories about his golfing success," Phillip, Marketing Manager for the Northern division said. He was holding the half-eaten cupcake. He shoved it into his mouth, took a gulp of coffee and held the mug to his lips with both trembling hands.

"He tried to play squash with me a few years ago and I thought he was going to have a heart attack. If he'd collapsed on the squash court, I was planning on standing back to watch. No way I was giving him mouth to mouth. You don't know where his mouth has been," Tony the Payroll Manager said. He shoved the remainder of cake on his fork into his mouth. He giggled nervously and put his head in his hands.

"I've a fairly good idea when his mouth has been. Have you heard he regularly picks up hookers... two or three at the one time... and takes them to a seedy hotel to watch them have sex with each other, cos he can't get it up any other way. I followed him on one occasion and paid one of the working girls later to spill the beans, just so I could have something on him, the next time he messes with me," Raul, the warehouse Manager said. He filled his coffee mug up to the brim and tried to drink it all at once. Then coughed and spluttered cake crumbs and coffee all over the paperwork in front of him.

"My wife nearly committed suicide because of his continued sexual harassment at work functions and family team building events. She left me when I wouldn't quit my job. I'm only here for the money, and now she's gone I'm taking as much money as I can from the sleazy prick, to land myself a young trophy wife," Edward, Human Resources Manager said. His plate was empty. He tried to stuff the napkin into his mouth. His face was bright red.

"No one in this room understands what I've had to do to keep my job. The underhanded dodgy deals I've had to make, the kickbacks I've had to provide, the people I've had to blackmail to make sure we could do business. It's not going to touch Jeff or the company. It's going to come back and bite me. He'll throw me under the bus, I know it," Stephen the Sales Account Manager said. His lips were covered in frosting. He shook his head violently and burst into tears.

Jeff stood up and began to walk around the table. His eyes focusing on those who had dared to say those terrible words out loud. The fury was evident on his face, his color heightened, his dry lips formed a hard, thin line. Judy had been taking notes on her laptop, but pulled her mobile phone out of her pocket as soon as she realized that conversations were turning nasty and hit record. She noticed that every one of the remaining three staff members who had not spoken, were all squirming in their seats, with their hands firmly over the mouths. They had all eaten a little of the cupcakes in front of them and appeared to be in a tug of war within themselves, their faces scarlet.

"Well, well, well. This has been a most interesting meeting. It hasn't escaped me that I've had some negative comments made about me over the years. Everyone in power deals with jealousy and back-stabbing. But this takes the cake! If you pardon the pun. While you are all stuffing yourselves with cakes and coffee that I have provided, sitting on chairs that I have bought, and surrounded by a building that my money has renovated, you have the audacity to tear down my character." He returned to stand by his seat. "You will be happy to know you are all fired, effective immediately." He stabbed the cupcake in front of him with the fork, lifted the whole thing up to his mouth and took a huge bite, chewed and swallowed. He grinned at them all and licked the frosting off his lips. The chocolate trident fell to the table.

"You are all worthless pieces of shit. I will be so happy to be rid of all of you, with your average everyday lives, and dowdy wives, uninteresting partners, and boring children. I need some new blood in this office. Some young attractive people I can use and abuse to feed my ego before I retire. As for you Judy, you useless unattractive old hag, the only reason you're still employed, is the fact that you know too many of my dirty little secrets. But I'm thrilled to let you know it's all going to end for you when I walk out that door. I hope you're recording all of this because I am going to sue each and every one of them for defamation. These people are going to lose everything they old dear." He gleefully picked up the chocolate trident and stuffed it and the rest of the cupcake into his mouth and swallowed. "Cheers losers!"

He raised his coffee mug to his red frosting covered lips and took a large swig. He grinned grotesquely at those around the table, showing teeth covered in red coloring. He suddenly dropped the mug, and sat down heavily on his chair, his body spasming, forcing the chair away from the table. His torso began to shake, his eyes rolled back in his head, and as he continued to fit, he slid to the floor.

No one moved from their chairs until he stopped twitching and lay perfectly still for a few minutes. You could've heard a pin drop. Judy rose from her chair and walked slowly to Jeff's side still clutching her mobile phone. She pressed some buttons, raised the phone to her ear and told reception to call an ambulance as Jeff was having a seizure. Then she took her place at the head of the table and addressed the Managers.

"He's dead. Before anyone arrives, I want you all to know, I've deleted the video. I heard nothing unusual, saw nothing unusual. I'm sure you will all agree. We had only just begun to have a board meeting discussing his retirement, until he began to look unwell and had a seizure. The agenda is in the paperwork on the desk if they want to see it. No one touched him. Nothing unusual happened here today. No questions need to be asked. Understand? We all still have our jobs, and our dignity has been restored." Judy pointed to the lifeless body on the floor. "I'm sure you will all agree, no matter who is appointed as the new CEO, anyone would be better than him. May he rot in Hell."

30

LUCIA

Judy Sledge called me when I arrived at the hotel.

"How did it go?" I asked.

"Better than I could've hoped. I was invited into the meeting to take notes. Nearly everyone around that table told Jeff what they thought of him. It was like the words couldn't be held inside their mouths for a second longer, they spewed out. He wasn't impressed. I thought he was going to explode he was so angry, and then he told them he was firing them all. He picked up his cupcake, took a huge bite, told them what he thought of them, and had a seizure. Although I wasn't expecting that, I'm glad he's dead."

"What happens now?"

"They'll appoint another CEO, I get to keep my well-paid job until they retrench me at the end of next year, and everyone can breathe easy knowing they don't have to work for Jeff."

"He can't hurt or humiliate anyone again."

'Thank you."

"I'm happy I could help."

"When I heard through the grapevine that he was trying to get rid of me without paying me what I was due, I knew I had to do something."

"It was fate that we met. You helped me and I helped you."

"When you approached me to find out more about Jeff and offered to help me, I couldn't believe my luck. All I wanted to do was get my substantial retrenchment package, buy a house by the beach somewhere and paint my watercolors. I though the cupcakes were only going to make people tell the truth, and he was just going to be humiliated and retire early. I wasn't expecting them to be deadly. Jeff dying was icing on the cupcake if you pardon the pun."

"Only one cupcake was deadly. It was designed to be ingested by Jeff and to react with his current medication. I wasn't sure if it would have the desired effect."

"As soon as he ate the cupcake and drank his coffee, he had a seizure."

"Needless to mention to you this conversation stays between us."

"Of course. And I owe you one soul when I die."

"I'm prepared to tear up the contract in lieu of acquiring Jeff's soul early."

"No, a deal's a deal. I signed on the dotted line."

"May you live a long and happy life by the beach, Judy."

"Goodbye. Take care, Miss 'Devil-In-Training'. I will see you in Hell."

I called Rachel on my way to work to tell her about Jeff Hollis. I had already shared what I knew about Stella's truth formula, and we'd both agreed Jeff needed a little pay-back.

"How did it go?"

"You'll be pleased to know it went rather well. The truth formula worked. There was an added little bonus of a dead body. But you don't have to worry about it. That was all down to me, not Stella."

"A dead body! One of the test subjects?"

"Yes, but not from the truth serum. I added a little extra something special of my own."

"A little extra?"

"I have an old book of witches' potions I wanted to try. The guy was prone to seizures, I helped him have one. He was a selfish, greedy narcissist, so I added something special to the chocolate trident for his cupcake, knowing he had a sweet tooth. He died. But don't be sorry, he was the scum of the earth. A bit like your ex-husband."

"How do you know it went well?"

"I arranged the test with a woman I met when I was investigating one of our rather nasty male hotel guests, who liked to beat up hookers. She just called to tell me the truth formula test went well, and although she was surprised that he died, she was happy with the result. Now it's our little secret."

"Did she sign on the dotted line too?"

"Yes, she did. I got rid of Jeff, and she gets her beach house when she's retrenched."

"How did you know he'd get the deadly trident?"

"I told her to make sure the greedy bastard got the biggest cupcake. That was where I placed the special trident."

31

LUC

*T*here was a marked shift in the atmosphere on Earth. I was spending more quality time with Harper, and more time with Domenic, Sophie, and Daisy when I could. Lucia in fulfilling her probationary period was making me proud of her independence and lateral thinking. The bakery was doing well, making money, and bringing in new customers. It would take a while before I got a return on my investment, but it went without saying that I didn't need the money. I just needed to make sure Lucia understood that running a business wasn't easy.

Now I'm thinking it's time for Lucia to learn more about life in Hell.

Lucia, I think it's time to move you out of the night manager's position and return to Hell.

Really? I was sort of getting used to the long hours and the quality clientele.

You've proved yourself to me. I need you to spend time with Rourke.

Why?

He's my right-hand demon. He manages everything in Hell when I'm on Earth. He needs to know what you would expect if you're taking over.

Can't he just pretend that it's business as usual?

I thought you would prefer to put your own stamp on things.

Rourke won't like it.

Then it's up to you to work with him. Your replacement will be arriving tomorrow, so pack your things and say your goodbyes tonight.

So soon?

Is there any reason you want to draw this out?

No. Well not really. But I'm going to miss Rachel, and I think I've been helping some people with their... problems.

Your revenge scenarios?

Yes. I enjoyed them very much.

I could tell. You can still help people. You won't be in Hell 24/7. You are expected to be on Earth working your devilish magic.

Talking about magic, I found some spells and potions in the book I borrowed from Daisy. It was very helpful in getting rid of that despicable CEO, Jeff Hollis.

You'll have to show me the book.

I left it with Sophie to give it back to Daisy. She has a fascination with that old book.

It wouldn't surprise me. Magic is in her DNA after all.

Can I at least have a night at home with Mom?

Sure, take a couple of days. I'll expect you in Hell on Monday.

"Rourke, Lucia is returning next week. Please help her to get adjusted into the daily routine again."

"Of course, My Lord." Rourke's words did not match the expression on his face.

"I do understand your reluctance, but I really need you to make the effort and spend as much time with her as possible."

"Your daughter is not like any other human female I have met."

"She certainly is unique. But I'm counting on you to overcome your initial discomfort that working with a woman obviously causes."

"I shall do my best My Lord."

"I have always been able to count on you Rourke. She needs guidance and you are ideally suited to provide it."

"Drake's a younger demon, closer to her age. Wouldn't he be better suited, My Lord?"

"She needs to learn from the best."

"Then you should be training her, My Lord."

"Are you questioning my judgement, Rourke?"

"No, My Lord. I'm not sure that I have the... fortitude."

"Interesting word to use in this circumstance. Does Lucia cause you to doubt yourself?"

"She doesn't take direction, is willful, demanding, and argumentative. I'm afraid I might do or say something to her which will cause you to disintegrate me, My Lord."

I laughed out loud at this confession.

"Rourke, you needn't worry on that count. Dealing with Lucia on a daily basis, and teaching her the ropes is punishment enough."

"Very well My Lord." Rourke appeared visibly relieved.

3 2

LUCIA

*T*he screams of the inmates became fainter the higher the
elevator rose to my office on the top floor of the tower. As
the doors opened, I slung the backpack over my shoulder, took a step
into the corridor and smacked straight into Rourke's chest, bouncing
back a few inches. *Oh. My. Lord. He's solid muscle.* I couldn't help but
smile because I had an image of a semi-naked Rourke in a toga flash
into my brain from that small physical touch, and he didn't disap-
point. He looked down his nose at me and his expression deepened
from surly to annoyed in an instant, as if he had just stepped in something unpleasant.

"Good morning, Rourke. Fancy meeting you here. Just the man I
was looking for. My father tells me I'm working with you for the time
being. You're going to give me all the intel, show me the ropes, and
have me up to scratch with all this Devil stuff in no time at all."

Rourke looked even less impressed. *What is his problem, doesn't he
ever smile?*

"Get rid of the backpack, get changed and meet me in my office in
five."

"Could we make that ten I have to…"

"Five."

"But I've got to…"

"No."

"Really?"

"Four."

"Okay, okay."

I took the hint, sprinted up the corridor, dropped the backpack in my office, and quickly donned my uniform. When I returned, still buttoning up my leather waistcoat, he was waiting by his desk, holding a cattle prod.

"We just received new cattle prods. These ones cause searing, burning, and scarring at the contact point, when applied continuously to the skin. With the fornicators, pedophiles, or rapists, we want them to be used on the genitals for maximum effect."

"Why do I have to know how to use one of these. Don't we have a team downstairs to do this?"

"You need to learn how to use all the equipment. It's part of the training. You need to know how bad each type of torture affects the human body to determine the appropriate punishment. I had to learn all this. Now it's your turn."

"Who taught you?"

"Your father."

"Really? Why would he not delegate this task to someone else?"

"Your father took me under his wing. He said he saw something in me and wanted me to learn from the best."

"Ah. Now I see why *you* are teaching me. He's trusting you to make sure I get it right. That's a lot of pressure… on you I mean." I smiled. He looked displeased so I got rid of the smile.

I noticed his eye twitch. His expression was still glum, but I had obviously hit a sore point.

"Come." He commanded. Rourke strode off and I trotted after him as fast as my legs would carry me.

As it happened, we passed by a group of new inmates in Hell, and I spotted Jeff Hollis.

"Well, isn't this your lucky day, Jeff. Can I take this one?" I asked the demon guard.

"Do I know you?" Jeff asked.

"No. But you're going to remember me after today." In my real body he wouldn't recognize me.

The guard brought Jeff to the torture chamber and shackled him to the wall.

"Strip him."

The guard did as I asked. Jeff didn't appear phased by the fact that he was now naked. He still had a certain look of superiority on his face. I presumed that was because I was a woman and he had always taken every opportunity to belittle women. How far he'd come from the lofty heights he'd once enjoyed as CEO.

"You are my test subject today, Jeff."

I pressed the cattle prod into his stomach and held it there. The pain shook his body and he dropped to his knees. I moved the prod to his shoulder, then his back, witnessing the skin searing and scarring, the smell of burning flesh permeating the room. After twenty minutes had passed, listening to the sounds of his pain, I handed the prod to another guard and left the room. Rourke was standing in the corridor waiting for me.

"You're finished?" Rourke asked.

"I don't see the point in continuing. Surely there are other guards down here who enjoy this sort of thing? I prefer intellectual or emotional torture, or straightforward death, rather than inflicting physical pain."

"But it's part of the job."

"It's not my thing."

"Not your *thing*?" Rourke appeared stunned by this remark.

"I'm an intelligent woman. Surely there is something I'm better suited to perform. Let's leave the torture implements to those who enjoy them. Boys and their toys if you know what I mean."

"Your father said…"

"I know what he said, but I'm just not feeling it. Let's move on. What else do you have to show me?"

"Pretty much everything on this level is set up for torture."

"Well, I've seen the upper levels and spent my first months in Hell on the administration floor leaning about admissions and contracts. There must be something else? Surely?"

"Do you understand the concept of Hell? There is nothing else. Hell is supposed to be torture, pain, and suffering."

"For the inmates, yes. But surely there is something more for the guards? Even prison guards in the real world have downtime. What do you do for entertainment."

"Entertainment?"

"Fun?"

"There is no room for fun in Hell."

Now I understood why my father wanted to leave.

Father?

Yes Lucia.

I'm not cut out for this.

What are you talking about, Lucia?

I'm not going to spend all my time underground searing flesh, cutting off appendages, or poking people with cattle prods.

I see.

I'm intelligent, I'm not a barbarian. Please give me some other job.

Torture wasn't going to be your everyday job. Rourke was giving you an insight.

Rourke's enjoying my discomfort. He doesn't like me, that fact is obvious.

We all are required to perform tasks that we don't enjoy when we're new to the job.

You're doing this deliberately, aren't you?

What do you mean?

Trying to put me off. Change my mind.

Is it working?

No. But I do have an idea I would like you to consider.

An idea?

A suggestion. How about Rourke runs the day-to-day processes in Hell for you. And I concentrate on a job on Earth? I think I could be more useful above ground. You were happy with my progress at the Hotel. How about another Hotel? Maybe something busier, or overseas? An international hotel would have a lot of undesirables. Then I can quickly fly to take care of matters that need a devilish hand.

No.

No? You aren't even going to think about it? Give my idea a chance?

I knew I should have insisted on Domenic taking over.

And I should have been born a boy. Maybe I would have loved torture and being cruel.

This conversation is over, Lucia.

I closed my eyes and raised my hands to my temples, massaging the headache that had taken hold. I really didn't think this through. I should've had a better plan to talk to my father, a cleverly constructed strategy, instead of just blurting out what I was thinking. Now he's angry with me, and he won't listen to anything I have to say.

I opened my eyes and suddenly remembered where I was, stuck in the bowels of the earth, and turned to see Rourke watching me from a distance in the dark and dingy cavern. *Nope, I don't need his condescending opinion.* I don't want to deal with him right now. I headed in the opposite direction, walking fast, turning left, then right, I started running with no idea of where I was going. I just needed to get as far away from every other soul as possible.

The passage came to a dead end, and I had to admit defeat. I couldn't escape Hell, and it looked like I was going to have to go back and apologize to Rourke. An unfamiliar rumbling noise sounded from above. Small pieces of clay and dirt tumbled down on my head, the ground beneath me began to shake.

I began running back in the direction I had come. I arrived at a fork with two tunnels ahead. Did I come down the right or the left? I took the right, running faster, unsteady on my feet due to the earth trembling beneath them. The walls were cracked, steam escaping around me, large rocks littered the path ahead. I came to another dead end. I had chosen the wrong tunnel. I ran back down the tunnel jumping out of the way of rocks falling from the roof above but dodged left instead of right and a rock hit my head disorientating me, another hit my shoulder, forcing me to my knee, and pain shot up my thigh. I rolled onto my back, cradling the injured knee. The shaking and shuddering around me intensified in the tunnel.

Suddenly Rourke appeared and threw himself bodily on top on me, flattening me to the ground, trapping my arms at my sides and knocking all the air from my lungs. I tried to move him, to catch a breath, but it was impossible as a large boulder was wedged between his back and the wall pinning us both to the ground. The realization that he had thrown himself into the path of the boulder to protect me wasn't lost on me.

"Stay still," he commanded.

I couldn't move even if I wanted to.

"I can't breathe. You're squashing me with your gigantic body!"

"This gigantic body as you put it, saved you from the rock pinning us down, which would surely have killed you."

"You're hurt!" I was shocked to see blood pouring from his shoulder and back, dripping onto me and the dirt beneath us.

"Are you okay?" he asked.

"I'm okay. I'll get help. I'll call my father."

I prayed my father would hear me and answer my call.

Father!

Nothing. No indication he heard me.

Father, please.

More boulders crumbled above us, dirt and earth and small rocks filled in the empty spaces around our bodies. The realization came swiftly that within minutes, maybe even seconds, we were going to be buried within this space. I looked into his eyes and knew he'd come to the same conclusion. The inevitability of death brought with it a type of calm I had never experienced before. They'd never find our bodies. If another fissure opened below us, we could be consumed by lava. The rumbling continued, the floor and walls shook.

33

LUCIA

*W*ell, if I was going to die, I wasn't going to die alone. But being face to face with someone who hated me wasn't the ideal scenario.

"This wasn't how I pictured dying."

"Stop talking," Rourke said through gritted teeth.

"Don't tell me what to do. My life is flashing before my eyes."

"Shhhhhh."

"Don't shush me."

Rourke's lips came down on mine, stopping all crazy thoughts of dying, and sending a totally different message to my brain. My eyes fluttered closed. His mouth may have been intent on stopping conversation, but now I had a totally different impression of this powerful demon. His lips were surprisingly sensual and remained still but now mine were moving and I deepened the kiss enjoying the sensation of his mouth on mine. If these were my last minutes and I was about to die, it was going to be on my terms. As my last act of She-Devilish pleasure, I attempted to crack the hard shell of the man wedged securely on top of me, to see if he had any emotions.

My tongue danced along his and I heard a moan deep in his throat. But I couldn't tell if he was in pain or if my kiss was working. I doubled down on the kiss, putting every ounce of emotion and pent-up passion I could into it. Then I felt the unmistakable erection wedged between us, hardening, pushing into my stomach, and I wanted to cheer. *Rourke does have feelings like any other male!* I finally broke the kiss and opened my eyes. The surprised expression on his face was one I was taking to my grave, and I smiled in return, delighted by the fact I had managed to give him even a few seconds of pleasure.

The boulder pinning us down rocked a little and seemed to be absorbed by the wall behind it, then sucked through an opening in the tunnel wall, along with the dirt and debris surrounding our bodies. Through the gaping hole I could see my father and several other large demon guards standing on the other side beside a vehicle. Rourke was lifted and placed face down on a stretcher on the back of what looked like an elongated golf cart. A demon with a medical kit helped me to my feet, quickly checking me for injuries. My father's strong arms lifted me, placed me beside him on the seat of this vehicle, and we were all moving at the speed of light through the tunnels, leaving the crumbing earth and the blackness behind us.

Once back at the tower, the vehicle with Rourke aboard disappeared down a corridor. My father carried me to his office and called the medics to check me over thoroughly. A few minor cuts and bruises, a sore head, perhaps a minor concussion but otherwise fine, I accepted the glass of brandy my father gave me.

"Thank you." I took a large gulp and coughed and spluttered.

"Take it easy. You've had a nasty shock. Sip the brandy, Lucia."

"What happened down there?"

"There was an earthquake. Anything that happens above will ultimately affect us down here. Why were you so far away from the Tower?"

"I was upset. And you ended our conversation. And you were angry with me."

"I had every reason to be angry. You keep changing the plan."

"And you didn't answer me when I needed you."

"Lucia there was a lot going on above earth. Thousands have been killed or lost to the earthquake. I was caught up in something else. But I'm sorry I didn't answer right away."

"Rourke saved me. He threw himself in the path of that boulder. I would be dead by now if he hadn't followed me."

"I shall see that he's rewarded."

"I need to go and see him. Where did they take him?"

"To the hospital. But you need to take a minute to get your breath."

"No father. I need to see him to make sure he's okay."

"Very well."

My father took my arm and we walked to the back wall, and he opened The Veil. He found the pinprick of light that was Rourke, enlarged it, and we saw them working on his injuries in what looked like a hospital theatre. He was unconscious laying on his stomach, and his back was ripped open. But what shocked me even more was the network of scars he had on the skin unaffected by the boulder.

"He's been beaten," I said, amazed by this realization.

"Yes, he was mistreated, during his time on earth."

"There are a lot of scars."

"He was a slave. He was incarcerated for killing a man, which resulted in him being put to death. We met the day he arrived in Hell. But he should never have been sent here. He killed his abuser to protect others less fortunate than himself. I saw a lot of positive qualities in Rourke, and that was why I trained him to be my second in charge." My father closed The Veil and we returned to his office.

"You trust him."

"With my life. And now as it happens, with yours. He's a good man."

"I have a new appreciation of him. I thought he hated me and wanted me to suffer in Hell. Maybe he really wanted to prove to me that this life is not for me."

"Is he correct, Lucia?"

"As I told you earlier. I think that staying one hundred percent of the time in Hell is not for me. But I want to help you, Father. I want to give you the opportunity to be with Mom, to live a life away from here. To enjoy Daisy and other children that may come from Domenic."

"What about you, Lucia? Do you want children?"

"Life on Earth has so much darkness. There are so many cruel and wicked people walking amongst the innocent. I would worry for any child I had, knowing who I am, knowing my lineage. I am not even sure that I'm maternal, although I do love my family and warm to the thought that I'm an aunt, a sister, a sister-in-law, a daughter. And of course, being the Devil's daughter has brought me a new insight into human behavior."

"You've amazed me with your dedication in the last year, Lucia. You've managed to collect many souls, and you've helped women who've been badly treated. The bakery is doing well, the refuge you adopted is benefitting from Rachel's and your help. I'm very proud of you."

"Are you?" My breath caught in my throat. I was finding it hard to breathe.

"Very much so."

"I was so hoping to prove to you that I am as good as any boy."

"Lucia, my darling girl. You are more precious to me because *you* are *you*. Headstrong, determined, intelligent, dedicated, passionate, and caring, all those qualities I admire. You are unique. There is no one in Hell or on Earth like you, and I can make an informed guess that there never will be. I don't want you to try to be a boy. You are perfect just the way you are. Although you do cause me to worry. But only because I love you with all my heart. And of course, so does your mother. We would lay down our lives for you."

"I want you to be proud of me," I sobbed.

Now the tears flowed. My father put his arm around my shoulders and pulled me to his strong chest. I sank into his embrace, absorbing his love for me, and his strength. I needed to feel his arms around me. Suddenly I was aware of how close I had come to never experiencing this again. He moved to hold me at arms-length and looked into my eyes.

"I've given some thought to your proposal. When Rourke has

recovered and if he is amenable to the suggestion, we will work out a solution. Nearly losing you has caused me to reconsider. I want you to be happy, Lucia."

"Thank you, Father. That means a lot to me."

"Now I'm going to suggest a few days, on Earth with your mother. Aimee will make all your favorite foods, and spoil you. You can visit Domenic, Sophie, and Daisy and when you return, hopefully Rourke will be recovered, and we can talk. What do you think?"

"Won't the other demons think you're playing favorites, giving me a leave pass so soon after Paris?"

"Do you honestly think I care? You are my child. Nepotism at its finest down here. Now go get your things and give Daisy a hug from me. I will mind the fort whilst you are gone."

34

LUCIA

I left my father and headed to my office to pack a few essentials, but I can't leave without seeing Rourke. I picked up my bag, turned and bumped into Drake coming in the door.

"Drake! Can you take me to the hospital? I need to see Rourke."

"He's with the medics."

"Then I'll wait."

"He's unconscious."

"I understand that, but I need to see him." We are at a stand-off, but I can see the cogs in his brain working overtime. *What happens if he takes me, and what happens if he doesn't.* "Please, Drake. He saved my life."

"Follow me."

He took me to a room several floors below the Tower, where we could watch the operation unobserved from a balcony of sorts. The medics were cleaning his wounds, removing the dirt and debris, and I had a lump in my throat witnessing how badly his back was damaged.

"He lost a lot of blood. They think there's spinal damage," Drake whispered.

"No. Surely not."

I covered my mouth with my hands praying that was not the case.

Below us the door opened, my father appeared and had a word with the medics, who then covered Rourke with a bloodied sheet and left the room. My father approached the table and pulled the sheet down to Rourke's hips. He placed his hands on his back, and bowed his head, almost as if in prayer. Then he picked up a scalpel, cut the palm of his hand, dripped his blood into the wounds, then ran the bloodied hand down and around the edges of the wounds on Rourke's back.

We watched in amazement as the wounds began to pull together, attempting to close.

"You can come down, Lucia and Drake. I'm aware you're up there."

When we finally entered the room, my father was standing near Rourke's unconscious form, with his arms folded, and a stern look on his face.

"Lucia, I thought I told you to go back to earth? And what were you thinking bring her down here, Drake?"

"She wanted to see Rourke, My Lord."

"Don't blame, Drake. I made him bring me. Rourke saved my life. I wasn't going to just leave, without at least telling him I appreciated what he'd done."

"He's unconscious. They've given him something to keep him immobile."

"I would've waited. What did you do to him?"

"I helped him recover."

"You care for him." It wasn't a question. It was obvious that Rourke means more to my father than he'd been willing to share.

"There was a possibility he wasn't going to be able to walk. I couldn't have that. Rourke is essential to the running of Hell."

"Will he recover fully?"

"Time will tell."

I wanted to communicate with him. I clasped the right hand of the unconscious Rourke between mine, to show him that I appreciated what he had done for me, and I was sure I felt him flex his fingers a little in return. I received another glimpse of his tragic life on earth.

"Please keep me informed and let me know how he is." I turned to Drake and made eye contact. He nodded.

I stepped under the rain shower in my family's Hollywood home, sighing as the hot water flowed over my head and down my body, washing away every vestige of dirt and grime. My long dark hair, which now reached my hips, became plastered to my skin. I wanted to stay there forever luxuriating in the steady stream of clean, hot water, coupled with the early morning sunlight pouring in from the skylight in the bathroom. The darkness which almost consumed me was in my past. The incident clarified my proposal to my father in my mind. Somehow, we needed make this work. Rourke had to get better to continue his work below ground, and I could most definitely work above ground and surely between the two of us the family business could still go on.

Reluctantly I shut off the faucets, stepped out of the shower, wrapped a towel around me, twisted my hair up on top of my head and walked through to my bedroom to dress for the day. A blue linen shirt over jeans was perfect attire for a day at home. I folded back the shirt cuffs to just below my elbows, towel dried my hair, combed out the snags, and left it to dry naturally. It fell down my back in soft waves, leaving wet patches on my shirt.

Mom wouldn't approve, as she always liked things to be perfect, but I didn't care. Being home meant comfortable clothes, no shoes, no make-up and untethered hair. Being home meant the aroma of good food wafting from the kitchen that someone has made for me, relaxing and sinking into soft cushions on the couch to read a book or drink a cup of coffee. Being home meant choosing peace and quiet in my own bedroom. Or wandering downstairs looking for someone to talk to if I felt inclined, as there was always someone at home, or Cameron outside working in the garden. I wasn't ever going to take home for granted.

❧

The house was quiet. I enjoyed this time of day, when everyone was still in bed and I could walk around the house barefoot, like I did when I was a child, and not make a sound. I made a cup of coffee and took it outside to sit by the pool. The gate was open between the two properties, and I could see Domenic and Sophie's house bathed in early morning light. We were so lucky to be living close, to be able to help each other, and to support each other. I imagined they were getting ready to start their day too. Maybe Daisy was having breakfast or playing with her toys. I'm glad my mother had a grandchild to love, and to spoil.

My father's words replayed in my head. *What about you, Lucia. Do you want children?*

Do I want children? I'd never really longed for children like some girls do. Maybe because I was a spoiled little princess. Oh yes, I knew I was spoiled. But I'd grown up a lot in the last year and changed in ways I could never have imagined.

"Lucia! You're up early," Aimee called out from the patio door. "I'm making breakfast. Would you like waffles?"

"When have I ever turned down your waffles Aimee?"

"Your mother will be down shortly. We're going to visit Sophie and Daisy this morning. Are you coming?"

"You couldn't keep me away." I laughed and joined Aimee in the breakfast room while she set the table.

"You seem very cheerful this morning. I'm surprised you're not in bed, resting, after your ordeal."

"My ordeal, as you put it, has made me appreciate things more. Like clean water, and sunlight, and breathing!"

"Of course. Have you heard how Rourke is recovering?"

"No, not this morning. I'll ask Father."

Good morning, Father, can you tell me how Rourke is today?

Good morning, Lucia. I hope you slept well. Rourke has shown marked improvement.

Can you tell him...

What?

Can you tell him I'm glad he's recovering.

I will.

And that I was thinking about him.

Yes.

To tell the truth, he'd been on my mind constantly since the moment he placed his lips on mine. Of course, I wasn't oblivious to the fact he'd been trying to shut me up, but a tiny part of me thought there was more to it. And when I kissed him back his body did respond.

I poured a glass of freshly squeezed orange juice from the pitcher on the table and took my seat. The tantalizing aroma of home-made waffles drifted out from the kitchen and made my mouth water. I tried to think but couldn't honestly remember the last time I ate anything. My stomach rumbled in reply to my query. Aimee appeared with a plate of piping hot waffles, topped with mixed berries, the melted butter and honey dripping down the stack onto the plate.

"This looks delicious, Aimee. Thank you."

"I hope you made some for me, Aimee," my mother called out, sailing into the breakfast room in a pale peach kimono, her hair perfectly styled. "And not just for your favorite girl."

"Hi Mom." I looked at Raven by her side. "Where's Max?"

"He's with Cameron at the Gatehouse. We're expecting a delivery."

"Something new for Daisy?"

"How did you guess? It's a dual-level cubbyhouse, with a swing set attached."

"Isn't she a bit young?"

"Oh, I'm not giving it to her yet. But I saw it and couldn't resist."

"You're having the best time spoiling this little girl, aren't you Mom?"

"Actually I am. She's a delight, and such a smart child. When I hold her and look into those big blue eyes, I imagine she understands every word I say. She knows I love her. That we all love her."

"Here you go." Aimee placed a plate containing two perfect waffles, and berries, in front of my mother.

"Only two waffles, Mom?"

"I'm trying to watch what I eat. Aimee's food is too good."

"Do you want me to make a pot of tea now?" Aimee asked.

"After I eat thank you. Unless Lucia wants some."

"No, I'm happy with juice, thanks." I stood to take the plate and glass back to the kitchen. "I'll be in my room. Call me when you're ready to leave."

I wanted to use The Veil to check on Rourke. I had to be alone to achieve that. My father had instructed me, but this was the first time I had put it into practice. Once in my room I faced North, closed my eyes, and concentrated very hard on opening The Veil. I stepped inside the void, brought the image of Rourke into my mind, and very soon a pinpoint of light became bigger until I had the vision of Rourke stretched out on a bed before me. He looked much better. A medic came in and helped him to stand. He took a few tentative steps, then a few more confident ones. He was obviously improving, and he could indeed walk. This was a good result and made me feel less guilty about leaving Hell.

I closed the Veil, and pulled a brush through my hair, which had dried into waves cascading over my shoulders and down my back. My mother was calling me from downstairs. Just like she did when I was at school. It made me smile.

It was nice to be home.

35

DOMENIC

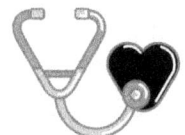

It caught me by surprise to see Lucia sitting with my mother and Aimee at our kitchen table. Luc had informed me about the near fatal incident in Hell. I was thankful Lucia was safely back home, and grateful that Rourke had been on hand to prevent a tragedy. I wasn't convinced that Hell was the place for Lucia, even though Luc had stated on more than one occasion that she was doing well. My baby sister and I haven't had many telepathic conversations over the last twelve months. Since Daisy came along daily life wasn't the same. Sophie and I were busier, and our focus had changed.

"Lucia, it's lovely to see you. I didn't know you were back."

"I only arrived late last night."

"Luc told me what happened. I'm glad you came out unscathed. Rourke is recovering, I hear."

"Yes. Rourke was the hero of the day."

"You'll notice a big change in Daisy. She's growing up so fast. She's walking and talking a little, although most of the time I have no idea what she's saying. She loves to play in the vegetable garden, wandering amongst the plants and picking up bugs to examine them. She seems to have a leaning towards nature, and the outdoors. We're very lucky to have such a big yard for her to explore."

"Spoken like a true besotted father," Lucia said.

"It's not only my opinion. Aimee also thinks she's gifted. She's noticed that when she takes Daisy with her to the vegetable patch, the plants grow better."

"It's true," Aimee said. "She toddles between the plants talking gibberish, and touching the leaves and they bloom. My tomatoes are bigger this year, the green beans are huge. She's my good luck charm in the garden."

I turned to see Sophie walking down the hall with Daisy on her hip.

"Dada!"

Daisy stretched her hands out to me, and I took her and threw her up in the air. She giggled and clapped her hands. I threw her up again.

"Be careful she doesn't spit up on your suit jacket," Sophie said.

"Can I have a hold of my niece?" Lucia asked.

I placed Daisy on Lucia's knee, noting the difference in their appearance. Daisy was fair-skinned child, with red hair and big blue eyes. Lucia had olive-toned skin and dark hair. Daisy reached up her chubby hand and gently touched Lucia's cheek. I know my daughter had the same ability as I do to calm people by touch. We knew she could move objects like Lucia did when she was a child, and Aimee was convinced she could help plants grow. I wondered what other abilities she had. Abilities that we were yet to discover.

"I'd better get moving. I have patients to see before my surgical list this afternoon. I'll be home a little later for dinner tonight. Hopefully not too late. Go ahead and eat with Daisy."

"You could come over to our house, Sophie, and we could all eat together since Lucia is home," my mother said.

"I'd like that." Sophie smiled. "I'll bathe Daisy before dinner and bring her pram so I can settle her after dinner."

"Lovely that's settled then. A family dinner. Domenic, I hope you aren't too late and can join us."

"I'll try. No guarantee."

36
ROURKE

*T*hey told me I was recovering. However, I'm not a good patient, and I've been forced to stay in this hospital room against my will. I'd rather be returning to duty because I don't know what to do with myself. The saying "idle hands are the Devil's playthings" keeps flashing into my mind. I've no idea why. The only benefit is that I have time to think about how far I've come.

Hell has been my home for centuries. On Earth, my existence as a slave was fraught with punishment and pain for even the slightest perceived wrongdoing. But when my master began abusing children, it was the straw that broke the camel's back. I killed him and I have never regretted my actions. His barbaric treatment of slaves meant my master was also sent to this scorching, sulfurous prison for eternity. I was happy to secure that place in Hell for him. The day I arrived here and was greeted by the Devil himself who took me under his wing, I was aware my fortunes were about to drastically change.

I learned from the best. I educated myself and made the effort to seek out those who could help me. Devil knows I have had plenty of time in Hell to accumulate knowledge. I built up my body and my strength, and have been a loyal servant to My Lord, Luc Nightingale. I have followed instructions, never questioned My Lord's decisions, have punished, tortured, and dealt with the scum of the earth who ended up in Hell. I have managed to recruit a band of loyal demons who, like me, were sent to Hell for trying to right wrongs done by mankind. We have maintained order as best we can.

However, the day My Lord informed me his daughter was coming to Hell to replace him, was the day I questioned his sanity. Having a female demon guard in Hell was unheard of. Men were required in this position because of their strength, their power, and the conditions in which they had to reside. The only women down here were inmates. Hell was run by a Patriarchy, always had been, and in my opinion, always should be.

The day she arrived I knew I was in trouble. Lucia Nightingale was the most beautiful creature I had ever seen. When My Lord gave me the task of showing her all the ins and outs of the day to day running of Hell, I tried to fob her off to Drake. Looking back, I should've been more insistent, and perhaps I wouldn't be in a hospital bed and trying to learn how to walk again.

Of all the women I have ever met, she was the most infuriating, exasperating, headstrong, willful, stubborn, and yet thoroughly intoxicating. When she'd said she didn't want to torture the inmates and took off down the tunnels I had no choice but to follow her. Babysitting wasn't a task I enjoyed. I thought of letting her cool off, but the tunnels were dangerous to someone new in Hell, full of dead ends. I had no choice but to follow at a distance.

The cave-in had come as a surprise. It was fortunate that I arrived at that moment, or she would have been crushed. Instinct had taken over when I threw myself on top of her, yet she still argued with me! I warned her to be quiet, and she wouldn't, but I do not know what possessed me to lay my lips against hers. As soon as I did, I knew it was a foolish move, but I couldn't take it back. She seemed to enjoy it. That kiss changed everything, and now I can't stop thinking about her, can't stop the thought of her body beneath mine in that cave and what I wanted to do at that moment, even though I knew we were about to be buried or burned to a crisp in lava.

I had to learn to control my thoughts because if My Lord found out, there was no knowing what he will do.

37
LUCIA

I was aware that I was dreaming, but it was so good that I didn't want to wake up. Rourke was kissing me passionately and my body lit up from within, cleaving to him, wanting his hands on me, desperate to feel him plunge deep inside me. My nipples were painfully puckered, rubbing against his bare chest. I imagined I could feel him grinding against me. My hips rose, my breathing was labored, I was aching for release, and I knew he could give that to me. Just a little more, a little harder, a little to the left. Stars flickered and lit up behind my eyelids and I was coming and the moan erupting from my throat startled me awake. My hands were firmly clasped between my damp thighs, and I realized I'd brought about my own release.

Damn this man... or demon, or whatever the Hell he was. He was a male, had all the XY chromosomes and he had become a problem. Why was I attracted to someone who had done everything he could to show me he wanted me gone from Hell? To show me that women are weak and have no place in a man's domain. He was aloof, dismissive and a know-it-all. *So why the Hell am I wasting even a second of my time thinking about him?*

❧

It was time I checked on Rachel and Sweet Devil Bakery. I hadn't been a very good friend or business partner lately, and I needed to remedy that fact. When I opened the door and saw the tables full of smiling customers, with plates of cakes and mugs of coffee in front of them, it made my heart swell with pride. Rachel and I had created something wonderful from an abandoned shop front. Sure, Rachel has the creative talent, and my family gave us the start-up money, but I was proud of my part in steering this business to fruition.

"Hey Rachel."

"Hi. I was wondering when you were going to grace us with your presence."

"I see our café is full."

"We had to turn away customers. But some were willing to buy coffee and cakes to go."

"Maybe we need to look at expanding the café?"

"There's no room for more tables in there."

"What about the shop next door?"

"I don't think they do much business, but I haven't heard that they're ready to vacate their lease."

"Maybe it's time for me to have a chat to the owner?"

"Hang on, can we afford to take on more space?"

"Let me at least enquire. Then I'll work out the cost and we can discuss. Okay?"

"Sounds fair."

"Is Stella working today?"

"No, she's studying."

"I'll drop by her place later."

I thought it prudent to talk to my father before I made any enquiries about expansion.

Father, have you got a minute?

Yes Lucia.

The café is doing well, and we've had to turn people away due to lack of seating. I think we could add more tables if we had the space.

Really?

I'd like to talk to the shop owner next door and see if he's willing to give up a little of his space. I think there's a storage room on the other side of our shared wall. He doesn't seem to be very busy. He might be happy to pay less rent for a smaller space.

That's extra expense for your business.

Sales will make up the difference.

There's no harm in trying, but don't get your hopes up.

We might take longer to pay you back.

I've already come to that conclusion.

You're not going to talk me out of it?

I'm giving you a chance to prove you can make this work.

I appreciate it.

I pushed open the door to "Little Treasures", the toy store next door, and was immediately enchanted by the fairy displays, the wooden trucks and doll houses, and the variety of soft plush toys scattered about the shop. On the counter, a music box played Claire de Lune, a little toy ballerina "on pointe", turned in a circle on the lid. I was the only customer in this children's fairyland. I placed a bakery box with cakes on the counter, picked up the tiny brass bell sitting there, and jiggled it. No one appeared, so I juggled it again.

Someone tapped me on the shoulder, and I spun around. A short elderly man, leaning on a walking stick stood behind me. He was wearing a cherry-red, velvet suit, a white shirt, and a black bow tie. I noticed he had carpet slippers on his feet, which was probably why I hadn't heard him. His long, curly, silver hair sat on his shoulders. His lips curved into a wide, endearing smile and his pale blue eyes twinkled with mischief.

"No need to ring it twice. I'm not deaf, just a little slow on my feet."

"Sorry, I thought... it doesn't matter."

"Can I help you find a toy?"

"No. I'm Lee Edwards, one of the business owners of the bakery next door." I pointed to the pink Sweet Devil bakery box I had placed on the counter. "I wanted to talk to you because I'd like to expand the café. I'm not sure what is behind our adjoining wall. Are you able to give up some space?"

"Why would I do that?"

"I've noticed you're not very busy. I thought you might be happy to pay less rent."

"You mean this room over here?" He walked to the door and pushed it open. There were cardboard boxes stacked on shelves, an old table and a couple of wooden chairs, but most of the room was empty. "I guess I could spare the space."

"We would be very grateful."

"If I do it, I would like you to do something for me."

"If it's cakes or pies you need, I'll see you get a good discount."

"No, that's not it. I'd like you to give my granddaughter Zoe a job waitressing. She was helping me, but as you've pointed out, business isn't going very well."

"Is she here? I'd like to interview her."

"She's out back. But I need to tell you something before you meet her. She is not like any other eighteen-year-old girl you meet. She's special."

"I understand. Everyone loves their grandkids."

"No. I mean she's a very quiet and sensitive young woman, and she has a special way about her. She was in a bad automobile accident when she was young, and she sustained a brain injury. The accident killed her parents. My wife and I became her legal guardians, and we home-schooled her. My wife passed away recently, so there's only me now to take care of her."

"Can I meet her?"

"I'll go bring her out. And there's something else."

"Yes?"

"Occasionally when Zoe touches something you own, or you've touched, she gets a reading. Sometimes she sees things that are going to happen, like a fortune teller. Some people can't handle that, but she doesn't understand to keep it to herself. She says it needs to come out."

He disappeared into the back of the shop, reappearing a little later holding the arm of a slight young girl with short dark hair and large hazel eyes, wearing blue jeans and a green sweater.

"Hi, Zoe. I'm Lee. I'm part-owner of the Sweet Devil bakery next door." I held out my hand.

Zoe looked at her grandfather who nodded. She shook my hand. I had a flash of the accident, resulting in her brain damage. I felt her shock when her parents were both pronounced dead at the scene.

She locked eyes with me, and I had the feeling she knew I was something more than human. She quickly withdrew her hand. *She sees me!*

"Hello," she said quietly.

"Your grandfather would like you to come and work for me in the bakery. What do you think?"

"You're sweet devil."

"Yes, that's my bakery."

"*You* are a sweet devil."

No doubt about it, she knew who I was, but I was wondering if she would be able to perform the tasks required of a waitress.

"Can I have a word with you, Mr...?"

"Farthing. Thomas Farthing. Call me Thomas."

"Okay, Thomas, can we have a word in private?"

"Are these cakes for us?" Zoe asked, glancing at the bakery box with the clear lid.

"They sure are. Would you like to take them into the kitchen and try some?"

I watched her face light up. She picked up the bakery box and went behind the counter to the kitchen.

"I know what you're going to say. She can take orders, and she can manage customers. She is just a little slow, and shy," he said.

"Thomas. Please understand. I am not discriminating, but your granddaughter has brain damage. It gets busy in the café. I'm worried she may not cope."

"Can you please try her out. Even for a few hours?"

"Okay, how about this. Before we make any deal, Zoe comes to work a couple of hours in the afternoon tomorrow. After the lunch rush. Say two until four o'clock?"

"Sounds good to me."

"Then if that works out, we can try another longer day. I'm not going to hold you to anything, and I don't want to be forced into anything, or stress Zoe. She needs to agree to this."

"I'll talk to her."

"She needs to do it because she wants to do it. Not just to please you."

"You want this space. I want the best for my granddaughter. She needs to spend time with people. She spends too much time with an old man."

I really hoped I wasn't making a mistake. Zoe had some difficulties, but I totally understood what her grandfather was trying to do. Everyone needed to feel useful in this life. Now I was going to have to explain to Rachel that we had another casual staff member to look after. With Rose helping in the kitchen and Paula waitressing, Stella helping with the baking and introducing the new frosting flavors and now Zoe, the numbers were climbing.

"Okay Thomas, I'll talk to my business partner. I'll drop off a uniform and she will need to wear flat white sneakers. No trip hazards. I'll see her tomorrow in the shop at 1.45pm to introduce her to the other girls before her shift."

"Thank you."

We shook hands. I had a flash of his life. He missed his wife Beverley very much. He was a kind man who loved to make children happy, which obviously was the reason for opening a toy shop. Thomas and Beverly only had one daughter, had always wanted more children but were never blessed with others. Joyce, Zoe's mother, would have been forty-five this week if she hadn't passed away in that collision. Thomas and Beverley believed God had saved Zoe in that crash, to keep them going.

38

ROURKE

*D*uring my recovery, Drake had accepted many of my responsibilities and I was impressed with what he'd done. According to the feedback I'd received, he'd been a wonderful stand-in. Today I was back in charge, and thankful to have returned to my desk outside My Lord's office. I wasn't good at taking orders, I preferred to give them. Of course, that did not apply to My Lord.

And as for Lucia Nightingale! That damned woman was constantly on my mind. Even when drifting off to sleep at night, she gave me no peace, invading my dreams with her sassy attitude and inappropriate ideas about how Hell should work. Excessive exercise normally cleared my head of worry, but today no matter how many weights I lifted or how many miles I pounded out on the treadmill, she still returned.

I dropped to the floor to perform my usually push up routine, but she was there, beneath me, smirking and daring me to kiss her again. I had to ditch my training early today, but I was determined to regain my strength and flexibility as soon as possible. A Demon Guard in my position needed to be feared, needed to be looked up to for his strength and fortitude. Not pitied because he was less capable after an injury.

"Rourke!"

"Yes, My Lord." I stood to attention at the door.

"What are you doing back at work? The medics told me you're not fully recovered."

"I believe I'm capable to work again."

"Come in here, shut the door and remove your shirt, I want to inspect your back."

I did as I was asked. I was aware my wound had closed, and the medics had obviously done a good job. Whenever I reached my hand around, I could feel the puckered skin along my spine amongst the scarred tissue, but it didn't feel the same as it used to feel. I was unwilling to look at the scar in the mirror until sufficient time had passed and it had fully healed.

My Lord stood behind me and inspected the damage. I felt his hand running over the puckered skin, extreme heat from his palm suffusing the tissue and muscles beneath. My body stiffened as pain shot up my spine, and my head began to thud in unison with my pounding heartbeat. Then he removed his hand and told me to put my shirt back on.

"What did you just do?"

"Since you are determined to be back on duty, I wanted to speed up the recovery."

"You can do that?"

"Well, let's see. It's not conclusive. Let me know tomorrow if you notice an improvement in stamina. You can go."

"Yes, My Lord." I returned to my desk, collected some new admission files, and went in search of Drake.

39
LUCIA

Rachel was icing cupcakes when I returned to the bakery. The commercial beater was switched on beside her, whipping up another batch of butter cream. She looked contented and completely in her happy place. Would my news wipe that smile off her face?

"How about taking a break for five minutes?"

"No can do. This is a special birthday order and pick up is in twenty minutes."

"I need to discuss something with you."

"Talk, I'll listen."

I glanced around and noticed Rose cleaning counters and washing up cake tins. I lowered my voice.

"I spoke to the shop owner next door. His name is Thomas Farthing. Isn't that a cute name? He said he'll let us expand the café through the wall and take over the storeroom space."

"That's good news. It's what you wanted."

"But he has a favor he wants from us."

"A favor?"

"He wants his eighteen-year-old granddaughter Zoe to work in the café."

"Back up the track. You want to increase the space for the café which will be more expense, and now you want us to hire another worker. How is this going to benefit us?"

"The café will mean more paying customers, eating our food, drinking our coffee. The granddaughter has learning difficulties, so it's only a few hours of casual work. Not full time."

"What kind of learning difficulties?"

"She was in an automobile accident which killed her parents and left her with mild brain damage. Her grandfather says she's slow, but she can serve customers. I met her and I believe she's a kind person. I want to give her a try, Rachel. She needs to feel useful."

"You're just one big bleeding heart aren't you, Lee! Okay, let's give her a chance. Heaven knows I'm not one to judge."

"Good. That's settled then. And oh, another thing. Sometimes Zoe can tell fortunes by touching an article that belongs to someone ese. Or someone has touched."

"Something has just occurred to me."

"What?"

"Everyone working in this bakery and café has been dealt some pretty bad cards or has had a rough time with life in general. It's become a refuge for lost souls. A second chance, a place to feel useful and to fit back into society."

"I hadn't really thought about it."

"And that's down to you, Lee. *You* are helping people. So much for your 'devil-in-training' gig."

I guess it was true. The café had become a safe space for Rachel, and Rose and now Zoe might find connections with other people nearer her own age. But did that make me any less my father's daughter? Hadn't he always been opposed to the job allocated to him. Maybe this apple hasn't fallen far from the tree at all.

Daisy sat on the rug in her playpen, holding the ragdoll I'd brought her, and gibbering in her cute baby talk to the toys scattered around the floor. Sophie turned on the television and selected a children's educational program to keep the little one amused while we chatted.

"How about a coffee? Aimee made some coffee cake yesterday, and I'm sure there's some left."

"Coffee would be wonderful, thanks. Hold the cake. I've eaten enough at the bakery the last few days. I'm gaining so much weight."

"Nonsense you look as gorgeous as ever. Domenic told me what happened. You had a lucky escape. How's Rourke?"

"He's better. Father says he was determined to get back to work."

"When do *you* have to return to work?"

"I'm not sure. I'm making the most of my time here with everyone."

Out of the corner of my eye I noticed Daisy dancing to the music on the big screen, and the ragdoll is dancing too. Dancing on its own. Daisy was giggling.

"Don't look now, but I think Daisy has another talent."

"That's not new. She's been bringing her toys to life for a while now. They dance and move about, but it only lasts for a short time. So far, it's been harmless. But I still feel I need to watch her like a hawk. Where did you get the beautiful doll?"

"I was in a toy shop yesterday, next door to the bakery. We're thinking of expanding the café, and I needed to approach the owner of the shop next door to see if he would be open to us extending our premises into his storeroom. It's funny but I never really paid attention to the shop before. It has some beautiful and unusual kid's toys, so I picked up the doll for Daisy on my way home, hoping she would like it.

"Your café is doing well then? Was he able to help?"

"Yes. On both counts. He's asked that we hire his granddaughter Zoe in the café, as part of the deal. She has brain damage, but she's a gentle soul. I'm trying her out this afternoon to see if she can manage a couple of hours work. Mornings are busier."

"I hope it works out for you."

"Getting back to Daisy. Maybe she's lonely and needs a playmate. When are you going to give her a brother or sister."

"Oh. Not you too. Your mother keeps dropping hints about that very subject."

"And?"

"I'm not ready to have another baby yet. But Domenic would like us to start to try soon. It might take ages, but I'm afraid it will happen with the first attempt."

"It's good to know you're open to having more children. I loved having a big brother. I'm sure I would've been even more spoiled if I'd been an only child."

"Yes, I see the benefit of having more. I guess I'm concerned about the special talents of any other children we have."

"Don't let that stop you. Talking about talents, Zoe can tell fortunes from touching something someone ese has touched. I'm telling you this because there are lots of so called 'normal' people out there in the world who have abilities which are considered strange."

"I guess you're right."

I turned to see the doll laying limp on the carpet. I guess Sophie was right, Daisy's ability was short lived. Daisy stood up and walked to the edge of the playpen and raised her arms to me.

"Up," she said.

I lifted her into my arms. She buried her head in my neck and wrapped her arms tightly around me. The warmth of her little body and the smell of baby powder was intoxicating. A surge of happiness flashed through me. Was this just Daisy's special talent. Or was I more maternal than I thought? Damn my father for putting these ideas into my head.

"You have a true friend there. She obviously loves her Aunt Lucia."

"Her hair is so soft. It's such a pretty shade of red, just like yours."

"I used to get teased for my red hair."

"Well, I think it is beautiful on you and on Daisy. I wonder if the next one will have red or dark hair?"

"I would love a little mini version of Domenic."

"As much as I would love to stay and cuddle with her all day, I have to get to the bakery soon."

I handed Daisy to Sophie and took my leave. They walked me to the back door. I kissed Sophie on the cheek, and then kissed Daisy too.

I was at the bottom of the steps when I heard her.

Goodbye, Aunt Lucia.

I turned and smiled in answer to this child who, like my father and brother, had the ability to communicate telepathically with me. No point in mentioning that to her mother yet, she has enough to deal with.

Zoe arrived at Sweet Devil Bakery at 1.45pm as instructed. I introduced her to Rachel and Rose, who was on duty in the café, and left Rachel to show her the ropes. I could feel Zoe's excitement, being in a new place and meeting new people. Her eyes were as big as saucers when she was shown the commercial equipment in the kitchen and the large cold room and freezer filled with cakes and pies. I noticed she had a notebook that she pulled out of her pocket from time to time to scribble in.

"I'm off now, Zoe. Rachel and Rose will show you how to take café orders. I've ordered an official name badge, but I made this temporary one for you today." I handed over the badge and Zoe looked down at the badge sitting in the palm of her hand.

"He's thinking about you, and he'll contact you soon," Zoe said.

"Who?"

"The big man who doesn't smile."

The hairs stood up on my arm. Did she mean Rourke? How could she know? I had no answer to that comment. I brushed it off.

"I'll await his phone call then."

"No phone call. A gift."

Ah, this girl was barking up the wrong tree. If it was Rourke she was taking about, he was not going to be sending me a gift.

"Thanks."

I left the café.

Rachel called me later to let me know that Zoe had managed her two-hour shift with ease. She said Zoe had brought a breath of fresh air into the busy café, was courteous and kind with customers, remembered all the orders and helped clean the kitchen before she left.

I could see no reason to deny Thomas his part of the deal. We agreed that the wall would be removed as soon as possible, and that Zoe would work three full afternoons per week in the bakery until we finished the renovations.

40
LUCIA

I poured a glass of wine and settled my long body into the comfortable pillows on the sofa to read a book. I enjoyed not having to maintain Lee Edwards body within these walls, or when I was around my family. I could dress as I pleased, and I could be myself.

Max and Raven dropped beside my feet. They'd been very protective since my return, as if sensing I needed their continued presence. Aimee had also been very kind, filling the fridge with comfort food she knows I enjoy. Simple pleasures like these had been few and far between for me over the last year or so. I appreciated my family even more these days. I guess a near death experience will do that to you.

I opened the book and began to read, but my thoughts returned to the cave-in and then of course to Rourke. Was he fully recovered now? Both dogs sat up, their ears picking up movement well before I could. My father appeared, standing by the drinks trolley. He poured himself a glass of red wine.

"Father, how lovely to see you. Mom is over visiting Sophie and Daisy."

"Yes, I know, I stopped by to say hello before I came here."

Max stood and went over to my father, who placed his hand on the dog's sleek head in greeting.

"Max has been keeping me updated on your wellbeing. I'm pleased to see you're relaxing. I thought this might be a good time to talk about your proposition."

"I think I'm much better suited to work here on earth, amongst the living. Inflicting pain and torture aren't my areas of expertise... well, not physical torture anyway."

"I see."

"Don't take this the wrong way, but you would not be using me to my full potential keeping me locked up in Hell. I know you want me to know how Hell works, but it's not my forte. I'm a people person, and they respond to me. You must admit my quota for souls was great when I was working at the hotel. Maybe not as good as yours but it's getting better. And I get a kick out of helping people. I've felt more alive in the last few months setting up the bakery and making sure some low life degenerates have had their payback, than I've felt in a long time.

"I'd like you to return to Hell tomorrow for a meeting with Rourke. He's back at work, but not back to one hundred percent functional."

"Okay." I wasn't sure if I'd made any impression with my plea to stay on earth.

"I'll take my leave now. Your mother and I have plans for the evening."

He finished his wine and stood to leave. Max and Raven also stood, prepared to go with him.

"No. Stay with Lucia." He placed his empty glass on the side table and handed me a small package wrapped in brown paper. "Rourke wanted me to give you this."

The hairs stood up on my arms. Zoe's words came to mind. *I had indeed received a gift.*

I peeled open the wrinkled brown paper, and inside was a piece of green crystal. It was rough, as if just pulled from the earth, and appeared to have dried blood still embedded in the crevasses. The lines of varying depth of color running through it were distinct, even in this rough state.

"It's malachite. This was part of the debris they removed from Rourke's wound. The boulder that held you captive was full of malachite, and very valuable," My father said.

"Can you use the malachite in the boulder?"

"Yes. malachite is sought after, and that quantity will be worth a lot of money. It has healing qualities. One of the benefits of being underground is that I can mine all the earth's treasures when I need them. Where do you think I amassed my fortune?"

"I hadn't really thought about it."

"The necklace you're wearing is lovely, but this crystal would make a nice pendant for that silver chain. May I?"

He took the crystal from me and cupped it in his hand. He blew on it, closed the other hand on top and squeezed his palms tightly. As he rubbed them together, bright light filtered through the gaps in his fingers for several seconds, then disappeared. He opened his hands, and a polished teardrop of malachite sat in his palm. He slid it into my outstretch hand. The polished surface highlighted the lines in varying shades of light to dark green and almost black. It even had a tiny hole near the point to thread a fine chain through.

"It's beautiful. Thank you, Father."

"Yes, it is a stunning piece. You see the small red dot at the base of the teardrop. That's Rourke's blood. I thought it appropriate to seal his blood inside to remind you of his sacrifice."

"But he's going to get better, isn't he?'

"Time will tell if he'll ever regain his optimal strength, but every day I witness an improvement. You do realize that no other demon would have had the strength to support that boulder in the cave-it, to stop it crushing you."

"I wasn't aware of that."

"That was why I helped him. He saved your life, and it was important to try and give him back his ability to walk again."

"I hope he recovers fully. I would hate to think I was the reason he was suffering."

My father looked thoughtful for a moment, and I wondered what he was thinking. He has the best poker face.

"Tomorrow," he said.

"Yes tomorrow."

My father disappeared as quickly as he had arrived, leaving me holding the crystal. I removed the bauble from my chain and replaced it with the malachite pendant. It nestled against my breast, over my heart. The heat emanating from it was comforting, and I clasped my hand around its smooth, polished surface and closed my eyes, breathing deeply, allowing the healing qualities of the crystal to flow through me. *Green crystal and demon's blood, what a combination.*

I was back in the cave running, running, with no way out. I turned and Rourke was there waiting, beckoning me to come to him. He reached for me and pulled me to his chest as the cave walls came tumbling down, his strong arms encompassing me, shielding me from harm. I raised my head to thank him and pressed my mouth to his. I opened to him, allowing his tongue to search for mine. My body cleaved to him, feeling every muscle, every ridge on his torso as he held me tightly. He broke the kiss and whispered the words. *"You are mine Lucia. I will always protect you from harm."*

Then he licked my face and kept on licking, and I opened my eyes to see I had slid down on the sofa and Max was licking my face with his big slobbery tongue.

"Yuk, Max." I wiped my face with the back of my hand. 'I think it's time for a shower and then an early night. I've a big day tomorrow."

Both dogs cocked their heads to the side listening to me. Max lifted his paw to shake.

I laughed. "I wish I knew what you're thinking, Max."

I turned off the table lamp and headed for the stairs. Max and Raven followed me up and dropped outside my bedroom door.

"I've got an early flight to Hell. Wish me luck, guys."

41
ROURKE

I stepped off the treadmill and took note of the distance I'd run today. It's encouraging to note my stamina's improving, and my strength's returning, although I know it has a way to go. I finished my work out early because My Lord's requested a meeting and Lucia would be there. This would be the first time I saw her in the flesh since the accident, although she'd been constantly with me, inside my head, day in and day out.

Maybe this was punishment for all the wicked thoughts I'd had since that kiss. Was this my state of Hell? No, I didn't think it had come to that yet. It would be far worse if My Lord guessed I was having these fantasies about his daughter. He'd make my days in Hell much worse if he knew.

"Come in, Rourke. Take a seat."

My Lord gestured to the empty chair to his left. Lucia sat to his right.

"Good morning, Lucia."

"Good morning, Rourke. I'm glad to see you're back on your feet."

"Let's get to the point of the meeting, shall we? Lucia has indicated that she doesn't want to spend all her time in Hell. She would rather spend her time above ground collecting souls. She's made the suggestion that you perform one half of the job in Hell, and she performs the other half of the job on earth."

"Job-share the position," Lucia said.

"Job-share? What job?"

"Being the Devil of course," Lucia said.

"You can't job-share the position of The Devil."

"Why not?"

"Because *he* is *The Devil*." I pointed to My Lord.

"It's time for a change," Lucia said.

"Why. It's worked perfectly well since Hell began."

"But my father... sorry... The Devil, wants some time away from Hell, and that was why I offered to step in as his successor, instead of my brother."

"And you did step in. And look where it's got us. You've made changes, angered the guards, changed shifts and responsibilities, and... never mind." I stopped before I crossed the line.

"And you were going to say, nearly got us both killed! Were you not?"

"Stop!" My Lord held up his hand. "You've both shown me that you're good at what you do. Rourke, you've been invaluable as my second in charge down here in Hell. And Lucia, you've impressed me with your independence, your quota for soul collection, and business acumen on Earth. I've given some thought to the suggestion, and I'm willing to trial the two of you to fill the position. But in order to do that you have to agree to work together. Yes, I'm looking at you, Rourke."

"I'm trying to keep an open mind."

"Try harder," Lucia said.

"Enough!" My Lord stood. "I'm going to leave the two of you here to talk this through and work out your differences. I want to make an announcement soon. I expect someone to come to me with good news before the end of the day.

214

"Yes, My Lord."

"Yes, Father."

My Lord left the office and I stared into the eyes of the woman who has become my nemesis. How could someone be so frustrating, stubborn, opinionated, and so alluring at the same time? I wanted to strangle her for putting this idea into his head, but more than that I wanted to pull her onto this table and fuck her so hard, until I rid myself of this cursed spell which she no doubt had placed over me. My gaze travelled over her face, looking into those eyes which are so mesmerizing. I lowered my eyes to her lips, so lusciously red and inviting, and moved down to the creamy skin bursting out of the top of her leather waistcoat. Her uniform left nothing to the imagination, which was her plan all along. She wanted every man to desire her, to want to plunge his face into that cleavage, to want to peel away those skin-tight pants, and feel that flesh quivering beneath him.

The thought of any other man touching her was suddenly too much to bear, and I quickly rose from my chair and paced the room. My blood pressure was surely up and through the ceiling of this office.

"This isn't helping." Lucia swiveled in her chair to watch me.

"It's helping me."

"Of course. Because it's all about you, isn't it. Can you just sit down so I can explain how this would benefit all of us," Lucia said.

I reluctantly returned to my chair.

"I fail to see how this 'job-share' could be a benefit to My Lord. He needs one person on whom he can rely. Things would not run smoothly."

"You'd have more power down here. You wouldn't have to train me to do anything, which means you wouldn't have to spend so much time with me. You've made it perfectly clear that spending time with me drives you crazy.

"If only you knew how much," I said through clenched teeth.

"See. This plan would work better. You'd be down here in Hell, and I'd be up on Earth. I'd bring you the souls to process. I won't get in your way. My father can have some more time for fun. He can retire knowing we've got this."

"Do you honestly think that My Lord will be happy to retire and play golf like all those lazy humans on Earth, and not long for some excitement, some adventure. Do you think he'd be happy without the thrill of the chase, procuring all those souls?"

"He says he wants to spend more time with my mother. But now you put it that way, I guess I hadn't thought it through. But that doesn't mean we can't work together. And by we, I mean you and me, to at least remove some of his burden. Or is there some reason you don't want me here?"

"I'll do what I can down here, to free up some time for My Lord. You bring me the souls. I'm open to the trial."

"Great. Then let's shake on that deal."

Lucia stood up and leant across the table, her hand outstretched, and the malachite pendant swung out of her cleavage, and dangled in front of me. My eyes betrayed me and dove straight into the place the pendant had been, and I lost myself to the wonder of that creamy flesh rising and falling with every breath she took.

"Rourke!" Lucia yelled.

I snapped out of it and shook her hand. Her skin was so soft, her hand so small in mine. I could smell something sweet, something different lingered in the air whenever she was around. An ancient memory sprung to mind, of the fragrance of flowers in my master's garden.

I could tug on her hand, and she would glide across the table into my arms. I could peel away the leather waistcoat and feast myself on those luscious breasts. I could plunge my fingers deep inside her to feel how wet she was to receive me. I could...

"Rourke, what the Devil is the matter with you today? You're more spaced out than I have ever seen you," Lucia yelled, pulling her hand away. "Is it the drugs? Have they given you something to help with the pain?"

"No drugs. I'm just tired. Sleep has evaded me lately."

"It must've been the trauma. I'm not sleeping much either," Lucia said.

I locked eyes with her and I could have sworn I saw something there. A knowing look. An understanding. Was she thinking about that kiss in the cave-in too?

We walked around the table and headed for the door.

"Are you going to talk to My Lord? Or will I?" I stood back to let her go first.

"I'll talk to him."

Lucia stopped suddenly before we exited the room and turned. She was inches away from me. The fragrance was much stronger now, intoxicating. I inclined my head a little and inhaled. Her hand came up, her palm resting on my chest. My heart beat faster, the blood pounding in my head and ready to explode. *Was this She-Devil trying to kill me?*

"I am very sorry about the accident and of course your injuries, Rourke. I want you to know that. Regardless of our problems, I wish you no harm."

"Our problems?"

"*You* can't stand the sight of me, and *I* find your patronizing attitude to me insulting."

"I've never been patronizing."

"We agree to disagree then. See, we can't even agree on how much you hate me."

"Hate you?"

"Yes, hate me. Don't deny it." Lucia spat out.

I saw red. I don't know what came over me. I pulled her into my arms and ravished her mouth. She placed both hands on my chest and pushed me away with a strength I did not know she possessed and glared at me.

Then she grabbed the front of my shirt and pulled me down to kiss her again. She unclasped the shirt and entwined her arms around my neck and plastering her voluptuous body along the length of mine. I felt every muscle tense, every nerve ending alert to the sensation of this warm curvaceous woman attempting to climb up my body, and to position the juncture of her thighs closer to my obvious erection - which had sprung to life the moment I touched her lips.

This kiss was dynamite, igniting things in me long forgotten. All the blood in my skull headed south, no blood left for any reasonable thought. I was a goner.

42

LUCIA

J tore my lips away from the best kiss I had ever had in my entire life. I took a step back. "What are we doing? This is my father's office! Do you have a death wish, Rouke?"

"You drive me crazy. I wasn't thinking about location. Obviously!"

"Let's just pretend this never happened, okay. We're two adults working together toward a common goal. We are *not* sex-starved teenagers."

"It never happened." Rourke marched out of the office and didn't look back.

I sank onto the nearest chair and tried to work out what *had* just happened. I'd never been kissed with such passion, with such promise, and I didn't know what to do with that knowledge. *He hates me, but he kisses me like he wants to make love to me.* Ha! Listen to me. Make love! Demons didn't make love, they raped, ravished and plundered. They took what they thought was rightfully theirs, and to Hell with the consequences.

I fanned my face with a stack of papers on the table and tried to slow down my racing heart. Wow, that demon could kiss, and that demon had an appendage unparalleled to anything I'd ever encountered. Devil knows what it looked like when freed from the confines of clothing. That thought had my heart racing again.

I had to go, find my father, and tell him we'd come to an agreement to trial this working relationship.

Let the games begin.

***

I didn't waste much time returning to Earth after my father made his announcement to the population of Hell.

The first thing I needed to do was find appropriate accommodation. I'd given up the tiny apartment I'd leased as Lee Edwards, Night Manager, and I couldn't expect to live with my mother forever, now that my role had been established. I was thrilled I wasn't going to be living in Hell. Money was something to keep in mind though, so it would have to be modest for the time being. I hoped there would be a fair amount of travel with my new role. Degenerate souls were to be found in every country around the globe.

I jumped online and found a top floor apartment in a small building two blocks from the bakery, and not too far from the central business district. Two bedrooms and a study, two bathrooms, a spacious living area and modern kitchen. Not that I was planning on doing much cooking.

I made an appointment with the realtor to view it tomorrow morning. But on the way there I planned to check in on the Bakery.

***

The café tables were full and customers lining up at the bakery counter for coffee and cakes when I arrived and I was thrilled.

Rachel waved me over to join her in the storeroom with the cool room attached. "I want to show you something." She opened the door and removed a trolley on wheels, holding a tall, three-tiered cake. It was covered in aqua buttercream, and decorated with flowers and butterflies that looked so realistic I reached out to touch them but stopped myself in time.

"It's beautiful. Well done."

"It wasn't me. It was Zoe."

"Zoe. I didn't know she could decorate cakes."

"I knew she was artistic, but I had no idea to what extent. She keeps a small notebook in her pocket and she's always scribbling in it. She says it calms her down when she's nervous. She showed me yesterday and I couldn't believe the intricate drawings she can produce in minutes. Then after her shift yesterday she asked me if she could use the leftover fondant and she made the delicate flowers and the butterflies and added some of my edible paint. She worked on these in the kitchen, in her own time, after her shift."

"They really are stunning. She certainly has a flair for this."

"We attached them to the cake this morning, and we planned on putting this in the refrigerated display window. I think we'll get some orders, don't you?"

"I'm sure we will. I'm really pleased she's managing to fit in."

"She has the sweetest nature. The customers love her. Some even ask for her by name when they come to the café. I'm going to show her what I know about piping buttercream onto cakes, but I've a feeling that she will pick that up very quickly, and probably surpass anything I can do."

"She's working this afternoon, isn't she? I've an appointment to look an apartment near here, but I'll call back in to see her afterwards."

"What about the other apartment near the hotel?"

"I let that go when I finished my assignment. I'd rather be more central."

"Do you have a new assignment?"

"I do. But I need to leave now, so we'll catch up later, and I'll tell you all about it."

The brick building's facade looked as if it had been painted recently. It looked solid and had good bones, and it reminded me of a building in an old Hollywood movie. No elevator, a fourth-floor walk-up, but I didn't mind, as climbing the stairs would keep me fit.

Seth Jonas, the Realtor, was young and eager, and wasted no time in giving me the history of the building, and detailed instructions about parking and trash collection and information on the other facilities in the area. The spacious apartment took up the whole of the top floor. We walked around from room to room, and he pointed out the benefits of the air conditioning and fully electric kitchen and appliances.

"What's behind this door here?" I turned the handle, but the door was locked.

"That is the staircase to the roof. Because this apartment doesn't have a balcony like the others. This apartment has a roof garden."

"Do you have a key to this door. I'd like to see it."

Seth unlocked the door and climbed another flight of stairs ahead of me to unlock the door at the top. He allowed me through first and I was surprised when I stepped onto a roof with raised garden beds full of beautiful flowers, and miniature trees. There was a wooden outdoor table, and four wooden chairs. A folded outdoors umbrella poked up through the hole in the center of the table. It was a stunning oasis in a concrete jungle.

"Wow. I had no idea this was up here. You can't see it from the road. Who maintains this garden?"

"Well, that's another thing I was going to discuss. The owner would like whoever rents this apartment to maintain the garden."

"That's a big job."

"His wife was the gardener, and he doesn't want it to die. She passed away recently, and that's why he's renting out this place. It's self-watering, just needs a bit of TLC every now and again."

"I don't know. I'll think about it."

"There would be a reduction in the rent I believe."

"A reduction?"

"Yes, the owner would have to accept your application, of course.

But he did tell me that he would look at a generous reduction if the right person took this apartment."

"If you have an application form, I can do it now?"

He extracted a form from the paperwork he was holding and passed me a pen. I sat down at the table, filled in the form, and handed it back to him.

He tucked the form back amongst the paperwork. "I'll get back to you tomorrow."

We returned to the apartment locking the doors behind us. I left Seth and walked back to the Bakery, where I'd parked my car.

"Are you taking the apartment?" Rachel asked.

"I'm not sure. It's spacious and very close by. It has a roof garden and if I take it, I'm supposed to maintain the garden."

"Really? That's a big ask."

"I know. But it's a little oasis of flowers and a few miniature trees and would be great in the summer."

I watched Zoe take an order from an elderly couple at a table by the window.

"She's doing okay, isn't she?"

"She's doing more than okay. She's really coming out of her shell. I've asked her to make some more cake decorations. We have a birthday party order tomorrow for a six-year-old girl who's into puppies. I'm keen to see what Zoe can produce for the cake," Rachel said.

Zoe handed the couple's food order to Rose behind the counter, and I beckoned her over to us.

"You were right, Zoe. I did receive a gift." I unfastened the malachite pendant I was wearing.

She opened her hand, and I placed it in her palm. She looked down, a frown appearing on her face. She offered it back to me.

"Did you get a reading from the pendant?"

"Yes," Zoe said, quietly.

"Can you going to tell me what you saw?"

"Pain."

"Pain? Who's in pain?"

"The big man who doesn't smile," Zoe said.

"That's all?"

She nodded and turned away.

"What was all that about?" Rachel asked.

"This necklace was a gift from someone who's had a bad accident. She must be getting a vibe from that."

The shop door opened and Seth Jonas, the realtor appeared. I'd listed my current address as Sweet Devil Bakery and he was obviously looking for me as he glanced around the café and he smiled when he spotted me, sitting at a corner table, enjoying a cup of coffee.

"I'm sorry to bother you but there were a couple of questions on your application, on the back of the page, that you need to complete." Seth placed the form on the table.

"Not a problem. I didn't realize I'd missed any." I took the pen Seth handed me and completed the form.

"It's nice in here." He took a seat.

"We're pretty happy with how it looks."

"And it smells so delicious."

"Yes, you can't beat the smell of freshly baked cookies and pies."

I noticed Seth searching the room. When he spotted Zoe, he smiled. Zoe looked up and when she saw Seth her face lit up.

"Thanks, I'll talk to the owner and get back to you," he said. He took the form from my hand without taking his eyes off Zoe.

"Would you like a coffee? Or a cake, or a cookie. We have a great selection."

"A coffee would be nice. Thank you."

I beckoned Zoe to come over.

"Zoe, can your take Seth's order? It's on the house."

"What can I get for you?" Zoe's cheeks had turned an adorable shade of pink.

"Just a long black coffee, please."

"Nothing to eat?" Zoe asked. "We have some freshy made ginger-bread cookies."

"If that's what smells so good, yes, I'll have one. Thank you."

Zoe left to place the order and Seth finally turned around to look at me.

"Do you know each other?"

"We don't really *know* each other. I've seen her walking around the area. And in the toy shop next door."

"Ah yes, her family owns the toy shop."

"Mr Farthing is the owner of the apartment we looked at," Seth said.

"You are kidding me!"

"It wasn't until I was back in the office that I noticed the address you listed was next door to the owner's shop."

"I wasn't aware he owned the apartment either."

"He owns the whole building. He used to live on the top floor, but the stairs are becoming too much for him. He's moved into the ground floor apartment, with his granddaughter. That's why he's renting it out," Seth said.

"And it was his wife who passed away recently, and who loved to garden. Now it all fits."

Zoe returned with Seth's coffee and gingerbread cookie. It was adorable to watch this shy young woman basking in the admiration of this young man. I touched his hand to tell him I would be back in a minute and left the two of them to talk. I had a flash of his life in that second. He was also a gentle soul, not suited to the cutthroat business of real estate. He was doing this because his father owned the business and wanted him to take over one day. Seth was an artist. I saw him painting a beautiful portrait on an easel. I went to find Rachel.

"You will never guess who owns the apartment I looked this morning?"

"Who?"

"Our friendly toy shop owner, next door. He owns the whole building apparently."

"That's spooky!"

"He used to live in the top floor apartment and has moved into the ground floor of that building, because of the stairs. His wife was the gardener, and remember I told you she passed away recently."

"So, you're thinking of taking it?"

"It seems too much of a coincidence don't you think? Something bigger than both of us has guided me to this area for our bakery, meeting Mr Thomas Farthing next door and his lovely granddaughter Zoe, who has a talent for cake decoration, and now the apartment building, where we may all be living. Spooky does not begin to describe this."

"Zoe looks happy," Rachel said.

Seth and Zoe were talking quietly at the table in the corner.

"I think that Seth really likes Zoe, and the feeling is mutual apparently. If her pink cheeks are anything to go on."

"Young love. Isn't it wonderful."

I suddenly thought of Rourke and that kiss in my father's office. What would have happened if I had not pulled away. I was climbing him like a tree!

"Any chance we could meet up for a quick drink tonight? After you get the kids settled of course. I'll text you the address. Can you get a babysitter at short notice, and get a cab back to town?"

"Yes, the teenager across the road from me is always looking for extra pocket money. I'll check with her and let you know later."

It was time to show Rachel my real body. She only knew me as Lee Edwards, but if I was going to move forward into a long-term business partnership, I would have to be honest with her and show her the real me.

43

LUCIA

After dinner I showered and changed into a knee-length, sleeveless black dress with a plunging neckline and a small split up the thigh and added my Louboutin shoes with the highest heels. I pinned one side of my hair back off my face with a small red flower picked from my mother's garden and allowed the bulk of my curls to tumble down my back. When I fastened my malachite necklace around my neck, the pendant nestled comfortably into my cleavage. A red patent leather purse completed the ensemble. I checked the image in the mirror and was satisfied with my choice.

Cameron drove me to the hotel where I'd arranged to meet Rachel. He parked nearby to wait. He told me he was concerned about dropping me here and going home because of how fabulous I looked. I had to agree, I was feeling fabulous tonight. It was prudent to have him close by as there were low life thugs in every city who would try to rob you for your fabulous shoes, or your purse given the chance. And although I could take care of myself, these days there was always someone around with a camera ready to capture the incident. Best to avoid taking the chance of a She-Devil harming a human and being filmed.

The stylish interior was dimly lit, but I spotted Rachel sitting at the corner of the bar, with a glass of white wine in front of her. I approached and sat on the barstool next to her.

"Sorry, I was keeping that stool for my friend. She's arriving soon. Would you mind moving over to another please?"

"Are you sure you don't want me to sit here?" I called the barman over and ordered my own glass of white wine.

Rachel stared at me, her eyes wide, as my voice registered with her. "Lee?" she whispered.

"Yes. But you can use my real name tonight. It's Lucia."

"I don't understand. You're gorgeous."

"Thank you."

"How did you?"

"Become gorgeous?"

"Yes. And you're tall. How did you?"

"Become tall?" I laughed. "I am tall. My business suit is Lee Edwards. I created someone who would fit into the role of night manager for that sleazy hotel. Someone who wouldn't make an impression. My name is Lucia Nightingale, this is the real me. And I am pretty sure if I walked around like this people would remember me."

"Oh, my God. I can't believe it. If I looked this good, I wouldn't want to hide it."

"You're forgetting what I do Rachel. Don't you think someone would leak a picture of me to the media if they worked out who I am? My alias is my protection. But I wanted you to see me, meet the real version of me, because we're going to be in each other's lives for a long time."

"Can you change into other versions? Other people?"

"Yes. But it takes a lot out of me to maintain the appearance of the other body."

"Can you perform other tricks?"

"I wouldn't exactly call them tricks. I have other abilities if that's what you mean. But I try to not draw attention to myself."

"Like what, for example?"

"I'm strong. I'm half human but much stronger than a human

female. I can travel between Hell and Earth. I can sometimes read impressions of other people's lives though touch. I can make people tell me their heart's desire by looking deep into their eyes. I can communicate telepathically with my brother and father."

"The Devil?"

"Yes."

"And your mother is human?"

"Yes, but she has some of the Devil's DNA in her. She has some very minor abilities too. She was a stuntwoman when she was younger. She hardly ever gets sick but if she does, she heals quickly. Now she can communicate telepathically with my father."

"This is fascinating. I would never have guessed you were in disguise."

"I didn't always look like this. I changed into this form, became exceptionally tall and grew my wings when I became eighteen."

"Wings?" Rachel glanced toward my back.

"You can't see them at the moment." I laughed. "They're retracted inside."

"It's going to be hard to see you the other way, now that I know."

"Obviously this is between us, not something I can discuss. Our family is very private."

"You already have my soul. You also have my silence. Plus, we have our own secrets, don't we."

"We do indeed. I wanted to meet you tonight to tell you what's been happening to me lately. Remember the day I came into the bakery we talked about expanding the café? Well, the reason I was back in town and not in Hell was because there was a cave-in, and I was trapped underground with Rourke and..."

"Who's Rourke?'

"He's my father's second in charge. He was showing me around, and I didn't enjoy the torture chamber and..."

"Hang on! Torture chamber?"

"Standard Hellish practice. You must've heard the rumors."

"So, everything they say about Hell is true then?"

"Can I just finish my story, before we have the Q & A?"

"Sure. Sorry."

"I ended up in a dead-end tunnel and the walls started shaking and Rourke threw himself on top of me to save me from a boulder crushing me. We were trapped in that tunnel for a while."

"OMG. That must've been terrifying."

"It wasn't pleasant. I thought I was going to die down there."

"How did you get out?"

"My father and some other demons came and dug us out. I only had some cuts and bruises, but Rourke was badly injured. They thought he might not walk again."

"And did he?"

"Yes, he's walking." I took a sip of my wine. "I don't think working underground is for me. I had a meeting with my father and Rourke to see if we could come to some arrangement. Instead of me working in Hell all the time, Rourke is going to continue to look after things down there, and I'm going to take care of collecting souls on Earth."

"Since the night manager's job is finished what's the new assignment? I'm presuming your father agreed to letting you stay here in Hollywood, and that's why you're looking for a new place to live."

"He hasn't given me a new assignment yet. He gave me some time off. It helps to be related to the boss. But I think that we convinced him to try this way. Rourke is happier in Hell."

"Did Rourke have a choice to work on Earth?"

"No." I laughed. "Why would you think he could do that. He's a demon."

"So is the Devil, but he works on Earth. You are half demon, and you work here too."

"I've never considered that Rourke might want to work anywhere but in Hell or working for anyone other than my father."

"Sounds to me like you never asked him."

"Point taken. But I'm not suited to be in Hell all the time. I have intelligence and I'm more of a people person."

"Rourke isn't a people person?"

"Hell, no!" I laughed "The opposite actually. He never smiles, he's never happy to see anyone, never has a kind word to say about anyone. He doesn't get pleasure from anything…" I felt my cheeks burn with the memory of the one thing I was very certain he did get pleasure from.

"You just remembered something, didn't you?"

"Yes, but it's not important."

"It clearly is because you're blushing."

"I am *definitely not blushing!*" I gulped down the rest of my wine. Was it heating up in this bar?

"The lady doth protest too much."

"No!"

"Spit it out. Tell me about this guy?"

"What do you mean?"

"Tell me about this Rourke guy. There's something you aren't telling me, come on."

I was bursting to talk about it, and I couldn't discuss it with my family. I guess Rachel was as close to a best friend as I was going to get.

"When we were trapped by the boulder, he kissed me. He was really trying to get me to shut up, but I then kissed him back and he liked it. I could clearly tell by the giant dick pushing into my stomach and…"

"Giant? How giant?'

"That's what you're taking away from this conversation… his giant erection?"

"Sorry, that was indelicate of me. Go on."

"Anyway, I've been thinking about him in a whole new way since then. And after the discussion with my father in his office, he kissed me again…"

"Your father's office! And what did your father say?"

"My father wasn't there at that point, he'd left us to work it out, and we got in an argument, and he kissed me again!"

"Was he trying to shut you up?"

"No."

"Then he clearly likes you."

"You think?"

"Did the giant erection make an appearance?" Rachel's smile couldn't have been any wider.

"I'm not answering that." I remembered my attempt to get closer to that giant erection. "It was over quickly. Honestly, we should never have been anywhere near each other in my father's office, and he hightailed it out of there immediately afterwards. Devil knows what my father would have done if he'd seen us."

"So, Rourke is sweet on you. But you haven't told me how you feel? What does he look like, this demon?"

"He's very tall, taller than me, and has a body builder's physique, with huge shoulders. He's one of the strongest demons in Hell my father says, and he should know. His head is shaved but his skull has a nice shape to it, his ears are small and don't stick out like some people who have shaved heads. A pleasant enough face but he's always scowling. A strong square jaw, wide, straight nose and eyes that appear to take everything in. They're as black as coal and show no emotion.

"He sounds a bit terrifying."

"He would be to anyone else in Hell."

"But he doesn't terrify you?"

"No."

"Mmmm."

"What?"

"You like him, too."

"He's a co-worker, and he annoys the Hell out of me."

"You like him. End of story. Are you going to pursue it?"

"No!"

Rachel took another sip of her wine. I motioned to the bartender to pour me another. And another one for Rachel, too.

"This one's on me." I turned to see a man in a black business suit, and white shirt making himself comfortable on the barstool next to mine. He was leaning in toward me, getting too close.

"Could you move back, you're making me uncomfortable." I frowned at him.

He grinned at me and moved back a little. There was plenty of room in the bar, and no need to sit beside us.

I accepted the glass of wine from the bartender, took a sip and tried to tap my credit card on the hand-held device. The man pushed my hand away and tried to pay for our wine with his credit card.

"Let me buy you ladies a drink," black suit said.

"Thank you, but no thanks." I looked directly at the bartender and made him take my card.

We drank our wine and ignored black suit.

"Stuck up bitches," black suit mumbled into his glass.

I turned to the man and tapped him on the shoulder.

"What did you call us?"

"Stuck up. I was only trying to be a gentleman."

"No, you were trying to be an asshole." I locked eyes with him. "Tell me, what is your heart's desire."

"I want to get laid by two beautiful women tonight so I can boast about it to my friends who think I'm a loser, cos my wife left me." He stopped and shook his head like he was coming out of a dream.

"Well, clearly, that's not happening. You should call it a night. Go home and sleep it off."

Black suit grabbed my bare arm tightly. *That's going to leave a bruise.*

"Hey, who the hell do you think you are, telling me what to do? You women are all the same. You take everything a man offers the wrong way, then you throw it back in our face." The bartended headed our way concerned by what was happening. I held up my hand to stop him.

I pried black suit's fingers off me, pushing him away from me, and watched his face contort with the pain as I bent them back, making sure to break a couple in the process.

"Never lay a hand on a lady. You just don't know what will happen," I said. "Time to go, Rachel. Come on, I presume you came in by cab, we'll drive you home." I finished my wine and tipped the bartender. We left black suit cradling his injured hand and went in search of Cameron.

"Does that happen a lot?"

"As I said, I'm not usually walking around in this body. It seems to get too much attention."

233

Cameron pulled up parallel to the sidewalk. He jumped out and held the back door open. Black suit came charging out of the Hotel yelling abuse and waving his uninjured fist at us. "You bitch, you broke my fingers."

Cameron took one look at the man, raised his clenched fist, and punched him square in the nose, without even raising a sweat. Black suit went down like a sack of potatoes. Cameron motioned us into the rear seat, refastened and straightened his jacket, shut the car door, walked around, and slid in behind the wheel. We took off and left the man sitting on the sidewalk, holding his bleeding nose.

"Are you okay ladies?" Cameron asked.

"Yes, we're fine, thanks, Cameron. He was as asshole who thought he was Don Juan."

"That was why I insisted on waiting."

"I know, Cameron, and I appreciate it. We're dropping off Rachel on the way home please."

While Rachel gave the address and instructions to Cameron I thought about our discussion in the bar. Did I really like Rourke? Was I attracted to him? He had certainly gotten under my skin lately. And let's face it, not many humans were going to be able to cope with me in my real form. Maybe I needed to pay him another visit and explore this a little more. After all, that kiss in my father's office was sensational and who knows what else he can do with that wicked tongue.

44

ROURKE

I wasn't thinking about Lucia. Just because I could feel in my pocket the other two small pieces of malachite I'd found imbedded in my ruined uniform, didn't mean I was thinking about her. Although they would make perfect earrings to go with the pendant that she was wearing the day we argued in her father's office. The day I foolishly kissed her. The day she kissed me back and I thought I would lose my mind! *No, not thinking about her at all.*

The pile of admissions had grown overnight. What was happening on Earth to cause this influx, all of a sudden? Humans were known for their ruthlessness and greed. The rich get richer, the poor get poorer, that was a universal fact. But something terrible must be causing this, and so many humans of all ages, dying every day. When I think about it, do I really want to know? Probably better to keep my head down and worry about what was happening in Hell, not up on the surface. Except Lucia's working on the surface. Will she be safe? *Stop thinking about Lucia, she's not your concern.*

I pulled the pile closer and got to work allocating the inmates to their various torture cells. Demons entered my office, retrieving the completed forms from the "out basket", and I kept my head down in an attempt to get through this monumental task before the end of the day. The fragrance I had become accustomed to associating with Lucia, wafted in the air. I raised my eyes, and there she was, walking purposefully toward my desk. My olfactory senses had heightened since the cave-in for some reason.

"Rourke. You're busy I see but I wondered if you'd have some time to discuss some of the finer points of our agreement."

"Finer points?"

"I think we should have regular meetings to feedback our progress."

"With My Lord?"

"No. You and I."

"I hadn't considered we needed meetings."

"Somewhere private. Maybe in my office. What do you think?"

Somewhere private! Was this She-Devil crazy. Did she want to kill me. Was this an elaborate plan to get rid of me? Devil only knows what would happen in a private place. My carnal urges might take over and then…

"If you think that would be best." *No, no, no. You were supposed to say no.* I followed her down the hall to her office. She closed it firmly behind us, perched on the end of her desk and indicated I should take a seat in front of her.

"I feel I owe you an apology. I should've asked if you wanted to work on Earth, and not down here in Hell all the time. This is a job-share after all, and I wasn't sharing Earth time. Honestly, I never considered that option for you."

"I wasn't aware I had a choice. I was sent to Hell for eternity."

"But you could visit Earth. If you wanted to. Cameron and Aimee live and work on Earth, and travel through the portal in the Gatehouse at my family's home. Drake has worked on Earth protecting my sister-in-law and her best friend and supervising other demons to cater for my brother's wedding and renovate his house."

"I think that staying in Hell is my best option."

"But you've never even seen what it's like on Earth now. I'm sure everything has changed."

"Humans haven't changed. Evil and greed abounds on Earth, and that's why we're getting busier."

"So, you're happy down here? We don't have to worry about swapping. Me down here and you on Earth."

"That's a ridiculous idea." I folded my arms.

"Here we go again. I came here with an apology offering you a choice, and you're acting superior," she yelled.

I couldn't win. Little could be said now to make the situation any better. I remembered the malachite stones in my pocket and pulled them out.

"I'm not acting superior. Can we keep things the way they are. I'll stay in Hell, and you work on Earth. I found these and thought they might be useful to match your pendant." I placed the two small crystals on her desk.

"You're giving these to me?"

"Think of this as a peace offering. Now I must get back to work." I stood to leave at the exact moment she slid off the corner of the desk and stood.

Here we are again, inches apart. I'm breathing her air. I'm inhaling her perfume. I'm looking into her eyes, wondering what's going on behind those thick black eyelashes she's batting at me. Her lips are moving, but I can't hear her because of the blood pumping in my ears. Concentrate!

"I'm taking an apartment downtown. It's time I learned to live on my own. It's a pity you'll never see it if you're determined to stay in Hell. The roof garden's pretty amazing."

The memory of flowers came back to me, encouraged by the fragrance emanating from Lucia's warm skin. An imaged flashed into my brain of a garden a very long time ago, where I worked and tended to the soil, wearing an exomis, a shapeless tunic worn by Greek slaves.

"I'm glad we had a chance to talk. I'm sorry I yelled," she said softly.

"I hope you'll take the stones. They're the right size for your ears." I reached out and touched her earlobe. She inhaled a sharp breath, which drew my gaze to her slightly parted lips, and an unmistakable tremble ran through her body. *Kiss her, kiss her, kiss her...*

Someone cleared their throat behind me. I swiveled around to see Drake standing at the door.

"My Lord wants to see you, Rourke." He turned quickly, and left the door open to the room. But not before I saw the disapproval on his face.

45

LUCIA

ourke left the room, and I all but collapsed into the chair he'd vacated. When he touched my earlobe, I felt a tingling sensation all the way through my core. It was ridiculous that such a slight touch could elicit such a response. My blood was pumping so hard to a rhythm that whispered, "kiss me, kiss me, kiss me". I saw him looking at my lips. I sensed his hesitation, but I also sensed longing. If Drake had not arrived at the precise moment, I'm sure he would have kissed me again. Damn it, Drake!

Rachel was right. I am attracted to a demon!

What the Hell was I going to do?

I arrived back at the bakery in time to see Seth leaving the café carrying a large pink bakery box. He smiled when he saw me walking toward him.

"Hi Seth."

"I was looking for you. Mr Farthing has approved your lease. Can you call by the office, and we can sign documentation and hand over keys?"

"Sure. I'll come by this afternoon. Did you see Zoe?"

"I did. She made a special order for me. What do you think? Cool, isn't it?"

Seth opened the pink box to show me the birthday cake, covered in buttercream, and decorated with flowers, red ladybugs, and caterpillars.

"Very cool."

"My nine-year-old niece loves bugs. Zoe did a great job. My niece will be delighted." He closed the top of the box carefully. "Better get back to the office. I'll see you later."

I ordered two coffees and took them next door to see Thomas. I was pleased to see a few customers in the store, browsing and allowing their children to select toys. Thomas finished a sale and tied a small package wrapped in brown paper with bright red ribbon. The customer left the store, and I approached the counter.

"I caught up with Seth. I hear I'm now your tenant, Thomas. I thought I'd bring a coffee to celebrate. What a small world it is. We work next door and now we live next door to each other. Well, I live above you, but it's the same thing." We tapped our paper cups together.

"You could've knocked me down with a feather when Seth told me you wanted to rent the apartment. You know about the garden, don't you?" Thomas asked.

"Yes, I'll do my best to keep the garden alive and blooming. I have just the person to ask. My family has a gardener and he's wonderful with plants and trees."

"Excellent!"

"I also wanted to talk to you about Zoe."

"Has something happened? She's okay, isn't she?"

"Oh yes. She's fine. I wanted to let you know her artistic gift is working out so well. Rachel loves what she can do with the cake decorations, and she's willing to teach Zoe all she knows. You don't have to worry about Zoe. She's making friends and the customers like her. She's going to be fine working in our bakery. If she wants, she can have a permanent job there. Is it okay with you if I discuss this with her?"

"That's marvelous. Yes of course you can talk to her. Since Beverley died, I've been worried about Zoe not having many women around her. I didn't want her to spend all her time with an old man."

"Actually, she's made a friend in a young man. Seth, your realtor. He seems very fond of Zoe."

"Seth?"

"He's a kind young man. He has a good heart, Thomas, take my word for it. He would do nothing to harm Zoe. If I were you. I would encourage them to go out for dinner perhaps, or see a movie. I would trust Seth. Believe me I know good from evil. He's one of the good ones."

"Zoe looks just like her mother. Joyce, my daughter, was a beautiful young girl and she had lots of young men running after her. I was forever greeting new boyfriends. But Zoe has never had that chance. I guess we've protected her, we didn't want anyone to make fun of her, or hurt her."

"Well then, it's her time now, isn't it. We'll all look out for her. You don't have to do this on your own anymore." I noticed tears welling up in Thomas's eyes.

"Thank you. I'm not going to be around forever, and she needs to be cared for."

Thomas reached out and touched my hand. I had a clear vision of Thomas cradling a baby on his knee. I thought it was Zoe as a baby, but the woman standing beside him was indeed an older version of Zoe.

"Can I assure you, that I foresee you'll be around for a long time."

"I'd like to believe that. Maybe one day Zoe will have a family and I can pass on this toy shop to her."

"There will always be a market for toys. I'd better get back to the bakery. But I'd like to get a little something for my one-year-old niece. Can you suggest something? She is quite advanced for her age."

"How about one of those jigsaws. They have big pieces, shaped like animals. Easy for little fingers."

"Excellent. Gift wrap it please, with the special red ribbon."

I left with my purchase, with the intention of picking up my keys from Seth, and then visiting Sophie and Daisy. If I was going to visit Sophie, I should take some afternoon tea.

The lunchtime rush was over and only a few tables were occupied. Rachel came out from behind the counter.

"Hello, *Lee*," Rachel said pointedly. Her grin couldn't get any wider.

"Hello, Rachel." I returned a smile.

"Thanks for the entertaining evening last night. What have you been up to this morning? Seen anyone I know, or anyone we talked about last night, perhaps?" She winked.

"Very subtle Rachel. As a matter of fact, I did."

"And?"

"You were right. I do like a certain work colleague."

"I knew it." Rachel clapped her hands in glee.

"You can wipe that grin off your face. Nothing happened."

"So how did you work it out?"

"Because I really wanted something to happen. I wanted him to kiss me this time. But we were interrupted. Someone came looking for Rourke."

"Maybe you need to take him where no one is going to come looking for you."

"That's going to be difficult, because nowhere in Hell is private. And there is always someone looking for Rourke. He's a busy demon."

"What a pity you couldn't invite him to your new apartment."

It had never occurred to me until now that I could bring him to Earth. He could come through the portal at the Gatehouse.

"You know Rachel, sometimes you come up with really good ideas."

"You're going to do it? Invite him to Earth? Seduce him in your new apartment?"

"I don't know if seduction is the appropriate word here, because I've a feeling he wants this too."

"Go girl."

"The problem is my apartment will have to be furnished and set up…"

"Oh, for heaven's sake, all you need is a flat surface. Order a bed, the rest can come later."

I laughed. Typical Rachel, getting straight to the point. I guess she was right I didn't need to set up the apartment. But I desperately wanted to have my own things, show off my own style, before I invited him to see how I lived.

I selected a few cakes and pastries to fill a bakery box and left to collect the keys to a new and improved version of my life. One where I could entertain anyone I wanted to in my own space, be it man, woman or demon. Maybe I'll learn how to cook. Who am I kidding? I'll probably stock up the freezer with ready meals.

Suddenly the thought of all the freedom of choice was intoxicating. I knew exactly the person to ask about decorating the apartment. I called Sarah Wall. She answered on the third ring.

"Sarah, it's Lee Edwards. I need your fabulous decorator's eye. I'm hoping you might have some time to look at an apartment I'm leasing and come up with some ideas about transforming it into something fabulous. We'll be starting from scratch, so I need one of everything."

Sarah laughed. "Hi Lee. I'd be happy to help. When were you thinking? I have sometime this afternoon."

"I'm going to pick up the keys to go there now. I'll text you the address."

"Great. See you there."

❧

"This is a lovely spacious apartment. And so close to the Café." Sarah wandered from room to room. "It's been freshly painted, lots of closet space and a tub. You lucky girl. I would have killed for a tub in my first apartment. I can see lots of potential to decorate in here."

"I'm glad you have some ideas, because I don't know where to begin."

"My friend has a furniture store downtown, and I'm sure he'd have everything you need. And HomeGoods stores can supply all the basics."

"I have some requirements. I want a dining table to entertain. A big screen TV on that wall over there. Do you think I have room for a king-sized bed in here? Or would it be too overcrowded?" I walked into the master bedroom.

"You certainly do. That's the beauty of these old buildings. The rooms are so much bigger than some downtown apartments they're building now."

"Great, the bigger the better."

"Noted. A big bed." Sarah was grinning. She kept her eyes down on the notebook as she wrote down details.

"What?"

"I remember my first apartment. I remember my first bed purchase, that's all."

"And?"

"And I remember the first boy I wanted to share that bed with me. Is there a special someone in your life Lee? I haven't heard you talk about a boyfriend."

"I'd like a big bed because I like to spread out. I'm bigger than I look."

So much bigger when I'm Lucia.

"Okay if you say so."

"I'm doing this on a budget, so let's concentrate on the main items. Somewhere to sit, to eat and to sleep. Dishes, glassware, towels, and sheets."

"Let's go to my friend's store. I have some time before my next appointment."

"Are you sure? I'll pay you for your time."

"How about a trade. I'm having a birthday party, so I'm going to need a cake. Maybe some sweet and savory pastries?"

"Done. You tell me what you want. Better still tell Rachel, she needs to know what to make. We have a new girl working in the Bakery and she does wonderful things with cake decorations."

"Let's go. I'm looking forward to helping you decorate this place. How do you feel about neutral tones with a hint of sage green? It's very in vogue, at the moment."

"You're the expert. Lead the way."

I'd been in my apartment for one month, and it was hard to believe how easily I'd slipped into a routine. I stretched out my arms and legs under the cool cotton sheets in the super king-sized bed, the biggest bed I was able to fit into my bedroom. There wasn't a great deal of room for much else, but the bed made me very happy and that was all that counted. The headboard was studded cream linen, and the mattress was so comfortable, it was like sleeping on a cloud. But although it was tempting to stay in bed, the sun was rising, and a hot shower beckoned.

My new assignment would start today in an uptown boutique hotel, a definite improvement on my last working environment. The bar had live music in the evenings, and it had the reputation as a hangout for starlets, and new-to-Hollywood-wannabe-actors. The haves mingled with the have nots, the latter with the hope that something would rub off, or they'd hear about a casting call, or a new film in the works that hadn't reached the media yet, or casting agents. It was who you know that counted in Hollywood, and that was a fact.

My kitchen was filled with new appliances, dishes, glassware, and decorator items that Sarah deemed appropriate for a single woman who wanted to entertain. Although the notion seemed appealing, I could probably count on one hand the number of people I felt I could trust to invite into my home. Other than my family, of course. But there was one specific demon I wanted to invite. It was a matter of how I was going to explain it to my father, and picking when I could broach the subject. He'd been rather busy lately, and whenever I did see him, I'd lacked the courage to start something I couldn't take back.

I switched on the state-of-the-art coffee machine, my expensive indulgence, and prepared a light breakfast of toast and eggs-over-easy. When I was done, I placed all the dirty dishes into the dishwasher and entered the spare bedroom to select something to wear. The items of clothing I bought for my new assignment were kept in this room.

I was maintaining the outer appearance and body of Lee Edwards, which had worked well for me in the past, but I had changed her hair color to dark blonde over the last couple of weeks, and very subtly added sharper cheekbones and pouty lips, and given Lee some more curves. She's the new and improved version, for the new job.

The changes were made a little at a time. Nothing too drastic that anyone noticing might question. If asked, I'd say I had some work done. It was Hollywood, after all. But I didn't think anyone was going to ask. Humans were used to changing their look, that wasn't unusual. If I'd taken on another persona for the new job, there would've been too many questions when Lee didn't show up at the bakery.

When I left this building via the front door, I was Lee Edwards, businesswoman. I was still getting used to being recognized and greeted by a few neighbors on the street, but it was easier to start my day as Lee, and end it as Lucia in the confines of my home.

All of Lucia's expensive designer clothes and essentials were locked in the walk-in wardrobe in my bedroom, my private sanctuary. When I wanted to visit my family or go to Hell, I found the best way was to take off from my roof garden. The expression "to wing it" had taken on a whole new meaning for me. The take-off and flight were so fast, they weren't recorded by the naked eye.

My father was convinced by my mother that the move to a place of my own was inevitable. But to be on the safe side, as he put it, alarms and cameras were installed, which was monitored from our gatehouse by Cameron. I think my father was happy now to share the house with my mother, undisturbed, and they could walk about naked if they wanted to. Although, on second thoughts, that aspect of their life was not my concern. *Note to self: scrub that thought from your brain!*

I was eager to start my assignment as a junior manager at the prestigious Westland Boutique Hotel. The hotel employed twenty-five staff, including housekeepers. The trendy restaurant and bar had a good reputation, but I got the impression that wickedness lurked around every corner. Otherwise, why would my father have sent me here? The rooms may not be rented by the hour in this establishment, but the salacious sexual activity performed behind their thick closed doors and wood paneled walls, was no doubt the same.

The manager, Edward Norris, shook my hand when I arrived, and took me on a tour introducing me to other staff members. As we traveled from room to room, I smiled and nodded, but I probably wouldn't remember everyone's name at the end of the tour. I was thankful they wore name tags and at some stage their names would all click into place.

Attractive guests checked in, even more attractive guests sunbathed around the pool, and not surprisingly, the customer-facing staff also appeared to be hired for their good looks. I hadn't come across anyone yet who was less than a seven out of ten. I was glad I enhanced Lee's appearance, even slightly, but it appeared that to fit in with this Hollywood establishment she would have to have a few more tweaks.

I was shown to a desk, given a laptop, and a thick file of rules and regulations, which I was required to read and absorb immediately to perform as junior manager. They seemed to have the impression my first day would be spent at my desk!

"I'm finished. What would you like me to do now?"

"You can't be," Edward said.

"Why?"

"Because that was a very large file and there are many rules and hotel regulations to which we have to adhere."

"I'm a fast learner."

"Take it home and read it again."

"You don't believe me. Ask me a question, about any page in this file."

"Fire drill."

"(a) An unannounced fire drill shall be held at least once a month.

(b) A fire safety inspection and fire drill conducted by a fire safety expert shall be completed annually. Documentation of this fire drill and fire safety inspection shall be kept.

(c) A written fire drill record must include the date, time, the amount of time it took for evacuation, the exit route used, the number of guests in the hotel at the time of the drill, the number of guests evacuated, the number of staff persons participating, problems encountered and whether the fire alarm or smoke detector was operative."

He held up his hand to stop me. "Okay you've memorized the file."

"Yes. But I also understand and will adhere to the rules and regulations."

"It's probably a good time to break and have an early lunch. Then I'll email you a list of guest's names, which I want you to follow up. There was a party and some considerable damage to one of our suites, which was not disclosed when the guests checked out."

The restaurant was empty, so I took my chicken salad to a corner table and pulled a novel from my purse to read over lunch.

"How are you settling in?" I looked up to see my father standing beside the table. I hadn't heard him approach.

"I think I'm going to like working here. The staff seem nice. It's not too busy for this time of year."

"I like the new hair color."

"It's going to get a few shades lighter over the next few days. Have you seen all the beautiful people in this place?"

"Beauty is only skin-deep, Lucia. There are plenty of wicked people behind the pretty masks. People who will sell their souls for their big break in a movie, for a line of coke when they've sold everything else that they own, for their chance to marry a millionaire, and many other reasons. Don't worry, your quota will rise even higher in these lovely surroundings."

"Mr Nightingale!" Edward marched into the restaurant and held out his hand. "How lovely to see you again, sir."

"Good to see you, too." My father shook Edward's hand. "I was just introducing myself to the new junior manager."

"This is Lee's first day. I see great potential, though." Edward turned to the door leading to reception. Guests were arriving at the front desk, pulling suitcases behind them. "Sorry to leave so quickly. Important guests arriving. I hope you'll come back and visit us again soon."

"I certainly will."

Edward left and my father turned back to me, his right eyebrow raised, and a slight smirk on his face. "He's a pompous ass, but he's good at his job, and has connections in Hollywood."

"I'd already made that assumption. Will you join me for some lunch? Or a coffee perhaps?" I asked.

"No. I must get back to Hell. Rourke's been covering for more than his fair share of the burden since I've been overseas these last ten days."

I summoned up the courage to ask the question that has been ticking over in my brain for weeks now.

"I wanted to ask if Rourke has ever been back to Earth since he was sent to Hell? I know Drake has been working here from time to time, and some other demons."

"No. He's never put his hand up to return to work on Earth. I don't think he has any interest. Plus, I keep him exceptionally busy. Why do you ask?"

"I thought that since we're sharing the role, he should see what it's like on Earth in this modern day and age, see what he's missing. I mean, I commandeered the job Earthside without giving him a chance to..."

"You want him to see the world as it is now?"

"Yes." My throat was dry. "But I don't think he would come unless you gave him a good reason."

"You want me to fabricate a reason for Rourke to visit Earth?"

"For his own good. It might help him in his recovery too. You just said he's taken on more than his fair share."

"I cannot think of a good reason for Rourke to come to Earth. Unless..."

"Yes?"

"Maybe we could put on a party, your mother loves a party. Celebrate your... what did you call it? Job-share? Your mother's thrilled you're spending time on Earth instead of in Hell. He could be introduced to the family."

"If you think that would entice him."

"If I tell him there's a party, which he's required to attend. He won't argue."

"Then tell him."

"I don't think that bringing him here is going to make one bit of difference. He's happy in Hell."

"Please, Father. I'd feel better if I gave him the chance."

"Alright. I'll check with your mother, but I imagine she'll endorse it. She's all about fair play."

My father left, and I let out the breath I'd been holding in. I pushed away my plate. I couldn't eat another bite, and I was also having trouble maintaining what was already in my stomach. *Well, I've set this in motion. I'd better be prepared to follow through!*

46

LUCIA

I hovered next to the window near the front door, fiddling with the top buttons of my black silk shirt, trying to determine if my prim and proper ensemble of a shirt and ankle length skirt was appropriate tonight. I didn't want to be flashy. I wanted Rourke to see that I can be demure and classy like my mother. I turned and watched the Gatehouse for Rourke's appearance. My father told me Cameron had gone to fetch him through the portal and that he'd left clothes at the Gatehouse for Rourke to change into when he arrived. He said he didn't want Rourke to feel out of place with the rest of the party, but he must have had them specially made because nothing would fit Rourke straight from the rack.

I'd invited Rachel, now that I'd established that she was indeed my best friend, and I was interested in her opinion of Rourke. She was very impressed earlier when she entered our home, and so excited to meet my family. I thought she was going to faint when she held out her hand to my father, but he leant forward and kissed her cheek instead. However, my mother distracted her before she keeled over, and introduced her to Aimee. Rachel was delighted when she found out that Aimee was a fan of her work, and she could talk about cakes, buttercream frosting, and pies, to her heart's content. I handed her a drink and left to gather my thoughts. Domenic, Sophie, and Daisy were also in the living room, chatting with my mother and father. Everyone was waiting on Rourke and Cameron to arrive to pop the champagne corks.

A movement caught my eye jolting me back to the present. The door of the Gatehouse opened, and Rourke exited first. Rourke looked so different in a three-piece grey suit, white shirt, pale pink tie, and black leather shoes. Tall and imposing, he would surely strike fear in mere mortals, but he could also be considered handsome. *Hell, who am I kidding he is handsome!* He walked up the driveway with the same purposeful stride to which I've become accustomed, but the way the suit enhanced his body was different to the harsh black and red guard's uniform. My throat was suddenly dry. I took a sip of water, put down my glass and opened the front door to greet them. He climbed the steps pausing for a few seconds, staring at me before he crossed the threshold.

"Lucia." He gave a curt nod of his head.

"Hello, Rourke. Welcome to my family home. Hi Cameron."

I stood aside to let them pass and closed the door. He waited for me to walk ahead, down the long, wide hallway, and Cameron brought up the rear. When we arrived at the archway I stopped. Rourke moved to stand beside me, straightened, and clasped his hands in front of him.

"Everyone, this is Rourke, my father's second in charge."

Rourke walked forward to my father's side, to be introduced to my family. I noticed Rachel watching me, with a knowing look on her face. As Rourke approached her, she turned to shake his hand. His hands were huge, and they dwarfed hers. *I bet that I know what she's thinking now.* He moved off to shake hands with Domenic and Sophie. Rachel made her way over to stand beside me.

"He's huge," she whispered.

"Agreed."

"He'd be handsome if he stopped scowling."

"Agreed."

"He's wearing that expensive suit well."

"Agreed."

"Is that all you're going to say? He's sweet on you. I could tell the moment I saw him standing next to you. He leant in toward your body, like you were a couple, and he was protecting you." Her voice was low, but I kept my eye on the room, to make sure no one was eavesdropping on our conversation.

"He's used to having to babysit me as he puts it, and he hates it."

"No, this is different. I don't get the impression he hates being near you tonight."

"Come on, time to join the party." I took her arm, and we walked over to join the others. Canapes were being passed around before dinner. It was time to open the champagne.

"Can we raise our glasses and make a toast to Rourke, who selflessly put himself in danger to protect my daughter. You are always welcome here, Rourke," my mother said.

"To Rourke." My father raised his glass. Everyone followed suit.

Rourke had less of a scowl, and more of a surprised expression on his face now. He glanced my way and for a split second I thought he was going to smile. Then the stony face was back. *How am I going to crack this shell he's built around himself?*

"Dinner is served," Aimee announced, from the doorway to the dining room.

We took our places at the table. I sat on one side with Domenic and Sophie to my left, and Rourke to my right. Daisy was in her highchair between her parents. My father, mother, Rachel, Cameron, and Aimee sat on the other side of the table. The setting at the head of the table was unused, because that was the place my mother's first husband occupied, and she believed he watched over us. He wasn't sent to Hell, so I have never met him.

Serving platters piled high with succulent vegetables, plates of crispy roast potatoes, baskets of fluffy dinner rolls, and boats full of dark, rich, gravy were passed around the table. The conversation hummed as we dug into the roast beef and savory dumplings that Aimee lovingly prepared. Rourke ate his meal, taking in the conversation around the table, but said very little. I was very aware of his large form beside me, his thigh inches from mine, his forearms resting on the edge of the table, his hands and long fingers holding the knife and fork. I could feel the intensity of his presence, the vibration of his being, next to me.

When coffee and dessert had been served and eaten, the men left the table to take Rourke on a tour of the estate. Cameron was thrilled to show off what he'd created in the garden of both houses. Sophie wiped Daisy's hands, placed her on a rug with her toys, folded the highchair, and stored it in a closet. My mother, Rachel and I followed Aimee into the kitchen with dirty dishes but were quickly turned around at Aimee's insistence that she needed to tidy up the way she liked it.

Finally, when everyone was back together in the living room, I made my way over to Rourke and handed him a crystal glass filled with port.

"You have a lovely home." Rourke took a sip of the port. The glass appeared like a miniature in his hands.

"Thank you, but this is my family home. I don't live here anymore. I've recently moved into an apartment near the bakery that I own with Rachel."

"I wondered about the connection. I wasn't sure who Rachel was."

"I guess we've never really had a conversation about my life here on Earth."

"No, we haven't."

"You never gave me the impression you wanted to discuss anything other than what was happening in Hell. That's why it's good you have a chance to see what it's like on Earth now. Hell is all you know."

"Hell has been my existence for centuries."

"But for me coming from this life, and then going to Hell was very challenging. Look around you. They couldn't be any more different.

That was why I suggested the job share. But I felt I hadn't given you the chance to see what you're missing."

"This is not a place where I'm comfortable. I'm used to the dark caverns, and the torture chambers. I'm happy with my role serving My Lord in Hell."

I sipped my glass of port and considered how to phrase the next question.

"I'd like to take you downtown. I could show you the bakery. We could also swing by my apartment. The roof garden has a great view of the city lights. What do you think?"

His eyes gave nothing away. His head tilted very slightly, as if considering the questions that I'd posed.

"I'd like to see the roof garden. I used to tend to gardens, a very long time ago."

My stomach was in knots. That seemed too easy. But I wasn't going to question his answer. "Follow me."

As we drove downtown, Rourke stared out the windows at all the changes to a world he'd never seen or experienced. The billboards, the traffic, the neon lights were all new to someone who lived beneath the Earth. Classical music filled the space when conversation became awkward. Rourke was impressed with the bakery. I gave him the basic tour, but I was too nervous to stay there for more than a few minutes.

We'd left my family without saying goodbye, but I'd sent a tele-pathic message to my father to let him know where we were going, and I promised that I would bring Rourke back soon. I wasn't sure if I would keep that promise, it all depended on what happened next.

I pulled up outside my building and hoped I wouldn't bump into anyone in this version of my body. Thankfully no one was around. I unlocked my apartment door, put my purse on the chair, and switched on the table lamp by the sofa.

"I'll get the key to open up the roof garden." I removed the key from the hook in the kitchen and slid it into the lock. "The moon's out tonight. You'll have a fabulous view up there..." I turned and he was directly behind me. I looked up, into his unreadable eyes. "I want to..." *I really want to kiss you.*

"What," he asked, his voice a husky whisper.

I chickened out. I turned, unlocked the door, and climbed the stairs. "I want to show you my roof garden. What do you think?" I unlocked the second door and stood aside to let him pass.

He walked to the edge of the roof. His silhouette was huge and in stark relief against the illumination from the twinkling lights below.

"I never imagined all this." He yanked his tie loose, pulled it free from his shirt collar, and stuffed it into his jacket pocket. He flicked open his top buttons with one hand. I could sense he was relaxing a little.

"It's fascinating how far you can see from up here, on a clear day."

"I'm beginning to understand why you had trouble acclimatizing to Hell," he said.

"And the garden is so pretty, up here on the roof. I didn't plant it. The previous owner's wife built this garden from scratch. I have no idea about how to look after it but I'm going to ask Cameron to help me. You've seen what he can do with plants."

"I tended gardens. A very long time ago. It gave me great pleasure." Rourke reached down and brought a sample of the soil up to his nose to smell the composition. "This is good soil. But it needs compost."

"You see, I have no idea about all that. I'd rather leave it to someone who knows."

"I'm sure Cameron can help. I have good memories of working in the gardens." He rubbed his hands together to brush off the soil.

"Would you like a glass of wine? I have some downstairs."

He nodded his head. We secured the doors and returned to the living room.

"I'll be back in a minute. Make yourself comfortable."

I watched as Rourke removed his jacket and placed it over the chair. I walked into my bedroom and shut the door.

My phone had been vibrating in my jacket pocket for some time. I hung up my jacket, took out my phone and looked at the screen.

There were a few missed calls from Rachel and a text message. *"Where are you, and are you okay, Lucia?"* I sent a text back to Rachel to apologize, and to tell her I'd see her soon, and that I was sure Cameron would take her home.

I had a vague idea of what I was going to do, but I didn't know if I could pull it off without making Rourke angrier at me. I applied some more lipstick, fluffed up my hair and adopted a sexy pout, sent a kiss to the Lucia in the mirror, and prayed for a miracle.

I returned to the living room. Rourke was sitting on the sofa, reading Daisy's book. The red bookmark I'd placed in the section on Love Potions was on the floor. He held the book in the air pointing aggressively at the pages.

"Is this what you've done to me? You've bewitched me with elixirs? I've been losing my sanity, unable to get you out of my head, both day and night you're with me, taunting me, teasing me. I thought I'd no control over myself and my emotions, I thought I was going mad, but I've been tricked! You concocted a potion to make me fall in love with you, didn't you?"

"You're... you're in love with me?" I stammered.

"Yes! But obviously not of my own free will."

"I can assure you I did not trick you or give you a potion to *make you* fall in love with me."

"I don't believe you."

"Have you forgotten. As the She-Devil, I cannot lie when you ask me a direct question."

"Did you give me something to make me fall in love with you, Lucia?" he asked through gritted teeth.

"No."

"Did you do anything to cause this to happen to me?"

"I've tried to be nice to you. I wanted you to like me. I couldn't understand why you acted like I was a nuisance to you. Like I was garbage under your feet. Someone you merely tolerated. I brought you here to see if we could work it out."

"Work it out?" he yelled.

"Isn't it obvious I have feelings for you too?" I yelled back.

"You do?"

"Yes. And now you tell me you love me. So where do we go from here, I'm..."

Rourke dropped the book on the sofa. He launched up out of his seat, placed his hands under my arms, picked me up and rammed me back against the wall. I heard a thud when my head connected with the plaster, but I'd no time to think about it because his mouth was on mine, the heat from his body consumed me, the taste of his desire evident on his lips. His hungry mouth stole all the breath from my body, then travelled down my throat, kissing his way down to my cleavage. One arm still supported me against the wall, while the other hand tore the sedate silk shirt open to expose the black lacy 'bra' underneath. Buttons flew off, scattering on the floor around his feet.

His mouth enclosed one lace-covered nipple which was threatening to burst from its confines. I moaned, which encouraged him to tug on the flimsy lace between my breasts and the front of the garment ripped open. He had access now to both bare breasts and he wasted no time in giving each equal measure of his attention. His lips, his tongue, his teeth were all in play and I was dizzy with desire.

"You. Drive. Me. Insane." He punctuated each word with a kiss to my neck. "If you did not give me some love potion to cause this insanity, you are indeed a She-Devil, a temptress in every sense of the word."

"And you are the most frustrating male I have ever had the pleasure of meeting."

"Frustration is exactly what I've felt. Frustration, annoyance, anger, and the most intense passion I can ever remember feeling for a female. What have you done to me?"

"And yet you say you love me!" I pulled his head up to look at me. His pupils were large and black, but I could sense the depth of his desire without this visual aid.

"Yes. Devil help me. I love you."

"Well, I must also be insane, because I think I'm in love with you too Rourke." This was the first time I'd admitted, even to myself, the emotion that has been swirling around in my head, and my heart, for a very long time.

He lowered me down the wall to stand on my own two feet and took a step back.

"What are we doing?" He sat down on the arm of the sofa and turned the cuffs of his shirt up to his elbows. He was obviously hot, but I was on fire, ready to self-combust.

"Finally opening up to feelings we kept buried."

"Maybe these feelings should be buried."

"Do you honestly think we can walk away from each other tonight, and not wonder what if? Do you think you could go back to what we were?" I asked.

He shook his head and lowered it into his hands. I walked forward and pulled his head onto my bare breasts. His shaved head was smooth to the touch.

"I can't go back. I want to know what it feels like to be with you," I said.

He pulled away and looked at me, shock registering on his face. "You want us to..."

"Yes." I stepped out of my shoes, unzipped my skirt, let it fall to the floor, and pushed them aside with my foot. I discarded the ruined silk shirt and lacy bra, and finally slipped off the black lace panties.

"This is the real, unadorned me. Naked and completely vulnerable. Will you make love to me, or do you want me to beg?"

"I'm not worthy of this honor, You're My Lord's daughter. He will never forgive me."

"You are worthy. My father does not have a say in this. Do you want to make love to me, Rourke?"

"Devil help me, yes. I want you. Every molecule of my being is begging me to take you into that bedroom and bury myself deep inside you."

"No. That is fucking. I want you to make love to me. There's a big difference."

Rourke stood, lifted me into his arms and walked to the bedroom, never taking his eyes from mine. He lowered me on the bed, removed his clothes, which freed his enormous erection and stood proudly, hands by his sides, feet slightly apart, allowing me the chance to change my mind. I nodded my head.

He climbed onto the bed on hands and knees, moving slowly up my body until we were face to face.

"I do want to make love to you, Lucia. You're right. We cannot go back. I need to know you, really know you, and you need to know all of me."

I watched his face coming closer until his lips touch mine. My eyes fluttered closed. His gentle touch soothed the butterflies in my stomach. His heart was beating so loud I could hear it pounding in his chest. Or was that mine? He deepened the kiss and lowered his impressive body on top of me, baring his weight on his forearms. My legs parted and I reached down to judge his girth, guiding the head of his cock to my entrance. No need for prolonged foreplay, I was already wet and willing.

He flexed his hips and entered me slowly, a little at a time. His girth and length were both much larger than I'd ever encountered, but my body was quickly acclimatizing to him, and the fullness was exciting. He thrust his hips and I moved with him, although we hadn't established a rhythm yet. He hadn't broken the kiss, and his tongue was dancing with mine, causing my pulse rate to climb, and making me wetter than I've ever been with a human. I little voice inside my head whispered "condom?" And ignored it because it was too late for that. And anyway, he was a demon who hadn't been with a woman since he entered Hell centuries ago. And he was old. Very old.

My body accepted his girth and length, rearranged the muscles and tissue, and took him all in. The pleasure-pain threshold had been exceeded and now euphoria was clearly at the helm, guiding this ship home. He pumped harder, faster, and my head thudded against the padded headboard, but I couldn't stop. I wouldn't stop. The pleasure was building to heights I'd never experienced and could never have imagined in my wildest dreams. He sat back onto his haunches and grasped my hips taking me with him. He bent one of my legs and lifted it up and over the front of his body, all the while still pumping inside me. My legs were scissored open, and he was plunging into me from behind. In this position his hands were free to touch me and bring me to orgasm.

With careful precision, which I wasn't aware he possessed, he swirled his finger around my swollen nub, applying exactly the right amount of pressure. I floated free of my body, and wave after wave of pleasure zapped through every part of me for what seemed like an eternity. With one final thrust Rourke gained his release. In that moment I was one with Rourke, fused together on levels unheard of in human souls. I experienced his orgasm as if it was my own, shared his euphoria as if I was inside his skin, and I was flooded with the love that flowed between our hearts. In that moment I knew with certainty there was no other soul who could connect with me as Rourke had done, no other soul for whom I need ever search.

I glanced back at him over my shoulder, thoroughly sated, and I knew he felt this too. We were joined in ways no human could never imagine. Then I witnessed a miracle.

He smiled.

47

ROURKE

J was euphoric, exhausted, concerned, and confused all rolled into one... but I was the happiest I could remember being in centuries. It was a miracle to me, but I was aware our hearts were beating as one. I found it hard to come to terms with the fact that I was holding Lucia in my arms, and she was sleeping soundly, contentedly, after hours of intense physical pleasure. I knew beyond a shadow of a doubt that I would kill anyone who threatened her without a second thought.

The irony wasn't lost on me that I'd made love numerous times to the woman who had literally driven me to distraction, and the edge of insanity, for many, many, months. And she'd admitted she loved me. How was this possible? She was the daughter of My Lord and master, and I didn't know what would happen when he found out. But no matter what ensued, I could honestly say that this was the best night of my existence. No one had ever brought this intensity of emotion to my heart, either when I was alive as a slave, or in Hell as a servant of My Lord. I would literally die for Lucia right now if she asked me. Although the mere fact that I was in her bed, holding her naked body against mine, was probably cause for disintegration.

She stirred and reached up to touch my face. I looked down and watched her beautiful eyes opening and her smile made my heart jolt in my chest.

"Good morning."

"Good morning, Lucia. You slept."

"I dreamt of you."

"Was it enjoyable?"

"Maybe I wasn't dreaming. Maybe we did make love on the roof?"

"Dreaming."

"Next time then," she said with a smile, stretching up to kiss me.

"How are we going to explain our absence?"

"I haven't thought about it. I've been otherwise occupied," she said.

"Don't you think we'd better discuss it now?"

"I have to pee. I'll be back. Then we can discuss, okay?"

She slid from my arms and disappeared into the bathroom. I felt out of place without Lucia by my side. Sanity was rapidly returning and suddenly I was uncomfortable laying in this bed, with the sun streaming in through the gaps in the window coverings.

Earth is no place for me, I really think I should get back to Hell. I started to dress, pulling on my shirt and pants, searching for my shoes. I could only find one! *Where could it be?*

She opened the door to find me on my knees searching under the bed. "What are doing?"

"I can't find my other shoe."

"I meant what are you doing getting dressed?"

"It's time to go back to Hell. I don't think I can avoid your father, so I may as well take my punishment now. This might be the last time you see me."

"Don't be ridiculous."

"We've skirted around this issue, but we might as well face it. I'm not worthy. I have broken My Lord's trust, being intimate with you and My Lord will have me removed to the dungeons and tortured before he disposes of my broken body."

"If he's going to punish anyone, it won't be you. I did this. I forced your hand to show me your true feelings. But Rourke, I wouldn't turn back the clock. Last night was the first time since I transitioned into this body that I've felt I belonged, and that I was where I should be. Don't you feel it, too? We connected in more ways than with our bodies. I love you. You love me. Our hearts are one. That must mean something, even to my father."

Lucia walked over and began to unbutton my shirt. "Come back to bed. I want to show you how much I care for you, how much last night meant to me. You surprised me with your tenderness after we made love."

"You brought out a side in me long forgotten."

"I witnessed another phenomenon too. You smiled."

I smiled thinking about why I smiled last night.

"You're doing it again! You never smiled before. It was one of the things that irritated me about you. Even when I made a joke you didn't smile. You are very handsome when you smile."

"I had nothing to smile about before."

"I'm going to make sure I keep you smiling then. Come on big boy, make love to me again."

I laughed, and once I began, I couldn't stop.

Lucia sat down on the bed, her hand over her mouth, her eyes huge with feigned surprise. "Oh, dear. He laughs too."

I grabbed her around her waist and lifted her into my arms. "You have bewitched me. You are indeed a witch."

"No. That's another member of our family tree's ancestry. Sophie's great grandmother I think, was a practicing witch. You just happened to fall for my many charms. Some of which you are yet to discover."

I allowed Lucia to undress me. "You have many more charms?"

The smug expression on her face intrigued me, until she knelt on the floor at my feet. "Let me show you."

48

LUCIA

I would not let Rourke face my father alone.

"We're going back to Hell together."

"I don't think that's a good idea," Rourke said.

"I need to tell him how I feel. *We* need to tell him how we *both* feel." I jumped out of bed and grabbed some clothes from my wardrobe. "Come, join me in the shower, before we meet my father."

"Washing away the scent of you won't make any difference. He'll know I've been with you, and he won't approve. He can see inside my head."

"Can he see inside your heart? Because that's what we must impress upon him. You might not want a shower, but I do."

I threw a fresh towel over the rail and turned on the faucet. This shower wasn't as pleasant as I thought it would be. My swollen and tender nipples, and sensitive-to-the-touch thighs wanted it to end. Every part of my body was sensitive to touch. I turned off the shower, towel dried quickly and pulled on my clothes. My hair twirled into a bun pinned in place on top of my head, I walked into the bedroom. "Let's go Rourke."

Rourke wasn't in the bedroom, or anywhere in the apartment.

"Oh no! Damn it to Hell."

❧

I flew down to Hell and ran straight to my father's office, but he wasn't there. I called by Drake's desk, but it was empty too. Instinct took me down to the bowels of Hell to the torture chambers. Rourke had mentioned the dungeon, the worst of the worst. I ran along the corridors, not sure if I was heading in the right direction or not. One Iron door was slightly ajar, and it pulled my attention. I pushed it open to see Rourke, bare chested and kneeling before my father, who was holding a samurai sword in his hands, high above his head. The blade caught the light from the flames of several torches, burning on the walls. I was familiar with the sharpness of these swords. It wouldn't take much to behead a man, never mind a demon. Even a huge demon the size of Rourke wouldn't stand a chance if that blade descended. Instruments of torture covered the walls, and filled the room, including a medieval torture rack and an electric chair.

"Father. Stop!" I yelled. "What are you doing?"

"He's taken advantage of you. He must be punished."

"No, Father. Rourke is not to blame. I seduced him."

"He should've been strong enough and turned away from the allure of the flesh. Especially as it concerns my daughter!" The timber in my father's voice caused the walls to shake.

"Please, Father. I love him." I rushed forward, stood between my father and Rourke.

"Get out of the way, Lucia."

"No. Did you hear what I said. I love Rourke!"

"What?" My father's voice boomed in the hollow chamber.

"And Rourke loves me. Tell him," I pleaded to Rourke.

"Is this true?" My father lowered the sword and pushed me out of the way to glare down at Rourke.

"Yes, My Lord. I love Lucia. But I have transgressed. I have taken advantage of your trust. I should never have crossed that line with Lucia."

"You love her? And Lucia, you say you love Rourke?" My father turned and walked to the metal bench against the wall. "This is a situation I never thought I was going to encounter." He put down the sword, his back to us. Suddenly he turned around. "Stand up Rourke!"

Rourke stood to attention, eyes forward, not looking at me. My father returned to stand before Rourke. I remained by Rourke's side. *I hope he understands we are in this together.*

"You have sullied my daughter. Will you join your soul with hers? Are you prepared to protect her with your life, treat her with respect, care for her and keep her as your own for all time?"

"I am, My Lord."

"And you, Lucia, are you prepared to care for Rourke, love him for eternity, treat him with respect, and join your soul with his?"

"I am, Father."

"Then you have my blessing. I will not behead you today, Rourke. But if my daughter ever comes to me with complaints about your lack of care for her, I will strike you down. Do you hear me?"

"Yes, My Lord."

"And as far as the trial is concerned, I've made my decision. I think that Rourke should look after Hell, and you should collect souls on Earth, Lucia. It's the best outcome. I decree that Hell shall be managed jointly, by both of you. I will be a consultant."

"A consultant?" I was stunned by this news. I'd thought it was going to take longer to convince him.

"It's a modern world Lucia. I'm familiar with the term, and I think it fits with what I'm trying to achieve. I'll be happy spending more time with Harper and the family. I can step in at a moment's notice if required in Hell."

"And you are okay with Rourke and I... together now?"

"If you mean sharing a bed, then I will have to be. If, as you say, you love one another."

"Yes, I mean sharing a bed. Working together, sleeping together, collecting souls, and making sure the evil people are sent to Hell."

"Is it your heart's desire, Lucia?"

"You know I cannot lie. Yes, it is my heart's desire."

"I must return to Harper. She was worried about you."

"Thank you, My Lord. You will not regret this," Rourke said.

"You had better make sure I don't." My father cast his powerful stare on Rourke, who impressively held his gaze for several seconds.

Then my father disappeared, leaving us alone in the dungeon.

"Did you get the feeling that we are now betrothed?" I asked.

"Betrothed?"

"He pretty much said the words... "Do you take this woman to you, and do you take this man to me."

"Can he do that?"

"I have no idea. Does it bother you?"

"No. Does it bother you, Lucia?"

"No. Because I think I've found my soul mate in you, Rourke."

"I intend for you to keep thinking like that. Your father won't give me a second chance, remember." Rourke pulled me into his arms, and his lips found mine.

I wasn't afraid of a future in Hell, with Rourke by my side. Two immortal souls, who were lucky to be in the right place at the right time. If Domenic had decided that he'd wanted to be the Devil's protégé I might never have met Rourke. This way we could continue my father's legacy, working in Hell and on Earth, and ridding the world of as many evil people as we can.

"By the way, how did you get here so quickly? You don't have wings like me."

"One minute I was standing in your bedroom and the next minute, I was dragged through The Veil by Drake, and brought down here to My Lord."

"I wondered why I couldn't find Drake. He probably thought I would come looking for him to locate you."

"We probably won't find him today."

"What would you like to do now?" I asked.

Rourke smiled at me, and that was all I needed to bring out the little she-devil in me.

"These walls are thick, aren't they. Sounds won't penetrate, will they? I can make as much noise as I want to, and no one will come running. Sit," I commanded pointing to the chair. I closed and bolted the door with an iron bar.

Rourke sat as instructed on the edge of the electric chair. I straddled his thighs.

"Show me what you can do with a chair. Then show me what you can do with that rack over there."

We were both grinning because he didn't need much encouragement. Near death situations seem to bring out the desire in both of us. I turned my attention to removing my clothes, and unzipping his pants, freeing the part of him I have become very fond of. I climbed on top.

My screams of pure pleasure reverberated round the walls.

Maybe there was fun to be had in Hell after all.

49

LUC

*T*here were a few things I had to take care of in Hell before I left. I made sure Drake knew what was happening and would follow any direction from Rourke and Lucia. Harper was tucked up in bed by the time I got back to Hollywood. I slipped into bed behind her and pulled her into my arms, nuzzling her neck.

"You always smell so good."

"Oh, you're finally back. What happened?" Harper asked.

"I took Rourke to the dungeon. Lucia arrived in the nick of time before my sword came down on Rourke's neck."

"You are incorrigible."

"Why do you say that?"

"You are such a tease. You were never going to hurt Rourke."

"But Lucia didn't know that."

"Are you ever going to tell her that you selected Rourke for her."

"Never! She doesn't need to know that. But honestly, who else would have been perfect for her? Who else can run Hell as well as I can and can protect her with his life. He has proven that already, has he not? Who else can share the load with her, so that the miserable job of dealing with the scum of the Earth does not overwhelm our beautiful girl. Who else is immortal just like Lucia, therefore, they will have each other, and love each other for eternity."

"You are wise, my darling."

"I need to make sure she has someone to take care of her when we're no longer here. I'm making plans to grow old with you, Harper, to plead my case to follow you, if Heaven is the destination, for I cannot stay in this world without you. But if God wants to continue to punish me, and since you are too good to ever end up in Hell, then there is nothing for me to do but revoke my eternal lifespan and disappear into the stars. It's time for a new regime in Hell. And our girl has shown that the Devil can help people. Not just punish people. I'm so proud of Lucia, and what she's accomplished. And what she will accomplish with Rourke."

"No morbid talk tonight, please. I want to feel happy that our daughter is in love. Do you think we could have a small private celebration?"

"Subtlety is not lost on me. You mean a wedding, don't you? No need, I've already done that. They are joined. Plus, I've put the fear of the Devil into Rourke's heart. If he ever hurts her, he will no longer exist."

"But you are not ordained to perform weddings!"

"What the Devil has joined together, let no man or demon put asunder."

"Okay, if you say so. But I still want to give them a small private celebration."

"Whatever you want my love. Throw them a party if you think it's necessary. But you and I both know that the celebration is to make *you* feel better. Not them."

50

LUCIA

THREE MONTHS LATER

I wasn't sure how I would feel when I returned to work on Earth two months ago. I missed Rourke every single day, ached for him as you would a missing limb. But I kept a secret from him, and I wasn't sure how he was going to feel about it.

"I can never get enough of being held against your chest, with your arms around me. This is home now, and this is where I feel safe and loved."

"I've missed you, Lucia," he whispered into my hair.

"I've missed you, too. But I get a reprieve and can spend more time with you now that the hotel is having a renovation. I'm going to request to return to work in Hell for a while."

"Your father has made some changes in Hell. He's given me his office and moved down the hall. But I'm sure he'll be happy for you to return. You'll be impressed with the new schedule too. We've implemented some of your changes."

"I'm pregnant, Rourke." I blurted it out. I couldn't hold onto this secret any longer.

He held me away from his chest to look down at me.

"You're kidding, yes? That's impossible."

"That was what I said, but I feel different, and the medical professionals say I'm three months along."

"Three months. That would have been the first time we..."

"Yes, exactly."

"Three months! I'm going to be a father in six months?"

"Possibly."

"What do you mean possibly?"

"Twins usually come early."

"Twins!"

"I can hear two heartbeats."

"You said you thought you were just putting on weight the last time we were together."

"I thought that at first. But then I started to hear them. I didn't want to say anything until after the first trimester."

"I honestly don't know how this happened. I'm centuries old. I didn't think that I produced any..."

"I've been thinking about that too. Remember when you had the accident and my father helped you to get better? Well, I think whatever he did, didn't just fix your back. I think he healed other parts of you, like the scars on your back which have mysteriously disappeared. And it's also made you fertile."

"I'm stunned."

"But are you happy?"

"Yes. I'm going to be a father. I never thought I would say those words. How are you feeling?"

"Shocked. But I'm happy. I'm not sure if I'm ready for this."

"You'll made a wonderful mother. I'm sure of it." Rourke placed his hand on my stomach protectively.

"I wonder what we're having." I placed my hand over his.

"I don't care as long as they're healthy. Isn't that the traditional comment a father-to-be makes?"

"I predict a demon and a she-devil."

"You have insider knowledge."

"No, I'm just guessing like all mothers-to-be."

"Your parents are going to be shocked!"

"I can't wait to see my father's face. Let's tell them together tonight at the party my mother has arranged for us."

❧

I took my time getting ready and chose an ankle-length forest green dress that did not cling to my body but fell in soft folds from a halter neckline. My hair fell in loose waves over my shoulders and down my back to my waist. I pinned a small section up behind my left ear, fastened in place with pink rosebuds, which Cameron had carefully selected for me.

Mother and Aimee had not allowed us access to the garden behind the house since we arrived because they were setting up the outdoor table and wanted the decorations to be a surprise.

You can come join us in the garden, Lucia.

   Yes, Father. We'll be out in a minute.

I descended the stairs and made my way to where Rourke was waiting in the living room.

"How do I look?"

"You know my answer."

"I want to hear it anyway."

"You look stunningly beautiful."

"Thank you. Domenic and Sophie must have arrived. Father has asked us to come out. It's time to face the music. Are you ready?"

Rourke stood and I took his arm. We walked through the sunroom around the side of the house to the back garden. I was surprised to see a small marquee erected in the garden. It appeared we had under-estimated my mother's creativity. The curtains at the door were pulled back, draped open. I could see Domenic and Sophie, baby Daisy, Aimee and Cameron and Rachael waiting inside. My father, mother and Drake stood beside an older gentleman with snow white hair.

A long table sat in the middle of the room, beautifully decorated, with floral centerpieces, candelabras, crystal glassware and gold cutlery. My mother's signature touch of opulence and elegance was evident and very inviting. Beyond the table at the back of the marquee, I noticed an arch entwined with garlands of white roses and a small dancefloor and suddenly it all made sense.

"Oh, Rourke." I stopped, hugged his arm, pulling him closer and whispered, trying not to move my lips. "Do you see what they've done? This is a wedding marquee."

My father walked forward. He kissed me on both my cheeks and shook Rourke's hand.

"You look beautiful, Lucia. I see you've taken heed, Rourke, and making sure you're looking after my daughter."

"I try, My Lord."

"What's going on?" I asked.

"This is a gathering to celebrate your union."

My mother approached.

"Mother?"

"Lucia, your father told me you want to be together as partners, and he all but performed a marriage ceremony for you under duress. I wanted you to have something special to mark your coming together. I know you're both in love. Your father can be a bully, but he has seen the error of his ways and has allowed me to make it right."

"Make it right?"

"Come meet Charles. He's a demon, but also a celebrant and he's going to officiate at your wedding. If I haven't misjudged the situation, and this is what you want?"

My heart was singing with love for my mother, and the fact that she knew me so well.

"Yes, this is what I want."

"And you Rourke. Is this what you want?"

"Yes. I want whatever makes Lucia happy."

"Right answer." My mother patted his arm.

Daisy clasped a small posy of white roses and baby's breath, bound together with green ribbon, and toddled down the carpet to the floral arch where Rachel stood waiting as my Matron of Honor and witness. Drake stood beside Rourke, looking a little nervous but very handsome in a dark suit and tie. All eyes turned to me as my father handed me a bouquet of roses and took my arm to walk me down the aisle. My mother and Aimee had tears in their eyes.

My father kissed my cheeks and joined my mother a few feet away. Rachel relieved me of the bouquet of flowers. Daisy twirled in a circle, giggling, and enjoying the swing of her pretty dress and we all laughed. Sophie took her hand and moved her away to stand with Domenic.

Charles began to speak, and everyone turned their attention to him. "Dear family and friends of the Bride and Groom, we welcome and thank you for being a part of this important occasion. We are gathered today to witness the coming together of two souls, the joining of two hearts and to celebrate the joy of finding the love of their lives." He then addressed Rourke and me. "I am going to ask each of you to read out the words on this card. You may add to it if you wish."

Cameron handed the card to Rourke.

"I call upon the people present to witness that I, Rourke, take you, Lucia, to be my wife. I promise to love you, care for and respect you." Rourke returned the card to Cameron and took my hands in his. "Lucia, I will protect you from harm with my life. I wasn't whole until you came into Hell, stirring things up. Stirring things in me I had long forgotten. You are the missing piece I've been searching for. I love you."

Charles handed me the card.

"I call upon the people present to witness that I, Lucia, take you, Rourke, to be my husband. I promise to love you, care for you and respect you." I handed the card back to Charles. "Rourke, there is nothing I cannot achieve with you by my side. I love you with all my heart."

"By the power vested in me, I now pronounce you husband and wife. You may kiss your bride." Charles said.

Rourke's lips found mine, and I cried happy tears. I linked my arm in his and turned to the family gathered before us.

"I'm very happy, and very proud to be Rourke's wife. Don't mind the tears. I'm just a bit hormonal. That's what happens when you are pregnant, so they tell me. I'm still the powerful She-Devil you all know and love. There's just more of me to love now. And very soon our little family of two will be a family of four. We are having twins!

"Twins!" my father said.

"I predict you're going to be a Devil of a grandfather!"

THE END

EPILOGUE

LUCIA

*M*y father sent a telepathic message and asked Rourke and me to meet him and my mother in his newly refurbished study. Until recently this room adjacent to the sunroom had been a small sitting room. Now it was reimagined, with floor to ceiling bookshelves, leather couches and an antique partner's desk. My parents were standing in front of the desk, my mother's eyes sparkled, which indicated to me that she was excited about something. My father handed me a drawing, an artist's impression of a stunning house, smaller but similar in style to our family home.

"What's this?"

"It's our wedding gift to you both. This is your home if you want it. I had the idea before we found out about the pregnancy. I've bought the land adjacent to our property and I plan to move our walled estate to incorporate your house within the perimeter. And now that we know about the twins' arrival, you'd be near to your mother and have help from Aimee and Cameron when your time comes. With Rourke spending most of his time in Hell we felt this was a good solution. Our three houses within the enclave with be encircled by a higher wall. I've discussed bringing in extra staff to help Cameron and Aimee and have better security. What do you think?"

Tears sprung up in my eyes.

My mother placed her hand on my arm. "You don't have to say yes, if you think you would rather find your own home. And Rourke we don't want to take anything from you being the patriarch of your small family but..."

"Yes! A thousand times yes. I know I'm hormonal and emotional at the moment, but these are happy tears, Mom. I would love to live here with my family, within the safety of these walls. I want our children to know and spend time with the people who love them. To be able to express themselves without fear, especially if they have any unique gifts."

"Well, that's sorted then. I can't wait to see Aimee's face. You know she loves having little ones to look after."

Rourke put his arm around my shoulders and addressed my father. "This is very generous, thank you, My Lord. To be completely honest I'm grateful and relieved Lucia will be here with all of you. It has concerned me that she's not within my protection while she's working on Earth. And now that we're going to be parents, I'm even more grateful for your generous gift. I still can't believe this is happening. I have a family. I never thought I'd be able to utter those words."

"You are very much a part of this family, and soon you'll know the joy that children of your own can bring. I can't wait to spoil more grandchildren," my mother said.

"Construction will start immediately," my father announced proudly. "We shall have a home built before the twins are born."

"Come, Rourke, let's celebrate with a glass of champagne. And in your case, Lucia, a glass of apple juice. I'm going to find Aimee to give her the good news." My mother took Rourke's arm and led him back to party.

I locked eyes with my father, and we exchanged a smile. "Thank you. This means so much."

"You're welcome, Lucia. Your safety is very important to your mother and to me."

"I'm glad the twins will have a loving place to call home and the security you can provide. To grow up and to be who they are meant to be. I'm not sure what to expect. A half human with a demon? Will these babies be human or demon?"

"Does it matter? You only have to look in the mirror to see the combination of human and demon genes. You are beautiful, intelligent, and magical, and I expect your children will be likewise."

"I can hear them father! I can hear their hearts beating. Feel them moving inside me."

"It's a wonderful feeling isn't it. I was always very humbled when I could feel you moving inside your mother. To grow another being from love is a different state of magic in my opinion. Your mother and I could communicate telepathically when your mother was carrying you."

"Thank you for making Rourke feel part of the family too. He's getting better at sharing his feelings, but I know he suffered greatly over the centuries."

"Rourke has been my right hand since he arrived in Hell. Bringing him into the family seems natural. Let's go join the others."

FIVE MONTHS LATER

I reached down and touched the hands of my two tiny babies to let them know I was watching over them. Both have olive skin and dark hair and it's hard for others to tell them apart. But I know the difference. Theo was a few ounces heavier than Ruby at birth and has a bit less hair. And Ruby has a slightly smaller button nose, but no one else has managed to work out their differences.

My father's strutting about like he's produced this miracle, and I have no idea why he's so pleased with himself. My mother's breaking her own record of being the most smitten grandmother of all time. Rourke has surprised me by reading every book he could find on parenting so that he's prepared.

At first, I separated them into their own cribs, but they were unsettled. Now they are completely content when nestled together in an oversized crib Rourke made for them. They turn toward each other and hold hands, which to me is the sweetest thing. Rourke is completely in love and watching him care for these two babies so tenderly makes my heart ache. Their wellbeing is all I care about.

Who knew that motherhood would be like this. It was as if my heart was wrenched from my body and split into two individual pieces. I'd kill for them and die for them in equal measure.

The strong and caring heart of the Devil created me, and now I've produced these miniature devils-in-the-making. I'm proud to say my father's legacy lives on.

THE END… or is it the beginning? (insert evil laugh here)

ABOUT THE AUTHOR

Savannah Blaize lives in Melbourne, Australia, after emigrating from Scotland many years ago. She enjoys writing fiction of all genres, in which the reader can visualise and step inside the world she creates. When she creates a story, the scenes run like a movie reel in her head, and the consistent feedback is that they create the same visual experience for her readers.

Savannah is proud member of the Melbourne Romance Writers Guild, The Romance writers of Australia and the Sisters In Crime. She is passionate about reading across genres, about writing her stories in which her imagination can run free, and about connecting with her readers.

Devil Made Me Do It is the third book in the Heart Of The Devil Series. Devil In The Details, the second book, was published in July 2021. Deal With The Devil, the first book, was published in September 2020

Her first novel From Paris To Forever was published in 2017. Her second novel The Class Reunion was published in 2018. Her novellas If The Shoe Fits and A Tartan Christmas were published in 2020.

ALSO BY SAVANNAH BLAIZE

Deal with the Devil

Devil in the Details

From Paris To Forever

The Class Reunion

Novellas:

If the Shoe Fits

A Tartan Christmas

Short stories published in anthologies:

Baby Did A Bad Bad Thing

Knight In Shining Combat Boots

www.ingramcontent.com/pod-product-compliance
Lightning Source LLC
Chambersburg PA
CBHW070546120726
47909CB00007B/2251